THE
UPSIDE
OF
FALLING
DOWN

ALSO BY REBEKAH CRANE

The Odds of Loving Grover Cleveland
Aspen
Playing Nice

THE UPSIDE OF FALLING DOWN

REBEKAH CRANE

SKYSCAPE

SKYSCAPE

Text copyright © 2018 by Rebekah Crane
All rights reserved.

Published by Skyscape, New York

www.apub.com

Amazon, the Amazon logo, and Skyscape are trademarks of Amazon.com, Inc., or its affiliates.

ISBN-13: 9781503954250 (hardcover)
ISBN-10: 1503954250 (hardcover)
ISBN-13: 9781612187228 (paperback)
ISBN-10: 1612187226 (paperback)

Cover design by Adil Dara

Cover illustration by Leah Goren

Printed in the United States of America

For Drew and Hazel—may you be daring and embrace the adventures in life . . . and love.

Ladies and gentlemen, the captain has asked that you remain in your seats for the remainder of the flight. Please put away all portable electronic devices and return all tray tables to their upright and locked position. The flight attendants will be coming through the cabin one more time to collect any remaining items you wish to discard. Thank you for your help, and we appreciate you choosing Western Air.

We never believe we'll crash . . . until we're falling.

PROLOGUE

I was born twice. The first time was on July 9 to Paul and Mimi Haas in Cleveland, Ohio. My mother died six years later. My parents hadn't conceived another child, and my father never remarried. I was born with brown eyes and brown hair, and for eighteen years, I was, for the most part, healthy.

I was delivered again on June 18, just weeks before my nineteenth birthday. The nurses said I was born unconscious with ash tangled in the burned ends of my hair. Rescue workers pulled me from the belly of an airplane, where I was stuck between two seats, like a cushioned sandwich. There was no mother to gaze down at me in amazement or cradle me if I cried, but according to my nurse, Stephen, there were a plethora of camera crews and flashing lights.

Out of the wreckage of that day, which included thirty dead bodies, *I* was a miracle. Amid so much death and destruction, *I* was born.

For a day, I lay in the hospital, unconscious, before I opened my eyes to the world for the first time. I had bleached blonde hair and a nasty bump on my head.

When the doctor sat down gently on the chair next to my bed and asked me a question, I could only think to respond with these words: "There are four emergency exits on this plane—two at the front of the cabin and two at the back."

A handful of nurses and other staff broke into laughter, but my doctor didn't. She asked me another question, a puzzled expression on her face, to which I replied, "Please take a moment to locate your nearest emergency exit. In some cases, your exit may be behind you."

That's when the room went silent. All the laughter fell out of the air.

"Can you tell me where you are?" the doctor asked in an accent unlike my own. It took me a moment to understand her, partly because of the accent, but also because of the odd question.

"Where I am?" I said, feeling around. "Clearly, I'm in a bed."

A perplexed expression crossed the doctor's face as the others looked on at the miracle that I was. "Yes, but do you know where? Specifically, what country?" she asked.

I thought for a long while, touching the bump on my head. The bump was a flaw, and something told me that's not how this was supposed to be. People are born perfect, right?

"What happened to my head?"

"You don't remember how that happened?" When I shook my head and didn't offer an answer, the doctor asked me another question. "Can you tell me your name?"

It was a simple question, but at that moment, the complexity of it weighed me down, so much so that I had a hard time breathing.

"Or better yet, can you tell me anything about yourself?" the doctor asked.

"About myself?" I thought long and hard. As if the people gaping at me weren't clue enough, my confusion should have been. A person shouldn't have to think so hard about that question. It should come naturally. It's me. I know me, right? But concentrating so hard made my head start to ache, and I thought I might pass out. And for all that thinking, nothing happened.

Nothing.

The doctor glanced at the nurses, who stared at each other, but all the looking didn't find them any answers. I started to think answers don't come that easily.

I died and was reborn on June 18 in a plane crash in Ballycalla, less than eight kilometers from Shannon Airport, and I awoke to a new life a day later in the Mid-Western Regional Hospital in Ireland, not far away. When the nurse called me by name, I didn't respond.

He touched my arm. "Your name is Clementine, love."

"Clementine." I said the name over and over in my head, hoping one idea would stack on top of another and another and create something concrete. A person filled with a lifetime of memories.

But nothing happened. Instead, I said, "I have no idea who you're talking about."

CHAPTER 1

Day one. I have a tattoo of a green heart on my foot. It's on the inside of my ankle, down by my heel, like it's trying to hide itself. Who gets a tattoo they want to hide? This tattoo is small and totally lackluster, and its meaning is lost on me. I'm left wondering if I'm the kind of person who gets a tattoo only to hide it.

My hate for it is visceral. So much so that when I see it, my stomach turns, and I feel like I might puke. Hating this tattoo is one of the only things I know about myself.

When I changed my socks, I caught my first glimpse of it. Stephen brought me fuzzy blue booties because I complained that my feet were cold, and there it was—the world's most boring tattoo on *my* body. A high-pitched squeal tumbled out of my mouth when I saw it.

I can't bring myself to acknowledge it. All it does is remind me that I have forgotten my entire life. And I want it back. However, this tattoo isn't a good sign. Hate for something I *chose* to put on my body doesn't speak well for the person I was.

For now, my conclusion is to stay still and wear my booties to cover up my tattoo. Avoidance shouldn't be underestimated in these circumstances. Avoidance seems like a pretty solid idea right now.

In a way, losing my entire memory might not be so bad. Everyone has bad memories they want to forget. My situation wipes them all clean.

But there's the other side—the not so good side. All the pieces of my past I *want* to remember, the ones that explain who I am, are gone.

Like a breath. My life decided to exhale.

That's the part that gets me. I know I'm gone, even when Stephen shows me my chart and the minimal details he's collected about my life—all from a brief conversation he had with my dad.

"Cleveland, Ohio. Sounds lovely!" Stephen's voice is chipper. "I've always wanted to go to America. Do you think you know Justin Timberlake? *He's* lovely. I've always wanted to meet him."

"I don't think I know Justin Timberlake."

"Well, what's Cleveland like?"

Nothing happens, so Stephen tries another tactic.

"I spoke with your dad yesterday. He sounds like a lovely man, too."

"Lovely," I say.

"So you remember him?" Stephen's whole face brightens.

"You use that word a lot—lovely."

Stephen seems deflated. He pats my bootie-covered feet. "Your dad will be here soon. I'm sure once you see him, your memories will fall into place. Don't fret."

"What happens if I don't remember?"

"Let's not think about that."

But it's *all* I can think about. My mind has already forgotten so much, there's not much else to focus on. Who am I?

I'm a girl with a bad tattoo whose only memory is waking up in a hospital bed with a roomful of strangers. I try to cry for everything I've lost. Eighteen years. Vanished.

My doctor uses the term "retrograde amnesia." A loss of access to memories before the plane crash. So while I may know what a television is, I can't recall a single memory of actually watching television. Worse,

Stephen informs me that my mom died when I was six, and I can't recall a single thing about her. When my doctor sees the panic-stricken expression I must be wearing on my face, she's quick to tell me that the memories usually come back.

"Usually," I say.

"Yes. Usually."

"But not always."

She sits down on the bed, folding her thin hands in her lap. The scrubs she has on are too big for her waiflike body, and her brown hair is pulled into a loose ponytail at the nape of her neck. "Your memories might be gone, for now. But your soul remains intact."

"But what do I do?" I ask.

"Wait. That's all you can do," she says. "Don't lose hope, Clementine. You've survived worse."

It's a gentle reminder of the plane crash. Thirty other people didn't survive. I should have died with them. No one knows why I didn't. According to Stephen, whose accent is thick, making his words run together, the plane was flying into Shannon International Airport in western Ireland from Heathrow Airport, in London. A fire broke out in the cargo hold during the flight and burned its way into the electrical and fuel systems, causing a shutdown of the entire plane. The pilots tried to land, thinking they could make it to Shannon before the fire took complete control. But in the end, the plane went down just kilometers from the runway—there was just too much damage. I am all that remains.

The doctor leaves, and Stephen returns. I ask him, "Why was I on that plane?"

"Let's wait for your dad to get here." He bites his lip, busying himself with my blankets. That's when it hits me: What if the clue I'm searching for is so bad it would be easier *not* to know? I nod in agreement, feeling a numbing sensation overtake me all the way down to my tattoo. The more I search, the more lost I get in darkness. Crying isn't

7

even the solution. What am I crying for? *Who* am I crying for? As far as I'm concerned, what's lost never existed in the first place.

The memories mean nothing to me if I can't recall them. Except for the small fact that . . . they mean *everything*. No matter what people want to believe, life is locked in the past. It's all we are—a timeline of events that make up a person.

My father flew into Dublin early this morning and is driving across the country to take me home to Cleveland, Ohio, so I can get back to my life and out of the media chaos that's created a sensation around Ireland. Apparently, the mystery of a lone survivor of a plane crash garners a lot of attention, perfect for Irish tabloids. People are loving the sensational nature of it all, according to my doctor, but she repeatedly tells me that everyone in the hospital is working to keep me safe.

Oddly enough, it's not the public I'm most afraid of. It's myself. And the large, impending reality that going home to America means getting on another airplane.

Later in the day, Stephen walks into my room, pushing a rolling cart as I stare at my covered foot.

"No more tests." I cover my eyes and cringe. "I can't take it anymore."

Stephen chuckles, and I peek through my fingers to see what he's laughing at.

"I thought," he says in a bubbly voice as he wheels the cart over to me, "we'd have some fun."

"Fun," I say hesitantly, dropping my hand from my face. This feels like an odd time for *fun*, but it's better than wallowing. "I think I like fun."

"Here." Stephen hands me a notebook and a pen. "Write that down."

"Write what down?"

"Clementine likes fun." Stephen smiles and winks at me. "So you don't forget." When I don't laugh, he says, "Sorry. Bad joke."

I open the notebook and ogle at the blank page. This is me—*blank*. It would actually feel nice to fill in the space with something, even if it's just words.

"Actually, it's not a bad idea," I say, pushing myself up in bed and writing in the notebook *I like fun*. "OK. What else?"

"I figure we'll try a few things out. See if we can add more items to your list and maybe jog that memory of yours. You never know."

He sits on my bed and unfolds a gigantic map of the United States. "This is America."

I cock my head at Stephen. "I'm aware."

He chuckles again and points to Ohio. "This is Ohio." Then he points to a dot at the top of the state. "This is Cleveland. It's on"— Stephen squints as he reads—"Lake Erie. Lake Erie is one of the five Great Lakes in America."

I sit back in bed. "This is a *lovely* geography lesson, but how is it supposed to help me?"

"Close your eyes and think about water for a minute."

I take Stephen's advice, and for the next few minutes, I envision water, touching water, tasting water, the cool crispness of it . . . but nothing happens.

Stephen waves away the moment and gets out another map. "This is Ireland. Ireland is an island." And again, I cock my head at him, making Stephen giggle once more. "This is where Limerick is in Ireland. It's on the west side of the country."

"OK," I say, trying to take in exactly where I am right now. "What else?"

"It's the third-largest city in Ireland. And"—Stephen dusts his shoulder off—"the friendliest."

"Really?"

"You landed in a good spot, Clementine."

"I believe I crashed."

Stephen laughs. "You have quite a lovely sense of humor."

"I do?"

He nods. "Write that down."

I add *I have a lovely sense of humor* to my list, my spirit lifted slightly. Stephen starts reading off the names of the cities on the map to see if any strike a memory.

"Galway . . . Cork . . . Waterford . . . Dublin . . . Any of these sound familiar?"

The cities are easy to find on the map, but accessing a memory isn't so straightforward.

"Maybe maps just aren't your thing." He sets them both back on the cart. Stephen then holds up two books—one with a woman and half-naked man on the cover and the other with a man in a trench coat with a gun.

"Romance or suspense?" he asks. "Do you like a little sex or a little violence?"

I take the books from him and examine the covers. "I definitely prefer the half-naked guy over the violence."

"The guy," Stephen says. "So you're not gay."

I shrug. "I don't think so."

Stephen perks up. "A development. This is good. Write that down."

So I do. *I am not gay (most likely).*

On closer examination of the books, I notice the guy *is* pretty hot. "I definitely like this one more, and I might need a little distraction. Can I have it?"

An excited expression spreads on Stephen's face. "I think we've found your thing."

"What?"

"Clementine likes sex!" Stephen announces with enthusiasm.

"I'm not writing that down," I say with a small laugh.

"There's no shame in liking sex. It's natural."

"But I don't even know if I've had sex."

Stephen looks at me with a keen eye. "Oh. You've had sex."

"How can you tell?"

"A nurse just knows these things," Stephen says. My face heats.

"I'm still not writing that down." I smile.

We go through a few more items. I discover I like tulips over roses, broccoli over green beans, and I don't like balloons. At all.

"Knowing what you don't like is as important as knowing what you do like," Stephen says when we're almost done with all the objects on the cart.

"Where did you get all of this stuff?"

"I popped over to the shop next door." Stephen hands me a piece of chocolate cake. "But *this* I took from the cafeteria. Try it and see what happens."

My first bite of the cake is spongy and delicious. I shovel in more and speak with my mouth full. "Decent texture. Not too dry. Definitely made with butter, but it would be better with dark chocolate and applesauce. Cream cheese frosting is a nice touch."

Stephen seems impressed. "You can tell that just from a bite?"

"Is that unique?" I down another huge bite.

"Definitely." Stephen takes an extra fork and eats a bite of the cake. "Write that down."

As I do, Stephen instructs me to take another bite.

"Now," he says, "maybe there's a hint of a memory from a birthday party or a holiday hidden somewhere inside . . ."

A few tweaks to the ingredients, and this cake would be outstanding. I know it. But the food turns sour in my mouth as I shake my head and set down the plate. The truth is I don't know *why* I like it or *why* I know what it's made of. And I don't know *why* I think I could make it better. The only chocolate cake I can remember is the one I'm in the process of eating right now.

Stephen tries something else. He holds up a green sweatshirt with an Irish flag that says "Limerick" on it and a purple sweatshirt that says "When Irish eyes are smilin', they're usually up to something."

"Which one do you like?" he asks. "Green or purple?"

Both are fine, but I do prefer one. "Purple."

"Clementine likes purple." Stephen lays the sweatshirt down on the end of my bed as I write down *I like purple.*

"How is this supposed to trigger my memory again?"

Stephen's sight line falls to his hands, and he smiles in a broken kind of way. "Well . . . this one isn't. I just wanted to get you something. Everything you had was . . ."

He doesn't need to finish his sentence. He and I both know this. Everything I had burned in the plane crash. The clothes I was wearing were cut off me on the way to the hospital. I have no passport. No money. I literally have nothing. Not even memories.

This purple sweatshirt is the only item of real clothing I own right now. I put it on over my hospital gown and try to keep the panic out of my voice. "Thank you, Stephen. I love it."

He looks like he doesn't really believe me.

"Wait here," he says before disappearing out of the room. Alone, I fidget with my new sweatshirt and wonder how this is all going to end. Do stories like this even have happy endings?

Stephen comes back into the room minutes later with his arms full of clothes. He lays them out on the end of my bed and gestures to the messy pile. "Pick some."

"Pardon?" I sit up quickly.

"You can't feel human when you're dressed like a science experiment."

Shirts, pants, shoes, socks, bras, even a pack of new underwear are spread out before me. I sift through everything. "Where did you get all of this?"

"The lost and found."

"Lost and found?" I say.

"Well . . . not everyone who comes to the hospital is found, if you know what I mean."

12

I drop the shirt that was in my hand. "You mean these are clothes from dead people?"

Stephen rolls his eyes. "Not all dead. You'd be amazed what people leave behind here." He picks up a bra and holds it up to my chest. "Thirty-four C. That should fit." I snatch the bra from his hands, my face heating as Stephen chuckles. "It's better than a hospital gown."

He's right.

Minutes later when I come out of the bathroom dressed in a plain red T-shirt and a pair of jeans, my confidence has grown. The pair of black-and-white Converse even fit.

"How did you know my bra size?" I ask.

"I'm a nurse. It's my job to know the body." Stephen and I exchange grins. He hands me the purple sweatshirt. "For an American, I think you've got some of our Irish luck in you."

The word "luck" turns my brief positivity sour. I should be happy I'm alive. And I am. But I'm not sure how alive I actually am right now. Yes, I'm breathing. Yes, my limbs and my heart and my mind work, for the most part. But life should be about more than that, right? The story. The moments. And I've lost mine.

A chill comes over me even though I've put on the purple sweatshirt once again.

"Thank you," I say.

"Thank *you* for letting me help." Stephen goes to leave, pushing his cart with him, but before he does, I show him what I just wrote down in my notebook.

I like how Stephen says "tanks" instead of "thanks." It's lovely.

"You know," Stephen says, "the Irish accent is always ranked as the sexiest in the world."

"And as someone pointed out earlier . . . apparently, I like sex, so it makes sense I like your accent."

Stephen taps on the notebook. "I thought that might come in handy."

Even with all Stephen's encouragement and help, the unease of amnesia makes it hard to move forward, no matter how much I fight to keep going. I know I should press on, determined, unbreakable. A stronger person would do that. She'd fight. But all I feel like doing is curling up and disappearing.

"Keep adding to the list, and eventually you'll find yourself, Clementine." Stephen hands back the notebook. "And if that doesn't work, turn on the telly and watch *Coronation Street*. It always makes me feel better to see I'm not the only person with problems. Tracy is always up to something."

"But I don't know where I belong," I say. "Have you ever felt like that?"

"Love, I'm Jewish and gay. In *Ireland*. Story of my life." Stephen touches my arm, as if he can hold me together. "Stick to the list," he says again.

I nod, mechanically.

"I can tell you one thing, Clementine. If you're going to be lost, there's no friendlier place to get lost in than Ireland."

When he's gone, I add another item to the list in my notebook.

I hate tattoos.

CHAPTER 2

After Stephen leaves, I spend some time folding the clothes on my bed until they are stacked in a neat pile. The containers of cotton swabs and tongue depressors are now all turned the same way and organized from biggest to smallest. The bed is made with tight corners, the scratchy top blanket smooth with no bumps.

I write down something else about myself.

I like to organize. How lame.

My gown is in the garbage can. I will only wear regular clothes from this moment forward. When I meet my dad, I won't be a disaster. But a word hangs in my head at this thought, like a weight pushing me further into the ground, attempting to knock me to my knees.

I am *meeting* my dad for the first time. His daughter survives a plane crash only to not recognize him. How utterly awful. I have no choice but to cling to one possibility—the doctor said there is always the potential that seeing him will jog my memory. Seeing my dad will end this nightmare. I believe this. What other choice do I have?

When my room is tidy, and there's nothing left for me to organize, I turn on the television and sit down on my neatly made bed. The "telly" as Stephen would say is perched in the corner of the room and pops with static as it comes on. I'm not sure what *Coronation Street* is, but focusing on someone else's problems right now sounds like a good distraction.

Waiting for my dad is like waiting for the future and the past all at the same time. A few moments of diversion don't sound too bad, but unfortunately, that plan dissolves as the television comes to life.

"Workers are still trying to clear debris from the fields around Ballycalla. Airplane parts are scattered in all directions. For now, the victims' families remain silent as they cope with this horrific event."

I sit forward, biting my nails. The remnants of a black and burned airplane litter an emerald-green field.

"Eighteen-year-old Clementine Haas is the lone survivor of the plane crash that devastated the small town of Ballycalla. She was taken to Mid-Western Regional Hospital, Limerick, two days ago."

The scene changes to a shot of the hospital.

"Authorities have now confirmed that she is awake and talking. We'll bring you more coverage as the details of this horrific accident and its only survivor unfold."

I turn off the television and run to the window. The hospital is surrounded by television crews. Reporters stand outside with microphones and coffee in their hands, and burly men and women with big cameras are just waiting for me to "shed some light on this horrific accident."

The room closes in around me. Stephen said the media was following the story, but as if being trapped by my mind isn't bad enough, I'm also literally trapped in the hospital. There is no way out of this nightmare.

I sink to the ground, curling my knees up to my chest, my body rocking back and forth uncontrollably. Blonde hair hangs over my shoulders, and the smell of its burned ends makes me nauseous.

I'm losing control. The items I've added to my list are pathetic. They don't add up to a life. What is the point of cheating death if a life doesn't exist when you wake up? I'm not strong enough for this.

I crawl across the room to my bedside and press the emergency bell repeatedly. I might press it until it breaks, which makes me feel good. Then I won't be the only broken thing in this room.

Stephen rushes in a second later, alarmed to find me in a huddled mess on the floor. He races to my side. "What is it? Are you hurt?"

I want to scream, but all I manage to whimper is, "I can't stop biting my nails. I mean, look at these fingers. They're mutilated. Not a speck of polish."

"Maybe you're not a manicure kind of girl?" he asks, confused.

"Do you know how infuriating it is to do something and have no idea why you do it?"

Stephen sits down next to me. "I can't begin to imagine."

"Don't." I point at him with my dismal fingers. "Don't give me that pathetic voice."

I may not know who I am, but I cannot be pathetic. Being pathetic is just so . . . *pathetic*. I'm too angry for that.

"And my hair," I say. "It doesn't matter how much you wash it, it smells like a bonfire. Look at the ends. They're sizzled."

"We can fix your hair." Stephen gets off the floor and pulls me up to meet him. The room spins beneath me as I grab his arms to steady myself.

"I can't breathe in this room, Stephen. I *need* to get out of here." He shakes his head, unsure, but I bring his attention back with a jolt. "Please. Help me."

His answer doesn't come promptly, but eventually Stephen's stiff stance melts some, and he exhales. "Fine. I'll help you with your hair. And then maybe, *maybe*, we can discuss leaving this room for a bit."

"As long as there's a chance, I'll take it."

Stephen retrieves a pair of surgical scissors. He pauses before snipping the ruined ends.

"Go ahead," I say firmly. "Cut it. I don't remember the girl with this haircut anyway."

He trims my hair, slowly with care. "Love, don't be so hard on yourself," he says. "Most people your age do stuff and have no idea why they're doing it. It's called being young."

"I don't feel young. I feel . . . lost."

He touches my cheek. "Well, at least you know *that*."

When he's done, he dusts hair from my back and sweeps it up from the floor. I refuse to sit down. My feet itch to move and leave this bland, sterile place.

"So . . . ," I say, eyeing the window. "*Please*."

But Stephen just shakes his head.

"The fresh air and sunshine might trigger something," I insist.

This seems to get Stephen's attention.

"You never know." I shrug.

Stephen thinks for a bit. "Well . . . maybe just a short trip to the courtyard. Five, ten minutes at most, then it's back to bed with you."

"I'll take whatever I can get."

"And you have to ride in a wheelchair."

I roll my eyes, but say, "Deal."

By the time we make it down to the hospital courtyard, it feels like a different world. The day is mild and sunny. The fine weather eases my anger, though my nerves tingle as Stephen wheels me toward an empty stone table. I scan all the people around us, worrying someone might recognize me.

"No one knows who you are," Stephen assures me. "They haven't released your picture to the media yet."

"What about my accent? I'm clearly American."

Stephen waves the thought away. "There are more Americans in Ireland in the summer than there are Irish. It's tourist season. I've seen four Americans today already. Mostly hangovers and sheep bites."

"Sheep bites?"

"They all want to pet the sheep." Stephen rolls his eyes. "You should be safe as long as you're on hospital grounds. The media can't get to you in here. They're not allowed inside." He adds, "I won't let anything happen to you."

I take a deep breath. Ireland smells like rain and sunshine blended together.

After some negotiating, Stephen agrees to rid us of the wheelchair—which only reminds me of how broken I feel—and situates us at a table in the sun.

"I'm sorry I lost it back there," I say.

"In truth, I'm surprised it took you so long."

The sky is crystal blue with only a few meandering clouds. People laugh and talk, their lives moving forward. Even the wind blows in a steady direction, but me . . .

"It's just . . ." Words are inadequate to explain how disorienting this feels—how the world is moving, but I'm stuck. And my head hurts. "Thank you."

Stephen turns his face up toward the sun. "Just don't go talking to any weird strangers."

"*Everyone* is a stranger."

"*Weird* strangers. People carrying cameras and notepads and stuff." Stephen settles back in his seat. "And trench coats. Flashers, CIA agents, and undercover reporters always wear trench coats. You don't want to run in to any of them."

When everyone in the world is a stranger, who am I supposed to trust? For all I know, anyone could lie to me. The calm that I'd begun to feel slowly disappears as I realize how unsafe my life is now.

When I'm silent for too long, Stephen grabs hold of my hand. "I told you. I won't let anything happen to you. I promise."

"But how can I trust *anyone?*"

Stephen gets a look of resolve on his face and says, "You lived through a plane crash. That speaks to how strong you are, whether or not you can remember exactly *who* you are. The past is the past, but *presently* you are a mighty creature. Write that down."

I write *I am a mighty creature* in my notebook, though I'm not sure I believe it.

Stephen nods. "So start acting like it. Shoulders back. Thirty-four C chest out."

I sit up straight for Stephen's sake, but it's hard not to look at the people in the courtyard suspiciously. I am a stranger to myself, and the world is a stranger to me.

"Tell me something good," I say to Stephen.

He seems surprised. "Like what?"

"Something good about all of this."

Stephen thinks for a second and then lights up. "You're a born-again virgin! You get to have sex for the first time all over again."

"I'm not sure that's such a good thing."

"Think of it this way. You get to have your first kiss again. And first love all over again." Stephen gets a dreamy expression on his face.

That hadn't occurred to me.

"Do you really think I've been in love before?" I say.

Stephen thinks for a long while, like he's trying to remember my life for me. His care is evident, which feels miraculous since we just met this morning. But when his face falls, for just a second, he looks at me like I'm a sad creature, not a mighty one. Even if I was in love in my past life, in this life I don't even recognize my own name. And the heart tattoo on my foot isn't a good sign.

"Never mind," I say and tap the notebook in my hand. "Keep adding to the list and eventually I'll find myself. Right?"

"Right," Stephen says with a weak grin. A chill rolls through the air as a cloud covers the sun. Stephen glances up at the sky. "Time's up. I need to take you back inside."

"Do you have to?"

"Unfortunately, yes."

"Just a few more minutes?" I plead.

Stephen chews on the idea before explaining that he *could* go see one of his other patients for just a few minutes if I promise not to go anywhere. "But you have to promise."

"I promise." I cross my heart.

Stephen leaves. I settle back in my chair, closing my eyes, the sun sinking into my skin. I'm tired of thinking. My mind rolls and turns and doesn't seem to lead me anywhere. I'll let the wind do the moving and spinning for now, instead of me.

It's unnerving how much control I want and how little I actually have. Living in a state of chaos only makes a person want to hold on tighter. It's been one day, and I'm exhausted. Imagining a lifetime of this—gripping at everything like it might save me, only to be disappointed—feels unfathomable.

"Do you mind if I sit here?" a voice says. My eyes open to find a guy standing in front of me with a tray of red and orange Jell-O. He has bright blue eyes, and his shaggy black hair pokes out from underneath his baseball cap. He's a stranger among all the other strangers, but he's talking to *me* when no one else is. He plops down in the seat across from me, casually opening a container of red Jell-O.

"What are you doing?" I ask. With my mind already jumbled, riddled with the unexpected, I really didn't expect *this*.

He looks at me with a quizzical face. "Eating."

"Why?"

He rests his forearms on the table, a spoon in his hand. "It's a requirement for survival."

Stephen told me to be wary of people in trench coats, but this guy isn't wearing one. With his ratty old hat—"Paudie's Pub, Waterville, Ireland"—blue Trinity College T-shirt, and faded jeans, he doesn't appear . . . media-like.

"But why are you sitting here?" I ask.

He glances at all the other *full* tables and points to an older, grumpy-looking man sitting alone across the yard. "It was between you or him. Quite honestly, you're better looking."

He opens another container of red Jell-O and starts eating. His presence at my table is slightly disturbing, but he seems more interested in the Jell-O than in me.

"Aren't you a little old for Jell-O?" I ask.

"I'm not that old. And here in Ireland, we call it Jelly. Just so you know."

"Well, how old are you?"

"How old are you?" he counters.

"Eighteen."

"Twenty," he says, eating a heaping spoonful. "I win."

"Are you a patient here or something?"

His focus is down as he eats, barely paying attention to me. "You know, it's an urban myth that this stuff is made out of horse hooves."

"Pardon?"

"It's the bones and hides of pigs and cows."

"I'm not sure that's any better." When he takes another helping into his mouth, I say, "But you're eating the Jell-O . . . Jelly . . . anyway."

He examines his half-eaten container. "You can't be afraid of what's inside. And it tastes good. That's a life lesson."

"What?"

"If something tastes good, don't ask what it's made of. You might be disappointed."

"But you know what it's made of," I say.

"Never been good at taking my own advice." He eats another full container of Jell-O, and I marvel as I watch him. Then he turns his attention to me. "So you're American."

I nod, noticing again how blue his eyes are. They practically shimmer.

"Tourist?" he asks.

I nod again.

"Well then, I should tell you that leprechauns aren't real, and you're more likely to get herpes than the gift of gab from kissing the Blarney Stone." He points at my chest. "Nice sweatshirt, by the way."

"This was a gift." I pull on the bottom.

"And you accepted it?"

I groan. "The grumpy old man looks lonely. Go bother him."

"Old people are depressing."

"That's not very nice."

"But it's the truth." He takes a huge bite and then holds out his hand to me. "I'm Kieran, by the way." His eyes are distracting and mesmerizing at the same time. I'm distracted in ogling their unnatural brightness. "And you are?"

"Pardon?"

"I told you my name. Now, you tell me yours."

That's a really good question, and it only sparks more. With no answer to offer, my single option is to keep quiet. I don't owe this random guy anything. Kieran seems to take my rejection in stride and goes back to eating.

"So you're not going to tell me your name," he says.

How can I claim to be a girl I don't know? And if Kieran knows my real name—the girl-miracle from the plane crash—I'm pathetic all over again. Right now this conversation, which is odd on many levels, feels good . . . and normal.

"No," I say. "I barely know you."

He leans closer, his body taking up the space between us and causing me to back away from him. When I do, a cocky, intrigued expression pulls at his face. "Well, if you won't tell me your name, answer this."

"Yes?" I try to sound confident.

Kieran's smile is as distracting as his eyes. "Truth or dare?"

A momentary pause settles. "What?" I ask, confused.

"Come on. You know the game. Pick one. You can tell a lot about a person by which one they choose."

"Really?" Now I'm intrigued.

Kieran eggs me on. "Choose wisely."

With no past to go on and no idea of what kind of person I was, I'm stuck for an answer, and it feels awful.

"Don't think about it. Just go with your gut," Kieran says.

"Dare," I say.

"Dare," Kieran repeats. "Interesting."

When his face lights up, so do I. The answer felt honest. For the first time, it's actually plausible that I will be myself again. That living without my memories *is* temporary. This won't last forever.

Kieran pushes the last container of orange Jell-O across the table. "I dare you to eat the bones and hides of pigs and cows."

A laugh escapes my lips for the first time since I woke up in a strange room in a foreign place. Kieran rests on his elbows, waiting to see if I'll take the dare. I eye the Jell-O. How can something orange and fruity be made of cow and pig parts?

"Dare accepted." I grab a spoon and dig it into the Jell-O. Kieran sits back, a satisfied expression on his face, as I hold the spoon inches from my mouth.

But a split second before I can eat it, Stephen walks across the courtyard with another damn wheelchair. The spoon drops from my hand, and I stand.

"I have to go."

"What about the dare?" Kieran asks, but I'm back to where I started, with no answer to offer. I wish I had one. "Now you have to tell me your name. It's only right."

My name? Kieran doesn't realize that I don't know what I'm made of. The list in my notebook, presently, is small, less than one full page.

On the outside, I'm orange and fruity, but maybe on the inside I'm pig and cow parts.

It's not a lie if you don't know the truth, right? Clementine Haas doesn't exist. She died in a plane crash. I woke up in her body, and until I remember who she is, what she's made of, I can't claim her life. Instead, I go with my gut.

"Jane. My name is Jane."

CHAPTER 3

"You were right. The fresh air did you well," Stephen says as he wheels me down the hallway. "You're looking better. Lovely, really."

"I feel better," I say, though I'm still slightly disappointed that I failed at completing my dare. Being outside felt good—the sunshine, the grass, the normal conversation without a roomful of people gawking at me and waiting for something to happen. Waiting is awful.

But the clean hospital smell overshadows the freshness from outside, like a blanket of reality settling down on me again. The thought of sitting in my room and waiting for my dad to show up sounds miserable. I can't lie in that bed anymore. How am I supposed to add to my list if I'm stuck there?

"Can we go back outside just for a little longer?" I say.

"No," Stephen answers matter-of-factly. "You made a deal with me. Let's not push it. Your dad should be here soon. There are . . . decisions to be made."

"Like what?"

"Let's just get you to your dad, and we'll go from there."

Just as Stephen says "your dad," we round the hallway corner. At this point, I should expect the unexpected at every turn. This is the path of my life right now—twisting, turning, utterly unpredictable—and yet it still seems to surprise me.

My blood drops to my feet and paralyzes me in the chair. This is what I've been waiting for. My life depends on *this*.

Paul Haas from Cleveland, Ohio, stands in the hallway just outside of my room, talking to my doctor. I know it's my dad, like I know I'm in a hospital. By clues. Nurses. Doctors. Machines. Rooms filled with people hooked up to those machines. Uncomfortable gowns that open in back. All clues.

Paul is dressed in a Cleveland Indians T-shirt. That's my first clue. He appears tired, like a person who's been awake for a few days straight. Second clue. He's also listening to my doctor as he shakes his head and . . . bites his nails.

I glance down at my pathetic, nibbled nails.

"Stop," I say to Stephen. It's all I can manage to say.

Stephen brings me to a halt. My dad is here to save me, to bring me back to *my* life. I was sure I'd see him, and it would all come back to me—all the memories that make up who I am. I was sure that I would see him and *love* him.

Instead . . . I feel nothing.

Nothing.

When a girl sees her dad, she should be filled with emotion, right? She should feel a connection, because her blood is made of half of his blood, and nothing can ever change that. It's palpable, like a heartbeat. Or I think it should be, though I don't know for sure.

But as I sit in my wheelchair, I'm empty. Utterly empty. The only thing between us is space. Nothing connects me to him. I know it's my father based on the clues, but that's all. The clues don't fit together to make memories.

When he sees me, he'll know it. He'll see it on my face, just like the doctors did. He'll see that I don't love him like I must have before. He'll see that I'm vacant. He'll want a connection I can't give him. He'll want it so badly, and then I'll break his heart. I can practically see him holding himself together as he tries to process all of this. I'll shatter him again. How can I do that after everything he's been through?

"Bathroom," I say to Stephen as I stand up from the wheelchair.

"What?"

"I need to go to the bathroom."

"Clementine, I think I see your dad."

I give him a glare. "That's why I want to go to the bathroom. I just need a moment to . . . put myself together."

Stephen eyes me suspiciously.

"Please. I don't want him to see me a mess. I'll just be a few minutes."

"Are you sure everything's OK?"

"I'm fine." I can barely get the words out.

Stephen's brown hair curls around his ears, and the crinkles around his eyes are soft. I don't know anything about him. How old is he? Does he have a family? A lover? Children he cares for more than anything? But I don't have the luxury of time to get the answers. I'll have to remember him just like this—kind and helpful.

"I think you're lovely, Stephen."

"You're just trying to butter me up."

"No," I say fervently. "You're lovely."

He relents at my compliment. I didn't mean it as a manipulation, but it works that way nonetheless. "A few minutes," he says. "Then it's back to your room. Deal?"

When we shake on our deal, I wish I could be the person Stephen sees. A mighty creature. A strong person. That girl wouldn't do what I'm about to do. She would walk down the hallway and meet this challenge with bravery and confidence.

I am not her.

"Take it slowly," Stephen says. I walk toward the bathroom without a hug or a look back. I just made a deal with the person who's helped me the most, knowing I would break it. If I turn, I might falter.

My composure cracks when I'm safely tucked in a stall in the bathroom. Everything shifts, my real need coming into focus, like a caged bird that knows it doesn't want to live behind bars anymore.

I need to get out of here.

How can I see my dad and not *love* him? What is wrong with me? Everything I thought would happen hasn't.

I press my sweaty head against the cool stall door. I wish I could be who Stephen wants me to be, a fearless girl willing to fight through this. More importantly, I wish I could be who my dad wants me to be. Clementine Haas. But I can't. To go home with him like this would mean that every day he'll wake up and want Clementine there, and instead every day it will be me—whoever I am. We'll both live in a constant state of disappointment.

I can save him from that.

I come out of the stall, focusing on myself in the mirror.

"Jane," I say to my reflection. "I'm Jane."

Stephen surely won't help me get out of here. He wants to keep me safe in the hospital, which is still surrounded by camera crews and reporters. But there's another way.

The hallway is clear of my dad and Stephen when I poke my head out from the bathroom. My heart races as I walk swiftly away from my room and toward the staircase at the other end of the hall. Once the door closes behind me, and I'm safely tucked out of sight in the stairwell, a moment of relief comes, but it's brief.

The railing keeps me steady as I make my way down the steps and onto the first floor. My legs are weak, slow, but it's not an option to stop at this point. Stop and I get caught. Move and I might find freedom.

In the courtyard, Kieran sits at the table where I left him, his feet up on the bench, a book in his hands. I check out the cover. It's clearly a romance novel.

"You like romance novels, too," I say. "We have something in common. Though I wouldn't peg you as a romantic."

"I'm full of surprises." He squints in the sunlight. "I've never understood why guys go for fast cars and guns when these books have fast women and sex."

"Honesty again. That's a good thing."

Kieran dog-ears the page he's on and closes the book, setting it down on the table. "You ran away from the dare."

"I didn't run away." I take back my seat. "I had to do something."

"What was that?"

"It doesn't matter. I'm ready now."

"Are you sure, Jane?"

Kieran is just full of good questions, but debating the answer with myself would take too much time.

"Jane Middleton," I say, holding out my hand. "That's my last name."

"Very royal sounding." He places his warm hand in mine and says, "Kieran O'Connell. It's nice to meet you."

"Very Irish sounding, Kieran O'Connell."

"Half-Irish, on my mother's side."

"And your dad?" I ask.

"Technically, he's British, but he's more asshole than anything."

"Honesty again." I reach for the last container of Jell-O on his tray. "I'm ready for my dare. Spoon, please."

Kieran holds one up but doesn't hand it over. "Are you sure you want to do this, Jane? It's pig and cow parts."

This is so much more than Jell-O. This is my life he's holding in front of me.

"Where's Waterville?" I ask, pointing to his hat.

"South of here a few hours."

"Is it by Cork?" I ask, remembering the map and trying to sound like I know a thing or two.

"Not exactly. A bit more west."

"Is that where you live?"

"For the summer months."

I point to his T-shirt. "Then you go back to Trinity College?"

"Yep."

"And where is that?"

"It's in Dublin." Kieran looks at me oddly. "Have you not heard of Trinity College?"

"Of course, I have. I just forgot for a second. It's in Dublin. Right."

"What about you?" he asks. "Are you on break from college as well?"

The question throws me. I have no idea if Clementine is in college. But I'm also not sure it matters. The part of me that keeps searching for Clementine needs a break. Jane can be whoever she wants. "Yeah, sure," I say.

"What are you studying?"

"Undecided," I say quickly. "You?"

Kieran rolls his eyes. "Business."

"You don't sound happy about that."

"Not everything in life can be happy, Jane."

The spoon rests in Kieran's hand. No, sometimes life beats you down. Sometimes life deserts you, and your only choice is to find another path. "Are you going to give me that spoon or what?"

"You know, you don't have to do this," he says. His blue eyes hold mine. He knows this is more than just Jell-O, too. That's what a dare does. It taunts you to take a different direction, to do something you never thought you could do, to jump, knowing that a million consequences could be on the other side of that dare, but that if you don't do it, you'll always wonder. And sometimes wondering is worse than consequences.

"I'm doing it," I say. And I shovel a spoonful of pig and cow parts into my mouth.

Kieran sits back, a broad grin growing on his face. When I've eaten the container clean, he claps.

"I wasn't sure you had it in you."

I have to choke down the last bits of Jell-O, then I put my empty container on the tray with his, only partly satisfied.

"Why are you here?" I ask. "It can't possibly be for pig and cow parts."

"I come up to volunteer. Help out my fellow man and all. The food is just an added bonus."

"That's nice of you."

"People need help," Kieran says coolly. "It's the least I can do."

"People *do* need help," I agree. "And now it's my turn."

"For what?"

"Truth or dare?" I say.

A glimmer comes to Kieran's eyes. "That's my line of questioning."

"It's not fair that I answer the question and you don't."

"Life isn't fair, Jane. It's all Jell-O, remember."

I lean across the table. "Are you chicken or something?"

My confidence is surprising. Kieran seems to bring out something natural in me, or maybe he brings out more faith that the girl I was is still with me, just waiting to come out. Our eyes are fixed on each other's. Kieran crosses his arms over his chest.

The clucking starts first. Then I start to flap my arms like chicken wings. Kieran glances around at all the other tables, and then he starts to laugh.

"OK. OK." He holds up his hands in surrender.

But as soon as the clucking stops, someone drops an entire tray of dishes onto the concrete sidewalk. They break with a loud crash. I startle, freezing in my seat. It chokes the breath right out of me. A head rush comes on so suddenly that I'm worried I'll faint right in front of him. Blood sinks to my feet. My hands go clammy. I start to sweat.

"Are you OK, Jane?"

Kieran talks, but I can't see him. My head rests in my hands. Sound reverberates through me, and an intense pain creeps up behind my eyes. For a second, I swear I feel someone grab my hand. I expect to see fingers intertwined with mine, but they're gone, and I'm left with a horrible empty feeling inside my chest.

"Are you OK?" Kieran asks again.

"I'm fine." If I faint, this is over. With ragged breath and shaking hands that he can't see under the table, I say, "Truth or dare, Kieran?"

"We don't have to do this."

"Truth or dare?" I say again more forcefully.

Kieran shakes his head. "It's a Catch-22. Neither is easy. They both have consequences."

"Do I have to start clucking again?"

He pauses for too long, and then he says, "Fine. Dare."

The blood returns to my hands and head. The sweat dries on my forehead. This time, my voice doesn't shake as I speak.

"I dare you to get me the hell out of here."

CHAPTER 4

Pressure can make a truthful person into a liar, though I'm not sure whether I'm either. The line between truth and lies blurred the instant I woke up in the hospital.

I make sure to sound convincing as I tell Kieran that I was traveling alone in Ireland for the summer when I got mugged and robbed in Limerick.

"They knocked me around and took everything—my purse, my bag. My dignity."

"You do scream 'tourist' in that sweatshirt."

"I told you it was a gift."

He assesses me from head to toe. I can't tell if there's sympathy in his eyes or skepticism. My story gets more complicated from here, but I stick to it—a woman saw the mugging. She made me come to the hospital to make sure I didn't have a concussion.

"Which I don't," I emphasize, knowing that if Kieran thinks something is wrong with me, he's bound to say no. "But now, I have nothing." This little nugget of honesty pushes me forward, a reminder of how much I need this.

I tell him that I couldn't give my insurance information because I'm on my parents' plan, and they'd know something happened to me. It would cause them to totally freak out (this part isn't so much of a lie, either). Now I owe the hospital money, but since all mine was stolen, I can't pay.

"But I will," I ensure him. "As soon as I figure out how exactly."

"Are you asking me to pay your bill because—"

"No," I say emphatically. "I need something else."

Kieran takes in all that I've said. My story is strange, but the parts seem to fit together.

"Why come to Ireland?" Another good question that lacks a good response.

"Does it really matter why I came here? I did. And now I'm stuck."

"Why not just call your parents?"

"Because I can't," I blurt out. "This trip was supposed to prove to them that I can make it on my own. I didn't do so well my first year of college, and they're threatening to make me move home. I can't fail. My freedom depends on this trip." The lies trip off my tongue. "I thought Limerick was a safe bet. It's supposed to be the friendliest city in Ireland. I figured it was the safest place."

"And then you got mugged."

"Well, you guys are lying about leprechauns."

Kieran holds up his hands in defense. "Now don't go judging the whole of the country on some arse."

"All I need is a few weeks and a place to stay," I say. "To get myself together."

"Is that all?" he mocks.

"In the grand scheme of things, it's nothing. I'll stay out of your way. I'll practically be invisible."

"Who says I have a place you can stay?"

"You must know of *some* place," I plead.

Kieran sits tight lipped. Uncertainty creeps up on me. I can't let my mind drift from my goal. That won't help me. I *need* Kieran.

He finally speaks. "Call your parents. It's the sensible thing to do."

"This coming from the guy who dared me to eat pig and cow parts."

"I never said *I* was sensible."

"Look." I keep my eyes locked on Kieran, pretending I have the energy for this, though I'm losing steam. "I *need* to do this. My life depends on it. It's just a few weeks, maybe less. You said you came here today to help people. I'm people."

Forget the luxury of truth. Forget the deceit of lies. This is survival. Without this, I'm lost beyond words. Floundering. Falling.

I reach across the table and grab his hands. Kieran can keep me steady. He can keep me from crashing.

"Please." I can't keep eye contact for fear I'll be disappointed. I wish I could do this on my own, but I can't. "Please. From one human being to another. Please help me."

The silence between us lasts so long that if I wasn't holding Kieran's hands, I'd wonder if he was still sitting across from me.

Finally, I hear him say, "You're asking me to take you in for a few weeks, so your parents won't think you're a failure."

I peek out of one eye. "Technically, I'm daring you."

He shakes his head, mumbles something to himself that I can't hear, and says, "I *might* know of a place you can stay." I perk up, and we both realize simultaneously that I'm still holding his hands. He pulls away. "I have an extra room. But *only* for a few weeks."

I exhale for what feels like the first time in minutes. "I'll take anything."

He stands up, leaving the book on the table. "Let's go."

"You're not going to take it with you?" I ask.

"I have a feeling my life will be entertaining enough for a while." He shakes his head and then readjusts his hat. "You're gonna get me in trouble, Jane Middleton."

"You look like someone who isn't afraid of a little mischief, Kieran O'Connell."

He holds out his hand for me to shake, his eyes twinkling in the sunlight. "Consider this dare accepted."

CHAPTER 5

The thing with amnesia is that waking up in a strange place isn't actually strange. Doing it a second time should be less scary.

As it turns out, getting out of the hospital is easier than I expected. We just walk out, past a slew of camera crews and reporters drinking coffee and chatting, some in trench coats like Stephen said. With my eyes on the ground, I act calmly and walk casually. Moments later, we're at Kieran's old, beat-up truck.

I let myself take one more glance at the hospital.

"Are you getting in?" Kieran asks.

No more pausing. The goal now is to move forward. When this is all over, I'll make everyone understand why I did it, but I can't worry about that now. I'll make them see my side of the story—that I didn't want to pull them down with me. I didn't want to hurt anyone with my pain.

When the truck door closes, Jane Middleton sits in the passenger seat. My only reminder of Clementine is the tattoo on my foot. That's the unfortunate reality with tattoos—they follow you everywhere.

Much of the trip to Waterville is a blur of green patchwork countryside and winding roads. Kieran's truck is so old, the radio comes through as static half the time. There's no air conditioning, and the steering wheel is on the right instead of the left, which feels odd, even though I don't ever recall driving on the other side of the car or road.

The truck grumbles a weird noise. "Are you sure this thing is going to make it?" I ask.

"She hasn't let me down yet," Kieran says, and runs his hands lovingly over the steering wheel.

The road is twisty, and Kieran dodges gigantic tour buses, nearly hitting his side-view mirror on the hedges that line the road.

"The Ring of Kerry," he says. "You can't avoid it."

"Sure." A woozy feeling hits me as we go around another tight turn. "Of course."

The Ring of Kerry is a mystery to me. It wasn't on Stephen's map. For all I know, it's an actual ring worn by someone named Kerry. Kieran tells me he's spending the summer at his family's cottage, away from Dublin and school. When I ask about his parents—I forgot to ask about them when I devised this plan—Kieran tells me they aren't a factor.

"A factor?"

"My father won't come near the place this summer."

"And your mom?"

"Neither will she." He shifts the conversation in a different direction. "Waterville isn't a big city like Limerick, but your chances of getting mugged are slim." He smirks. "Where are you from in America anyway?"

"Cleveland," I say, with false confidence. "It's in Ohio. On Lake Erie."

"Lake Erie?"

I change the subject. "Look, sheep!"

After hours in the car, battling traffic and roads too narrow for two cars to pass each other safely, we reach Waterville. I'm exhausted.

"It's all just so green, Kieran O'Connell," I say as we pull into the town.

"Well, Ireland is kind of known for that."

"And the ocean." I rest my forehead on the window. The sun is setting, glistening off the water in iridescent colors. It's mesmerizing and beautiful and vast.

"We *are* on an island." Kieran teases.

"With sheep. Lots of sheep."

He pulls up a driveway to a large beige stucco house with white shutters, a sprawling, finely manicured lawn, and a large patio overlooking the ocean. Colorful flowers bloom everywhere.

"This is where you live? I thought you said it was a cottage?"

"It is," he says. "It's a really big cottage."

"But you drive this." I touch the beat-up truck's interior.

"The outside doesn't always match the inside." Kieran shrugs. "Always remember the Jell-O, Jane."

"Your insides are made of money."

"No," Kieran says with a laugh. "My *dad's* insides are made of money. And not much else."

"Well . . . what are your insides made of?"

Kieran comes around to open my door. "You're tired. You've clearly been through an ordeal. Let's get you set up inside."

"An ordeal. That sounds about right."

Kieran takes me inside and back to an empty bedroom. My mind tries to take in my surroundings—the living room and kitchen and all the fine decorations—but Kieran is right. I am more tired than I want to admit.

The bed in the spare room appears soft, with fine white sheets. When I sit down, it's like resting on a cloud.

"It's just the jet lag that's making me tired. That's all. And the mugging." I take off my shoes and settle back. "I promise I won't stay long. A week, maybe two. You won't even know I'm here."

Kieran draws the curtains closed.

I yawn, closing my eyes. "You're my spare tire, Kieran."

"What was that?"

Words come from somewhere deep in my brain, somewhere I haven't been able to reach all day, except for a few moments. "You always need a spare tire in Cleveland. For the pot holes of life."

Those are the last words I remember before sleep takes over.

~

When I wake up the next day, peeling my head off the plush pillow, light pours through the small crack between the curtains. I check the clock. It's past one in the afternoon.

My surroundings are still foreign to me. But the burden I felt yesterday has eased. I may not recognize this place, but it *feels* better than where I was. And I've accumulated one day's worth of memories. That's better than nothing.

My brain knocks against my skull when I sit up, still fully dressed, and check for Kieran. The house sounds and feels empty. My suspicion is confirmed when I get up and holler down the hallway, and no one responds.

The reality of what I've done hits me again. I ran away with a stranger to Waterville, Ireland, and I have no way of leaving. The weight of it is paralyzing. But the thought of going back . . . That's worse.

I owe Kieran my life. *Jane's* life.

It must be possible to push through the immensity of all of this toward freedom. I can't worry about what I left behind. When Clementine is back, we can all move on from this disaster, my time hiding in Waterville a blip.

A note sits on the bedside table, addressed to me, a stack of money next to it.

> *Gone for the day. Here's a little help for someone who's broke.*
> *Kieran*

He's left one hundred euros. Not only did Kieran get me out of the hospital, he's now left me money. Somehow in all of this, he's become a positive piece in this swarming mess. And what am I doing for him? Lying. About everything. And using him. Pretending to be yummy orange Jell-O when I'm really pig and cow parts. If I were more confident and capable, I would come clean before it goes too far. Even from the little I know about Kieran, he deserves that.

But at any moment, my life can turn upside down. I'm as inconstant as the wind, wholly unsteady. If I told the truth, he would send me back where people want to control me, and I can't go there yet.

I make it my mission to find a way to repay Kieran for all of this, before my lies destroy everything.

The cottage is one story, with fine furnishings, but quaint. It's large and smells like the ocean and burned wood. Windows line every room, exposing a stunning view of the water across the street. The living room has a large stone fireplace and wooden beams. A grand bay window overlooks the rocky beach that leads down to the sea. The view showcases large emerald-green hills, some steep with stone walls that make the land seem like a patchwork quilt. It's spectacular.

Four bedrooms are tucked at the back of the house. I snoop in the first and find a king-size bed with sheets that appear untouched. A few items hang in the closet—sweaters, jackets—all men's clothes. The taste is older and refined.

The next bedroom is slightly smaller. A mirror hangs on the wall, and magazines are scattered all over the desk—*Punk, Nylon, Dazed, Bazaar*. High-heel shoes are strewn all over the floor—peekaboo-style, T-strap, pointed toe, platform. And on the dresser are glass jars full of multicolored sea glass. The sun hits the containers through the window and reflects the colors on the wall.

In the attached bathroom, the mess gets worse. Toothpaste is caked in the sink. Towels cover the floor. The cabinet has a few packages of unopened toothpaste and toothbrushes and multiple boxes of hair dye in extravagant colors with names like "Magnetic Magenta," "Vibrant Violet," and "Lusty Lavender." Kieran never mentioned a roommate, and when I asked about his parents, he clearly didn't want to talk about them. I leave the bedroom, deciding it's probably better not to linger.

The kitchen is as messy as the bathroom. Used tea bags sit, staining the sink, and the counter is littered with crumbs and used plates and glasses. I realize the first chore I can do to help Kieran. This house needs to be cleaned.

The door to the last bedroom is closed. I casually push it open and turn on the lights. This room is relatively neat. The bed is made, and a pile of folded clothes is stacked on the dresser. A surfboard leans against the wall, and pictures are everywhere. There's a shot of two people dressed in full hiking gear, standing at the top of a snowy mountain with an Irish flag. A picture of someone skydiving, another of a person skiing, white powder flying up around his body.

Yet another sits framed on the dresser: a group of six boys, all dressed in school uniforms—blue sweaters, white button-downs, blue ties, dark slacks—huddled and laughing in front of a sign that says "Blackrock Preparatory School for Boys." I spot Kieran immediately. With his blue eyes, he's easy to find in the center of the picture. Judging by the mischievous expressions on the boys around him, Kieran isn't the only daredevil of the bunch.

My stomach turns sour as I set the frame down. This is Kieran's bedroom, his life displayed in pictures. His memories. Here I stand in an empty house, surrounded by other people's lives. And yet, I'm empty. It's numbing. But what did I expect when I left the hospital? I've known from the beginning I had to do this alone. Stephen couldn't help. My dad couldn't help. Even Kieran. He's given me moments when a life of some sort feels within my grasp, but even that hope is fleeting.

I'm alone and I deserve it, because I made it so. But I'm starting to think maybe I don't like being alone.

To ignore the numbness, I clean. Between the disorganized bedroom, the messy bathrooms, and the unkempt kitchen, there's a lot to occupy my time and distract me. And when the cottage is clean, I turn to myself. My teeth need brushing. My clothes are a day old, *and* I slept in them. I need an overhaul as badly as the cottage did.

After a sandwich of bread and Nutella, two of the only ingredients in the house, and a cup of tea, I sit with my notebook in front of me and write out a to-do list for my new life.

1. *Figure out what the Ring of Kerry is.*
2. *Buy some clothes and underwear.*
3. *Get groceries.*

It's painfully short, and the longer I sit alone in the kitchen, the more the paralyzing apathy threatens to come back. Kieran's old baseball hat sits on the kitchen counter. I grab it before I leave. It's a way to stay somewhat hidden in public, which I'll gladly take over being inside. I'm unwilling to stay still anymore.

Outside, the humid sea air comes off the ocean. It washes over me, the smell of salt water and fresh air a relief, the sensation similar to yesterday when Stephen took me outside for the first time. I feel more . . . capable.

The road is lined with hedgerows and stone walls on one side and the ocean on the other. Kieran mentioned during our drive that there's only one road into town. He went so far as to claim that I couldn't get lost if I tried. He doesn't know how wrong he is.

The green hedgerows are speckled with bright red flowers. Puddles glisten in the sunlight. The smell of earlier rain hangs in the air. Low, puffy clouds sit heavy in the sky, and the brisk wind feels good on my skin.

I cross the street to walk along the ocean. The beach is rocky, and the water is more murky than clear, like the bottom of the sea has been tossed around and brought up to the surface. Out in the bay, there are large, green rocky islands that look almost angry, with jagged edges and rough terrain. I sit on the sand, prepared to take my shoes off and feel how cold the water is, but instinct stops me.

My tattoo.

I'm not sure what's more frustrating: not wanting to see it, or not knowing why I hate it. My shoes stay on. I walk the beach, feeling the opposite of the mighty creature Stephen claimed I am. A tattoo shouldn't knock someone over, and yet mine attempts to repeatedly.

The small town of Waterville is decorated with multicolored houses and buildings—red, yellow, green, blue, pink. Tourists walk the streets, people carry grocery bags, moms and dads play with their kids.

For a while, I sit on a bench and watch the tourists in tennis shoes with rain jackets tied around their waists and cameras in their hands— all ready to casually capture the next memory, with no regard to how special that is. Each moment passes without much notice from anyone—a laugh, a kiss, a hug—each so easily etched in his or her mind. Not so easy for me. I have to fight for mine, which feels unfair.

With my notebook in hand, I leave the beach behind and head into town, checking out the shops and pubs. Each storefront is painted a different color, and signs out front advertise different specials.

FISH AND CHIPS €5

NO BUS OR COACH PARKING AND NO LOUD AMERICANS

LIVE MUSIC NIGHTLY

At the corner, a street sign points in multiple directions to cities and their distances.

TRALEE 73 KM

KILLARNEY 62 KM

CORK 120 KM

KILGARVAN 71 KM

Limerick isn't even listed, which makes me wonder: *Can I ever go back after what I've done? Is that even possible? It has to be. I can't allow an alternative.*

In the clothing store, most of the items are made of wool—wool hats, wool sweaters, wool skirts. Celtic crosses in all sizes hang on the wall for sale, and the music playing in the store is a mellow and bittersweet tune, all fiddle and fluttering flute. I browse alongside a handful of camera-toting tourists.

A woman with short brown hair and a friendly demeanor approaches me and asks in a thick accent, slightly different from Kieran's, "Can I help you, love?"

"That would be lovely," I say, thinking of Stephen for just a second before I push the thought away. "I'm looking for some shirts and pants."

"Do you have a specific style you're looking for?"

"A style?"

"What kind of clothes do you like?"

I should know this, and yet, as with everything else, my mind is a vast wasteland of nothing.

"Let's just go with plain." I can't keep the resignation out of my voice when I say it.

The woman shows me the white T-shirts, then the jeans. I mention that I also need underwear, and she shows me to the back of the shop.

"I don't have the stuff young people wear," she says, holding up a pack of granny panties, "but God likes you better in these."

I take them, content with anything. "Socks?"

She rings up my items, making conversation by asking if I'm just in town visiting. I nod, handing her money.

"Have you been in before?" She squints at me as she gives me my change. "You look familiar."

I shake my head. "It's my first time in Ireland." The first time I remember at least.

She shrugs and hands me the bag. "You have a wonderful day now. The sun is out. It won't be like this forever. The rain always comes. Enjoy it while you can." She winks.

Her reminder shifts my mood almost instantly. The sun is out. I should be happy I'm here. This is what I wanted. To stay in Limerick meant being trapped. No matter where I am, I can't allow myself to fall so far down into my own hole that I can't get out.

"Thank you. I will," I say with a determined voice. "Can you point me in the direction of a grocery store?"

Her directions lead me to the center of town and the Centra Market. The aisles of organized food are strangely comforting, adding to my improved mood. I feel more capable in here than I did in the clothing store, which feels notable, so I write in my notebook, *I like food more than clothes.*

There's a sense of freedom in taking my time, picking out items for Kieran's kitchen. Knowing that I'm being helpful on some level, my confidence swells.

With flour, eggs, sugar, milk, butter, chocolate, bread, cheese, fruits, and vegetables in my cart, I check out.

A book is on display at the register, *A Rough Guide to Ireland's Riches*, which completes my purchases for the day. There must be information on the Ring of Kerry in here. A sense of pride fills me. I've accomplished multiple chores today.

"Is that all for you, love?" the woman behind the counter asks. People are so nice in Ireland. Even her face is kind, covered in wrinkles that make her look like a sweet Irish grandma. I smile. Maybe I'm not as lost as I thought. Maybe Stephen is right—if you're going to get lost, Ireland is the place to do it.

"Yes." I say it with confidence. All I needed was a little freedom to get myself together. I went with my gut, and it's working. My memories are bound to come back quicker this way.

The woman behind the counter examines me after I've paid.

"Did I give you enough?" I ask, and then whisper, "I'm from America."

But she just keeps looking at me as she puts my food in a bag.

"America? Have you been here before?"

"No . . . Why?"

"You just look so familiar," she says, her eyes searching my face.

The woman in the clothing store said the same thing. I pull down on Kieran's hat, shielding my face some. I sense the clouds coming on.

"I swear I know you," the woman says. She dings the cash register loudly, the noise startling me.

"The captain has asked that you remain in your seats."

A flashback of the burned and crumpled plane I saw on TV pops in my head.

"Eighteen-year-old Clementine Haas is the lone survivor of the plane crash that devastated the small town of Ballycalla."

I step back from the counter. No one knows me in Ireland, and yet two people think they do. Stephen said my picture wasn't released to the public, but something is definitely off. A buzzing starts in my ears—like an engine. The woman behind the counter stares.

"Thank you." I grab my groceries and head speedily for the door, but my progress is halted when I come face-to-face with . . . myself.

Irish tabloids are lined up on the newspaper stand in the corner of the store—the *Irish Mirror*, the *Irish Daily Star*, and *The Irish Sun*.

My face is on the front page of each of them.

I gape at the pictures in disbelief, like the girl on the covers might start talking, telling me about myself. It's like gazing into a distorted mirror, the image clear and yet at the same time different than me.

Lone Survivor Escapes Hospital, Whereabouts Unknown

My finger touches one of the front pages, where my skin looks rosy, healthy. Then my hand reaches for my real face, and all I feel is a hollow cheek. I can't believe that girl is actually me. She's grinning, with long brown hair that's curled in loose waves draped carefully over her shoulder. My dirty, haphazardly cut hair is a sharp contrast to the silkiness of the hair in the picture. The color doesn't even match, though I have no memory of why or when I decided to go blonde.

The girl in the picture wears precise makeup, lips a bright red, mascara accentuating her eyes. She appears younger than me, less . . . damaged. Looking at her, I'm intrigued about her life, interested in what the article says about her. I almost pick up the paper to read it.

But she's just another person on the cover of a newspaper. She's not . . . me.

I practically stumble onto the street. My legs move fast as I retrace my path back to Kieran's cottage. *One road. It's impossible to get lost.* But Clementine is lost.

And now the whole of Ireland knows I went missing.

Clouds have rolled in, and the rain is coming, like the woman at the clothing store said. I fix my eyes on the ground, my face shadowed by Kieran's hat, until I'm back at the cottage.

No one is home. Where is Kieran? Possible scenarios play vividly in my mind. What if he's seen the papers? What if he recognized me and already called the authorities? He isn't here because he's in Limerick turning me in. My lies will be my downfall, and yet I knew this would happen.

At least no one is here to see me crumble. I sink into a chair in the kitchen, the weight of it all too heavy to hold, wishing I had an emergency button I could press so that Stephen would come running. He must have been so angry when I didn't come back. So scared. I broke my promise to him. I betrayed him.

And my dad . . . I did this to spare him pain, but the truth is that whatever I do will be painful for him.

My head rests in my hands, my hair falling around my face. The right decision is to go back to Limerick and end this. A good daughter would do that. A loving daughter. An honest person. But I can't erase the lies I've already told. And I don't know yet what kind of person I am.

I find a pair of scissors in a kitchen drawer and head straight to the bathroom. In the mirror, Clementine Haas reflects back at me. I pause, only for a moment. I don't know the kind of person I am, but I know I can't go back yet. Escaping the hospital wasn't enough. I need to escape Clementine, too.

After the first snip, there's no going back. I cut my hair short, to my chin, with jagged edges and blunt bangs across my forehead. Blonde hair falls in clumps on the ground. In the bathroom cabinet, a rainbow of color options is available. "Lusty Lavender" seems like a good color for my skin. The dye is cold on my head as I apply thick layers of color, the pungent smell tingling my nose.

When my transformation is complete, one of Kieran's white towels is soaked in purple dye. The girl in the mirror, with short lavender hair, is no longer Clementine Haas. No vague remnants of the person on the covers of the tabloids, other than my brown eyes.

I shower, my fingers running clumsily through my hair, purple dye swirling at my feet. As good as the hot water feels, l can't linger. My new clothes fit well, and once I'm done cleaning the mess in the bathroom, I throw a load of laundry into the washing machine. Moving is good. Thinking is the enemy.

I pick through the groceries on the counter, methodically moving around the kitchen. I turn the oven on and fill a bowl with butter, vanilla, and eggs. In another I mix dry ingredients—flour, baking powder, salt, sugar.

"And a dash of love," I say to myself, the words coming from somewhere unreachable. "It holds everything together." I'm not sure why baking cookies feels like the right thing to do momentarily, but putting the ingredients together, making something from nothing, seems right.

As the cookies bake, I read the book I bought. If my charade is going to work, knowledge is key. Jane would know a few facts about this place.

> The Ring of Kerry is the scenic route around the Iveragh Peninsula in southwestern Ireland. It boasts the best and most amazing pastoral and coastal views in all Ireland.

So it's not an actual ring.

> The most popular area is the Dingle Peninsula with the finest traditional Irish music in the country and where many of the locals still speak Irish.
> Killarney has impressive lakes and mountains.
> In Cork, it's popular to drink Murphy's Irish Stout instead of the more popular Guinness brewed in Dublin.

The oven buzzes—the cottage filled now with sugary smells. I set the cookies to cool and switch the laundry from the washer to the dryer. All the moving is working. My nerves have calmed. I might just avoid disaster.

Then I hear the front door open. I freeze next to the dryer. Steps echo through the house, getting closer and closer to the kitchen. I take a deep breath, ready to face Kieran for the first time today and deal with the consequences.

I step out from the laundry room into the kitchen.

But it's not Kieran.

"For the love of God, please tell me he didn't dare you to do that to your hair."

A gorgeous girl stands in the kitchen. Her long hair is hot pink. She's dressed in a tight black dress with red polka-dot tights. Her arms are covered in tattoos—tattoos she probably loves. But the thing I notice most . . .

She's pregnant.

CHAPTER 6

It's a stare-off. My mind spins for the right words to say to this stranger. After a moment of silence, she groans, setting her purse down on the counter with a thud. Then she picks up a fresh cookie from the plate and turns it around like it might be poison.

"Did you bake?" she asks.

"Yes," I say in a weak voice.

"Who the hell are you? Betty Crocker?"

"No . . . I'm Jane." I extend my hand, but she doesn't take it.

She runs a finger along the counter. "And you cleaned?"

"Yes."

"So you're Better Crocker and Snow Fucking White?"

"No. I'm *Jane*." I try again for the handshake, but to no avail.

"I know who you are," she says, like she's not happy about it. "Do all Yanks lack an understanding of sarcasm, or is it just you?"

"I don't know." My answer seems to annoy her further, but at least it's honest.

She opens the fridge and starts rummaging. With her head tucked inside, she says, "You bought groceries, too?"

My throat is a desert. "I was trying to help."

She slams the fridge closed. "We don't need your help." She takes a cookie and starts eating it, talking more to herself than to me. "He never thinks before he jumps. Bloody idiot." She shakes her head, chewing and not looking at me, which gives me time to take her in.

Both her arms are covered in tattoos, but whereas my tattoo is utterly lame, hers fit her perfectly, their colorful designs swirling together brightly, like her hair. She has a level of cool that, even without any memories, I'm sure I don't.

"I could kill Kieran for this," she says. "Some bloody payback I'm getting."

"It's my fault," I say. "I dared him to do it. Blame me."

"Don't worry. I *do* blame you. Are you a Yankee leech? Hoping to get your claws into a rich guy so you can freeload all summer?"

"No," I say quickly. "I didn't even know he was—"

She cuts me off. "Kieran never turns down a dare."

Her anger is palpable, but somehow it only makes her more beautiful, her blue eyes sparkling with rage.

"Maybe we can start again," I say. "I'm Jane."

"And I said I know who you are. Kieran told me everything."

"I'm glad he told *you*," I mumble, mostly to myself.

"Did he not tell you about me?" she scoffs and shakes her head. "That's because he knew how I'd react. Typical male."

She saunters over to me with a swagger that screams confidence. It only depletes mine. She's stolen my conviction for herself. I shrink away.

"I'm Kieran's twin sister. Siobhan."

"It's nice to meet you, Siobhan." I force a grin, but she comes at me with more aggression.

"Let me be clear. I don't want you here. I don't trust you. I already don't like you. As far as I'm concerned, you're taking advantage of a nice guy, and if Kieran won't watch his back, I'll watch it for him. Got it, Yank?"

"Got it." The words barely make it out, though I want to say so much more. She needs to know how grateful I am, how nice it is for them to open their cottage to me. I never intended to make anyone mad. I'll help out and earn my keep. But instead, I blurt out, "I used a bottle of your hair dye."

Siobhan scoffs again, taking another cookie. "So you *are* a bloody leech." She leaves her red heels in the middle of the kitchen. "Stay out of my stuff, Yank. I'm going to bed."

But I stop her before she leaves the kitchen.

"Do you know where Kieran is?"

She squares herself to me. "Our life is none of your business. As far as I'm concerned, you're a fly in my cottage that I have to put up with. Nothing more. So be a fly and buzz off."

Siobhan stomps down the hallway, but before her door closes, she yells, "Your hair looks atrocious!"

I slump back against the wall, stunned, and stay there until the dryer buzzes. Siobhan doesn't come out of her room, and Kieran doesn't show up. When the kitchen is clean and my clothes are folded neatly, my eyes grow too heavy, and the bed calls.

I sleep in the sweatshirt Stephen gave me and a pair of my new granny panties that look more like little shorts than underwear. I'm exhausted, but sleep doesn't come easily. My introduction to Siobhan replays over and over, making me cringe, my desire for a redo pressing. She can't dislike me so immediately.

Outside, the green fields are amplified as the sun moves closer to the horizon and changes from yellow to a rich orange. And Kieran still isn't back. Awake, I stew on all that I should have said to Siobhan to make her understand. Tomorrow, I'll rectify our first meeting. I'll make her like me. It's that simple. Kieran likes me. She can, too. I'll show her I'm not a Yankee leech. I can be helpful.

The moment before the sun sets, a lavender hue that perfectly matches my hair flashes in the sky. I run my fingers along the bottom of my uneven haircut. Siobhan is right—it's atrocious.

The bright spot in our awkward meeting is that she didn't recognize me. *That* I can be happy about, even if the rest was a disaster.

Eventually sleep comes. I drift off with my notebook on my stomach, but a loud thud startles me awake in the complete darkness. And then another. Without thinking, I get out of bed and tiptoe down the hallway to see where the sounds came from.

Kieran stands in the living room, rubbing his head.

"Shite. Bleeding door."

He's dressed in a black suit with a pressed white shirt unbuttoned at the collar and a crooked red tie. His attire is formal and crisp, a stark contrast to yesterday's worn-out jeans and baseball hat. The only similarity is Kieran's shaggy black hair.

And I am dressed in only a sweatshirt and granny panties.

Before I can back away, he sees me standing in the hallway. A grin pulls on his face.

"That sweatshirt is awful," he says, stumbling, grabbing the doorframe for support. "But you've improved it."

I pull down on the sweatshirt, hoping I can get it to cover more of me, but it's helpless. Kieran falls to the side, catching himself on the chair and nearly knocking over a lamp, and I rush toward him to hold him up. He glances down at me with glossy eyes. When he speaks, his breath washes over me in a cascade of alcohol. "What in God's name did you do to your hair?"

I struggle under his weight and the utter embarrassment of being half-naked. I walk him through the living room toward his bedroom, feeling that I can't desert him now, even if I want to crawl into a hole.

"I needed a new look. Something less . . . innocent. What do you think? Do I look like a badass?"

"Your purple sweatshirt matches your hair. You look like a painted Easter egg." Kieran grabs the ends of my hair to examine it. "But I like it. Change is good."

Kieran's head and arms flop as we walk. He moves like a marionette, making it hard to keep his body upright.

I get him into his room and set him down on the bed. His shoulders hunch over as he shakes out of his suit jacket. He holds it out to me.

"You can throw this out."

"Pardon?" I say.

"My father might like a suit, but no good has ever come of it for me. It's more like a straightjacket." Kieran shoves it toward me. I take it and hold it in front of my exposed lower half. He pulls the tie from around his neck and hands it to me, too.

"Are you going to take your pants off next?" I ask. "I feel like only one of us should be pantless right now. We've only known each other for a day."

Kieran laughs. "You're funny, Bunny."

"Bunny?"

"Because you look like an Easter egg."

"That doesn't make any sense."

"It doesn't make any sense that bunnies bring *eggs*, either. They're mammals." Kieran flops back on the bed. "Life doesn't make sense. We stuff ourselves into suits, and then we stuff ourselves into coffins. It's the 'pig and cow parts' of life."

Kieran breathes heavily. For just a moment, sleep seems to settle him, but then he grabs his head and closes his eyes. "The room is spinning."

I sit him up, worried he might throw up. He takes off his shirt, handing it to me, and now he's half-naked—that makes two of us. Heat flushes my cheeks, and I turn away from him. But when he bends down to untie his shoes, he loses his balance and begins to fall headfirst. I dive to catch him, ditching the clothes in my arms. He drags me down, and now we're both in a heap of tangled limbs on the floor. My hand lands on his chest—warm skin to warm skin. I yank it away, embarrassed.

"I'm drunk," he says, slumping back against the bed.

"Does this happen often?"

He blows out a long breath and says, "Only like"—he holds up three fingers—"two times a year."

After I've untangled myself from him, I offer to help him take off his shoes. When I hold them up to ask whether he wants me to keep or toss them, Kieran is staring over my shoulder at the dresser.

He pulls himself off the floor, walks clumsily over to the dresser, and picks up the picture I saw earlier, the one of the boys in school uniforms.

"Are those your friends?" I ask, pulling my sweatshirt over my knees.

Kieran nods. "From boarding school."

"You look like troublemakers."

"We were." His slight smirk fades too fast. "Ask me the question again, Bunny."

"What question?"

"Keep or toss?"

So I say, "Keep or toss, Kieran?"

He nods repeatedly. "Toss." Then he stumbles from his room, back down the hallway, and into the living room.

I follow close behind, wondering why he would want to throw out the picture and making sure he doesn't knock anything over as he moves, bouncing off the walls and the tables.

He stops in front of the fireplace, gripping the mantel. His attention returns to the picture. "Toss."

He throws it into the ashes, and it shatters. The noise startles me, and the sound of breaking echoes in my head, reverberating through me. A consuming pain overtakes my whole body, like I'm being pressed between two walls. Suddenly I feel helpless, like I'm falling and being crushed at the same time. My knees buckle.

Kieran turns around quickly. "Are you OK?"

I'm the unstable one now. Kieran grabs my arms to steady me, but it backfires. We stumble, arms flailing, bodies twisting, limbs intertwined, until we fall back on the couch, Kieran with a thud and me in a straddle on top of him, disoriented. I attempt to right myself, but it's too late. The damage is done.

"What the hell is going on?"

Siobhan's voice slices through the room. Kieran is passed out underneath me, without his shirt on. And me without pants. This entire scene looks horrible. When I try to climb off him, I do it clumsily, my hands pressing in places they shouldn't. My sweatshirt gets hooked in his belt, and I have to unbuckle it to remove myself. The process is long and embarrassing, and Siobhan watches it all with narrowed, vicious eyes.

She shoves me out of the way before I can explain, before I can make her understand that this is all just a mistake. She edges herself under Kieran's body and pulls him off the couch.

I move toward her. "Let me help—"

"Not taking advantage of him, are you?"

"I swear—"

"You're a bloodsucking leech with a bad haircut *and* a liar." Siobhan's words sting with full venom. "Stay out of our business, Yank."

When Siobhan slams Kieran's door, I lug myself back to my room and curl up in my own bed, pulling the blanket over my ears. There was no time to explain. Everything collapsed on me at once. I went from a bunny to a leech in an instant.

Pressing my head into the pillow, I try to erase the sound of glass breaking, of objects shattering and coming undone. But everything that happened tonight was a disaster. In one instant my knees became weak, my body rebelling. Then the chaos almost consumed me.

The harder I try to forget that—forget the sound, the pain, the moment when screaming didn't help—the more etched in my mind it becomes.

CHAPTER 7

Kieran's clothes are in the trash can the next morning. Another one hundred euros sits next to my bed. My sleep was restless, and my body is tired today. When I hear someone stirring about, I get up, hoping it's Kieran, hoping he isn't going to disappear on me again. But disappointment is all I find.

His bedroom door is open, bed made, like he didn't even sleep in it. The broken frame and picture sit covered in ash in the fireplace, shattered glass everywhere.

This time I'm fully dressed when I greet Siobhan.

A full scowl sits on her face when she finds me coming from my bedroom into the living room. For a time this morning, as I was waking from my light sleep, I allowed myself to think I just dreamed all of this, but like my purple hair . . . it's permanent.

"Good morning," I say warmly, trying to act calmly. "You look lovely today. *Lovely*. My friend Stephen likes that word. It's a good word, isn't it?" Siobhan is dressed in a tight gray shirt, black skinny jeans, and pale-blue T-strap high heels, her tattoos and pregnancy on display. She groans audibly.

My hair is a mess of tangles, my head still groggy. I wanted to see Kieran this morning, but right now there's still an opportunity to right myself with Siobhan. I move closer to her, running my fingers through my hair in an attempt to tame it, though I'm pretty sure I only make the mess worse.

"Can I make you some tea? Everyone seems to drink tea here. It's . . . lovely."

She doesn't acknowledge me with a response, but opens the closet. I'm repeating words like an idiot, my composure slipping away.

"Or maybe some breakfast," I say. "Do you like French toast? I like broccoli more than green beans. And romance novels over thrillers. I'd take sex over guns any day." When I realize that doesn't help my cause, I curse my slow brain. "Not that I'm obsessed with sex or anything." My pulse beats in my ears.

Siobhan closes the closet, putting on a raincoat.

"What kind of books do *you* like?" I say. "Oh . . . wait . . . you're more a magazine kind of girl, aren't you? I saw a few in your room."

Siobhan holds on to the door handle tightly.

"You went in my room." It's a curt statement. "Was that when you stole my hair dye?"

"I'm sorry . . ." At any second she's going to walk out, and I won't have explained anything. But where to start? Why couldn't it have been Kieran I found this morning?

I try another tactic. "I like your shoes. I'm impressed you can even walk in them."

Siobhan responds, bitingly. "What are you implying?"

Why does everything come out wrong with her? Why can't my head clear this morning? "I just mean they're really high, and it's impressive in your current state." I gesture to her belly. Judging by her sour expression, Siobhan doesn't appreciate my statement. "I'm not saying this right."

"My *current state* is none of your business," Siobhan says. "My room is none of your business. Our lives are none of your business. Stay away from me. Stay away from Kieran." She pauses. "Also, you look like a drunk Muppet with that haircut."

The door slams in my face before I've spoken a word about last night. All I've managed to do is insult Siobhan.

I'm alone once more.

French toast doesn't cheer me up. Neither does a shower. Neither does cleaning the kitchen and baking another batch of sugar cookies. Though after three cups of caffeinated tea, my head is feeling more centered.

I sweep up the broken glass and the picture frame, tossing the remains in the garbage. But when it comes to throwing out the picture like Kieran said to do, I can't. He doesn't know how precious memories are. How hard he should hold on to them. He may not want it right now, but he will at some point. That's how memories work. Even the bad ones. Without them, how do we know what feels good? I decide I'll hold on to the picture in my notebook for safekeeping. It's the least I can do.

The morning light doesn't help my haircut. While I like the color, Siobhan is right—the cut is atrocious. I'm not sure what a drunk Muppet looks like, but judging by my appearance and her disdain, it's not good. The image of her face as she glared at me on top of Kieran last night comes back in a wave of nausea. Why didn't I explain myself then? My head was just so cloudy in the moment. Same with this morning. Siobhan makes me nervous, jumbled. I've been spoiled with Stephen and Kieran, both of them easy to like and easy to talk to, but Siobhan is my reminder that not everyone is here to help. Some people would rather push you down.

She could barely look at me this morning. I'm just a bloodsucking Yankee leech and a liar to her. And she might be right, but not about last night. Last night was just a string of bad incidents. If she would just let me explain, I could change her mind about me.

I can't stew over it in the cottage all day. I'll go mad. Two cars sit in the driveway, so wherever Siobhan went, she must have walked in her high heels. If I find her and force her to listen to me, I can fix what happened last night. I wasn't trying to seduce Kieran. I was trying to help. It was just a big mistake.

One small problem stands in my way—I have no idea where she went. But as Kieran said, a person can't get lost in Waterville. All I need to do is look. There must be a clue somewhere in the cottage—a calendar or a datebook. For such a fine house, the place isn't laden with technology—no computers of any sort, no TV. People come here to escape the world. The lack of connections is a relief. I'm not tempted to turn on the television to watch news reports or search myself on the internet. After seeing myself on the covers of the tabloids yesterday and the disconnected feeling I had about my own face, the internet might put me over the edge.

Siobhan said to stay out of her business, and while it isn't completely lost on me that snooping in her room probably isn't a good idea, the risk will bear greater rewards when I find her and explain.

I'm not sure what I'm searching for as I go through her closet and the items on her dresser. I'm no good at finding my own memories, let alone someone who clearly doesn't want to be found.

Nothing pops out at me, and my caffeine buzz is wearing off. I sit in the kitchen with my fourth cup of tea, thinking and trying hard not to relive last night. Even in Kieran's drunken state, he was charming, a sharp contrast to Siobhan, and I'd be lying if I didn't admit how hot my cheeks were when I touched him. But when he broke the picture, the expression on his face was so sad, such a contrast to how I've seen him, even in the little time I've known him. Recalling Siobhan's words, though, squashes my intrigue—their lives are none of my business. She made that clear.

I banish the night from my mind and go back to my tea, when a magnet on the fridge catches my eye, its skull-and-crossbones design unique, dark—exactly like Siobhan.

THE SECRET BOOK AND RECORD STORE
248 SEAVIEW TERRACE
WATERVILLE, COUNTY KERRY, IRELAND

The sun seems to shine a bit brighter through the windows. My day may just improve. I write down the address listed on the magnet. While Siobhan could be anywhere in town, somewhere she's been before sounds like a good place to start. Maybe while I'm in town, I'll get a proper haircut.

~

Outside, the air is a bit warmer than it was yesterday. New buses full of tourists have unloaded in town, filling the quaint streets of Waterville with bustling energy. I stay along the beach, avoiding the crowds.

I stop only for a short time to search in the sand for sea glass—a peace offering of sorts for Siobhan, to show her that I'm not just here to take from her and Kieran. I may not have money, but I can offer friendship if she'll let me.

I search for a while down at the shore, where the waves are lapping only lightly today. A red piece of glass grabs my attention. Among all the gray, it's colorful. With it in my pocket and a place to start looking, I head into town.

The Secret Book and Record Store is harder to find, which isn't surprising, given the name. I walk past it a few times before a small blue door catches my eye. The address is barely visible, and no name is displayed on the outside. A poster reads, "Freaks, Sinners, Faeries, and Zombies, please proceed downstairs. Tourists, be gone!"

The yellow door directly next to the blue one is for Sheppard's Hairdressing. A sign in front on the sidewalk advertises the daily deal: "Haircuts, 20 Euros—Mind Reading, Free."

I take it as an omen—the two things I need. Today might be a success after all.

I push back the blue door quietly. The hallway is a bit dark. Steep stairs lead down into the basement of the building, which smells like old books, cardboard, and incense. At the bottom, bookshelves line a large room along with filled record bins. A man, probably in his midtwenties, sits behind the checkout counter sporting a black Mohawk that's at least four inches high. He glances up and eyes my purple hair, not a flash of recognition on his face. He goes back to intently reading a book. This store has none of the Irish charm of Waterville. No melodic Irish music with flutes and harps, no thick wool sweaters or Celtic crosses on the walls. But there's something comforting seeing this. It's out of place . . . just like me.

"Hi," I say to the man behind the counter. "Is Siobhan here?"

The guy gestures toward the back of the store, where wild clothes and costumes are on display. He doesn't linger on my face. Another good sign.

There's an entire section of wigs, hats, fishnets, vintage dresses, polyester suits, and sunglasses in retro styles. I make my way to the back of the store, acting casual, but feeling anything but, unsure of how Siobhan will react when she sees me, and also pretty confident I'm in for a fight.

This place is like the world's best dress-up bin. I try on an orange curly-haired wig and a pair of large round diamond-studded sunglasses that take up half my face. A stand with multicolored boas is next to the sunglasses. I wrap a blue one around my neck.

"Consider buying the wig. It's an upgrade from your current do." I turn promptly and see Siobhan.

"Found you," I say, hoping to sound chipper.

"That implies that I wanted to be found. Which I made clear I didn't. You can go away now." Siobhan walks over to a rack of dresses and starts organizing them.

I follow close behind her. "What do you think of the sunglasses? I kind of like them, but I need a girl's opinion."

"Are you hard of hearing?" Siobhan moves around the rack, keeping her distance from me and her eyes on the dresses.

"No . . . I don't think so."

"Again. You're missing my sarcasm, Yank. Now, get out of this store."

"Are you being sarcastic again?" I smile.

"No," Siobhan states clearly. She walks to the front of the store and behind the counter to organize a display of bubblegum and glow-in-the-dark condoms.

The guy with the Mohawk looks up at us. I lean on the counter and watch Siobhan, waiting, still wearing the wig, sunglasses, and boa. Being covered up so much escalates my confidence level. When Siobhan won't focus on me, I turn toward the Mohawk guy.

"What do you think of the sunglasses?"

"Totally wicked. Very glam-punk."

"Thanks," I say kindly. His brown eyes crinkle around the edges, making his face soften under his spiky hair. He reminds me of a punked-out Stephen, which is a comfort. "So what's the book about?"

He opens his mouth to answer me, but Siobhan cuts him off. "Are you going to tell Clive that you're addicted to sex?"

"What?" he says.

"Purple People Eater, here, is addicted to sex." Siobhan's voice is curt. "Though based on what I saw last night, she's not very good at it. Clumsy, really."

"All I said was that I like romance novels," I clarify.

"You're American," Clive says. He turns toward Siobhan. "Is this the wretched, slutty Yank you were talking about?"

"Is that how you described me?" I glare at Siobhan.

"You're the one who's addicted to sex, Abby Cadabby," Siobhan says callously. "I saw it with my own eyes, Clive."

I walk over to Siobhan and say, strongly, "I can explain that."

"I don't need the details. I saw plenty." She turns to Clive. "Her knickers are dreadful. Huge, ugly things."

Clive hollers over to us. "So where are you from in America?"

"Cleveland," I say, distracted by how badly this is going.

"Is that by Disney World? I've always wanted to go there. Do you happen to know George Clooney?"

"It's in Ohio. On Lake Erie." I rattle off the only information I know about Cleveland, then follow Siobhan to the back of the store again.

She stops in the used CD section.

"Please, let me explain what you saw last night."

"I don't need a play-by-play. Now go away."

I know I should just do as she asks. I'm being desperate, and this isn't helping my cause. But my whole life is desperate right now. Siobhan needs to know the truth. To like me. It would make staying here less . . . lonely.

I take the sea glass out of my pocket and hold it out to her.

"I found this on my walk over here. I thought you might like it. You can add it to your collection."

Siobhan eyes the red glass but doesn't move.

"Maybe we can be friends?" I offer.

"Friends? Why?"

I shrug. "Honestly, because I don't know anyone here, and I'm lonely."

Siobhan thinks I'm a liar, so maybe offering her this bit of honesty might crack her hard exterior. I *am* lonely. The only person I know, Stephen, I ran away from. And Kieran is nowhere to be seen. If he remembers last night at all, he might even be hiding from me.

Siobhan digs in a bin and pulls out two CDs. "This is me." She shoves a CD in my face. On the cover, a woman wears head-to-toe black, even her wild hair is black, and she's clutching an electric guitar—Joan Jett. "And this is you." This CD's cover has a woman in a flowing white dress and soft curls—Celine Dion. "Get used to being lonely, Yank. We all end up that way in the end."

Siobhan disappears into the back of the store, never taking the sea glass. Defeated, I walk to the register, putting the wig and boa back where I found them, but prepared to buy the sunglasses. It's the least I can do. This was a bust with Siobhan. Not only didn't I explain myself, but I'm pretty sure I made our relationship worse.

"I'll take these," I say to Clive, who's giving me a pained expression, like I'm pathetic.

"I love your hair," he says as he rings me up. "The unkempt style is totally in. And the glasses really do look gorgeous on you."

"Thanks, Clive."

"Your name's Jane, right?" I nod, and Clive's face brightens. "It's a sign."

"Take it from me—not all signs point you in the right direction." I feel the sea glass in my pocket.

Clive leans over the counter and turns his book, *Rip It Up and Start Again: Postpunk 1978–1984*. Hiding inside is another book, Jane Austen's *Sense and Sensibility*. "I love romance novels, too," he whispers. "Have you read Austen?"

I shake my head. If I have, I don't remember anyway.

"Bloody fantastic." Clive fans himself. "People love Mr. Darcy, but most people are idiots. Colonel Brandon puts him to shame. Totally swoonworthy." Clive takes the money for the glasses. "By the way, I've seen Celine Dion in concert twice in Dublin. Bloody brilliant."

"Really?"

Clive glances in the direction Siobhan disappeared. "Don't give up on her. She'll come round. She called me a punk poser once and told me David Bowie would be ashamed of hanging on the walls in this place. I almost fired her, but I kind of loved her more for it."

"Have you known Siobhan for a while?"

"Years. I make it a point to know everyone in town. Makes life . . . friendlier."

"I wish Siobhan shared your sentiment."

He leans over the counter closer to me. "If you push people away, they can't hurt you."

"But I don't want to hurt her," I whisper back. "I just want to get to know her."

"I think she's already been hurt enough. Some risks are just too big." Clive hands me the sunglasses. "Did she really find you half-naked, trying to shift Kieran?"

"Shift?" I ask. He demonstrates kissing. "No! I wasn't trying to . . . shift anyone. It was just a mistake."

"You'll get no judgment from me. I wouldn't mind a bit of a shift with Kieran."

When he says that, an idea dawns on me.

"So you know everyone in town?" I ask. "You wouldn't happen to know where Kieran is today, would you?"

He hands me my change. "He's working at Paudie's."

I remember Kieran's hat. "The pub?"

Clive nods and winks.

"Thanks, Clive. I'm really glad I met you today."

"Same here." He offers me a kind look. "Just don't tell anyone about my Jane Austen obsession. I have a reputation to protect."

"I guess we all have something to hide."

"If there's one thing I've learned from Jane Austen," Clive says, "it's that if we told the truth all the time, there would be no stories worth telling."

As I walk up the basement stairs, I hear him sing at the top of his lungs. Siobhan yells from the back of the store. "Seriously? The song from *Titanic*? Shut the hell up, Clive! You're a disgrace to everyone with a Mohawk!" But he only gets louder.

Outside, I take the door next to the blue one. Clive may think the messy look is in, but even though it pains me to admit Siobhan is right about one aspect of myself, my hair needs help. Inside the salon, two older women notice me and simultaneously say, "You're here for a haircut."

The sign wasn't lying. I better control my thoughts, or I'll be back in Limerick before the night is through.

CHAPTER 8

Paudie's Pub is crowded when I walk inside. People fill the wooden tables and booths, some looking at pictures on their phones, others at maps of Ireland. Some are just laughing, drinks in hand. It's warm and instantly infectious. The walls are stone. Old pictures make it feel like someone's living room. There's even a lit fireplace. The best part? I can't find a single TV.

I walk through the crowd, watching people interact, eavesdropping on their conversations, checking for lingering eyes. But no one notices me. Even Kieran, who's busily cleaning glasses and pouring beers behind the bar, doesn't look up when I sit down.

He seems tired today, back in his casual clothes—a green-and-blue striped Rugby shirt and jeans. His hair messy. Something shifts when I see him. A calm I haven't felt all day comes over me. It's as if I was drifting, and suddenly, I'm anchored. It makes sense, considering that he helped me, gave me a safe place to stay, and money. He's my reminder that this might all work out OK. I don't know how I'll ever repay him.

I nonchalantly take a seat at the end of the bar, wedging myself on the only open stool between two groups of people chatting.

Kieran wipes down the bar, his eyes fixed on it, and says, "What can I get you?"

"I hear it's popular to drink Murphy's instead of Guinness in this part of Ireland. I'll try a Murphy's."

At the sound of my voice, Kieran startles. His eyes come to attention on me, but I can't read his expression. For a second, it's almost like he's surprised, then that turns into nerves—or embarrassment—but it fades quickly, and the charm comes back. "Your purple hair."

"You remember?"

He rubs his temples. "Vaguely. Something about wanting to look like a badass so people won't mess with you?"

"Exactly." While I'm glad he remembers the excuse I gave, it means he probably remembers more—like what I was wearing . . . or not wearing. I put on my new sunglasses to hide my nervous appearance. "What do you think? Clive says they're very glam-punk."

"So you've met Clive."

"I'm making it my mission to befriend your sister."

"Von?" Kieran says. "You've met her, right?"

"She's a bit prickly, but that can change."

"A bit?" He stifles a laugh.

"I know she's not happy I'm staying at the cottage."

"She'll deal with it." Kieran wipes spilled beer from the bar. "We have an agreement. She owes me."

"I'm sorry if I caused a problem between you two."

Kieran fixes his gaze on me. "You're not the one who caused it."

"Either way, I'll fix it. I promise. I can be charming when I need to be."

"I'm well aware of this." Kieran rolls his eyes. "Just don't be disappointed if it doesn't happen, Bunny."

When he uses the nickname he made up last night, my stomach jumps. Visions of our half-naked bodies on top of each other bombard me, like little embarrassment bombs going off within me. Heat flushes down my body all the way to my toes.

"Is this where you work?" I ask, pushing the images from my head.

A customer orders a Carlsberg, and Kieran fills a pint glass with beer.

"Sometimes. When the owner needs extra help," he says over his shoulder as the beer foams over the top of the glass. He sets the full pint on the bar and smiles at the woman, who blushes.

I clear my throat. "Why didn't you tell me you had a twin?" I ask.

"It never came up." Kieran flashes the same devious expression he gave me at the hospital, making me think there are a lot of things he hasn't told me. But then again, I can't criticize him for keeping secrets when I'm doing the same. Worse, really. He's keeping secrets. I'm lying about who I am.

Kieran leans toward me across the bar. "In truth, Siobhan's sensitive about her . . . *situation*. I thought it best not to mention it. Better for you two just to meet and get on with it."

I almost ask for more details but then decide now isn't the time to pry.

I set my sunglasses on the top of my head. "So where were you yesterday? Other than a bar."

"Pub," Kieran clarifies.

"A pub." I roll my eyes.

A few guys get up, and Kieran collects their empty glasses, setting them in a sink with soapy water. "I'm sorry I wasn't around, but I had to go to Dublin for the day."

"You don't need to apologize. I'm the one invading *your* life."

He wipes his wet hands on his jeans and offers me a menu. "This place is known for the fish-and-chips. Tourists love it."

"No Jell-O?"

Kieran leans his forearms on the bar, his expression friendly. "You'll have to go back to Limerick for that."

I set the menu down. "How about a Murphy's?"

"No Murphy's here. Only Guinness."

"I guess I'll take one of those."

"Are you sure you want alcohol after what happened to you?"

"What?" I say sharply.

Kieran seems surprised. "The mugging? You hit your head."

"Oh . . ." I ease back in my seat, my heart pounding, and say the first thing that comes to mind. "The only therapy a Clevelander needs is beer. Takes care of all your pain at half the cost."

Kieran laughs, and I try not to act surprised at what just came out of my mouth. It was like someone else took over my brain for a second. Like Clementine came back but then disappeared in an instant.

"Cleveland . . ." Kieran says. "Sounds like a grand place."

I look away nonchalantly. "It's in Ohio. On Lake Erie."

"So you said."

I change the subject. "How about that beer?"

Kieran pours a pint and sets the dark beer with creamy foam, perfectly filled right to the top, in front of me. "Slainte."

I pick up the pint. "Pardon?"

"It's an Irish toast. It means 'to good health.'"

I hold the beer up to Kieran. *To good health. To staying hidden in Waterville until I get my memories back. To remembering who I was, so I can be who I am again.*

"Slainte," I say, and take a sip.

"Do you like it?"

"It's delicious." After a few more sips, I set the pint down on the bar. Kieran crosses his arms over his chest, the devious grin I've come to recognize painted on his face. "What?"

"Nothing."

I can tell he's lying.

"What?" I say louder.

Kieran reaches for my face, and I freeze. He undressed in front of me last night, before I straddled him on his couch, but he's not drunk now and, back in his casual clothes, Kieran is relaxed. It's becoming on him, handsome in an easy, natural way. He lightly cups my chin, his thumb running gently along my upper lip. My stomach tightens, and my head feels weightless.

"You have . . ." Kieran shows me the foam he wiped from my face. I hide my mouth and clean the rest of it, wholly embarrassed.

"Happens all the time." He laughs.

He leaves me be then, going down the bar and taking people's orders, refilling beers, collecting money and tips. His charm is captivating, the way he can smile at someone, forcing him or her to return the gesture whether they want to or not. He's smooth, effortless at times. But at other times, I think I see something different in him. Like maybe being effortless takes a lot of effort, especially the day after being drunk.

When my beer is gone, I hold up my empty pint to get Kieran's attention. "I'm ready for another one."

"Careful, Bunny. Those have a bite."

"I can handle it."

Moments later, he sets another full pint down on the bar.

"Slainte," I say. "See. I'm practically a local already."

Guinness has a milky quality upfront and a slightly bitter aftertaste, like dark chocolate. It's absurd, really, that I can pick out the intimate tastes of beer, and I don't even know if I've ever had one.

"So you said you're studying business at Trinity College, but you don't like it," I say to Kieran.

"I didn't say I don't like it. I said it was boring."

I take a big gulp of Guinness. "Well, what would you rather study?"

"It doesn't matter what I would *rather* do."

"Of course, it matters."

He stands in front of me, his forearms resting on the bar. "You can change the color of Jell-O, but you can't change what it's made of."

"That doesn't make any sense."

Kieran smirks, like he's confusing me on purpose.

"Come on. I'm trying to get to know you," I say. "All I know right now is that you're a flirt with a potential drinking problem."

"I don't have a drinking problem." And then he smiles at me, obviously flirting.

I take my sunglasses off the top of my head and put them over my eyes so Kieran can't see my reaction. "I think I need another Guinness," I say.

He soon delivers a new pint.

"I *am* sorry about last night, Bunny. I promise I don't have a drinking problem. Last night was . . . an exception."

"So what happened?"

Kieran gets a rag and wipes at the bar, though I don't see any mess. "Long story."

"My drink happens to be full. I've got loads of time." But Kieran doesn't reciprocate. He eyes the dirty rag in his hand. The flirting grin is gone. "You said you were in Dublin," I say, encouraging him.

He nods.

"Something to do with your father?" But he offers no response, so I try a different tactic. "Why is he an asshole?"

Kieran wipes the non-mess on the bar. "The list is long. I won't bore you with it."

"I won't get bored, I promise." But Kieran stays silent. It's deafening. "And you were dressed in a suit because . . ."

When he finally looks back up at me, the serious expression on his face gives me pause. Prying has done me no good lately. Have I learned nothing dealing with Siobhan? I can't make Kieran mad at me, too. He's all I have.

"It was a good choice to throw out the suit," I say. "I like you better this way."

"This way?" The tension eases in his body.

"Casual and slightly careless."

"Is that how you see me?" Kieran asks.

"Am I wrong?" Irritatingly, Kieran shrugs off my question. "Well, Clive says I'm glam-punk. What do you see?"

"I can't say. I barely know you."

Taking off my sunglasses, I reach over the bar and pull on Kieran's shirt to hold him still. "Just try."

My shoulders square to his, the corners of my mouth pulled into a little grin. Kieran exhales like he's begrudgingly playing along.

The space between us seems to lessen. Simultaneously, the air in the pub gets hotter and tighter. The stare we share is intense, almost palpable. Time seems to slow down. The more I want to turn away, the more invested I am in staying in this uncomfortable but utterly lovely feeling.

"Well?" I say.

Kieran moves first, sending time back into regular motion. "It doesn't matter. It's all Jell-O, Bunny. Looks are deceiving."

Kieran goes back to work. My head swims. I'm not allowed to be disappointed. *I'm* the intruder. I want to know Kieran, but when it comes to sharing anything about myself, it's a sham. Lies are all I have to offer, and yet I expect the truth. Or worse—I want Kieran to help me know *myself*. Until I can tell him the truth, I don't really deserve his secrets. And he can't tell me who I am . . . as much as I wish he could.

I leave my empty pint and twenty euros on the bar. The crowd has grown thick, people standing in what feels like every open space. I push my way through, searching for the door. The entire room feels heavy, like I'm walking through a swimming pool. My foot catches on a chair, and I stumble forward, bracing myself on a stranger.

"The Guinness really does have a bite," I say.

My legs are unsteady. I want to be strong, but all I find are limitations. It's infuriating. As if trying to remember my life isn't exhausting enough? The world is pushing me down, fighting against me, and I can't counter it.

My right foot catches on something again—my left. As I fall to the side, the irony that I can't seem to avoid hurting myself, let alone anyone else, comes to full light.

Kieran grabs my arm before I topple over. "I warned you, Bunny."

"It was supposed to make me feel better." I look up at him. "But I don't feel better."

"You're stubborn."

"Is that all you see?"

"And slightly drunk."

"You would know best." I try one more time, hoping Kieran will be able to see a truth about me, something I need to know, like he did before. "Anything else?"

Kieran takes his time, thinking, examining, finding what I can't see. How badly I want him to tell me everything.

"Come on." Kieran leads me back to the bar. "Let's get you a bite to eat."

Paudie's fish-and-chips are divine, but the residual tension between Kieran and me sours the meal a bit. He doesn't talk to me while I eat, but busies himself charming other customers. He wipes foam from another girl's face. She laughs and blushes. I cringe.

When I'm done eating, my belly is full, but an uncomfortable feeling is lodged in my throat. Kieran offers to get me a ride back to the cottage, but I turn him down.

"I need the walk," I say.

The rest of the night I spend hiding in my room, afraid of running into Siobhan. The sea glass I tried to give her sits on the nightstand. I review what I've written in my notebook. My list is still dismally small, but thanks to Kieran, I add another item.

I'm stubborn.

Two days out of the hospital and still no memories. I won't let myself think about a possibility that rattles me to my bones.

CHAPTER 9

"I can't believe this is happening. I should know better. I'm from Cleveland. Home of 'the Drive,' 'the Fumble,' 'Game Seven.' Even when you think you're winning, you're always one moment away from losing everything."

"Don't say that, Clementine."

"I can't believe you waited until now to tell me."

He grabs my hand. His touch makes me cringe, and I pull away. The buzz of the engines muffles our conversation, but I'm pretty sure 5A and 5B have heard everything. They'd take my side, no doubt.

"This doesn't have to be the end," he says.

"Then what would you call this?"

"Just a bump."

And as if on cue, we both lurch forward. I brace myself on the seat in front of me.

"The problem with bumps is when you don't see them coming . . . you inevitably stumble, and you usually fall."

I sit up in the dark. Something was just there in front of me. I search around my room in the cottage, desperate for what it was, remembering Kieran interrupting my sleep the night before. But the cottage is quiet. Not a single light is on.

I could have sworn I heard a familiar voice, but the longer I wait for it to come back, the more dreamlike it becomes, and soon it's gone.

That's what it was—just a dream, a vague figment the mind makes up to tangle with reality before it vanishes into the night.

~

When a person gets used to failure, it becomes much less scary. A person will walk into fire, knowing full well she'll get burned, but it doesn't hurt as much. When you're prepared for pain, pain loses power.

Or so I think when I show up at the Secret Book and Record Store. After hiding out in my room for a few days, afraid of Siobhan, it has become like my hospital room, just without the machines. I feel trapped, which defeats the purpose of leaving the hospital in the first place. If only Kieran was around—but he's gone every morning when I wake up and doesn't come home until I'm asleep. I'm beginning to think he's avoiding me.

Clive is the only other person I know in Waterville. He's the closest relationship I have to my friendship with Stephen, who I miss greatly after spending the past few days talking to myself, baking, and doodling in my notebook. On a positive note, I *have* managed to keep the cottage fully stocked with sugar cookies. They disappear rapidly.

My boredom outweighs my knowing that Siobhan doesn't want me at the store. I'll fight through her spikes and prickles for more time with Clive. He offered me friendship, and at this point, it's the only thing I have.

"Did you make these?" Clive asks, and he takes a bite of the sugar cookies I've brought him.

"Watch out, could be poison. You can't trust her." Siobhan's been taking little jabs at me since I arrived. I came mentally prepared. They barely register as dull pokes now.

"You didn't seem concerned about poison when you ate the whole batch I made yesterday."

"I'm made of poison. It has no effect on me." Siobhan gives me a pointed glare but speaks to Clive. "All I'm saying is be careful, Clive. People can surprise you."

He eats the last bite of the cookie, devouring it in record time, then licks each finger before picking up the crumbles and eating those, too. It makes me like him more.

"I would never hurt Clive or anyone," I say.

"Is that true?" Siobhan pops her hip out. Behind the counter, she's unloading a box of T-shirts that say, "Weird is a side effect of awesome." I want to come back at her with a resounding yes, but that would be a lie. There's a line of people behind me who I've hurt in just the past few days—my dad, Stephen, even my doctor.

I don't take Siobhan's bait, but turn away from her and offer Clive another cookie.

"Where'd you learn to bake?" he asks.

I shrug casually and examine a display of colorful headbands and scarves. "It just comes naturally."

I put on a bright mint-green headband, checking my reflection in the mirror.

"Gross. That clashes with your hair." Siobhan walks past me, carrying T-shirts. "It looks like you're wearing vomit. You should totally get it."

I take the headband off and try on a zebra-patterned one. "How about this one?"

Siobhan ignores my question, so I turn to Clive. He gives me a thumbs-up. The headband is a nice pop of color next to my white shirt and jeans.

"You have to pay for that, Muppet," Siobhan says.

"I know." I set twenty euros on the counter, but Clive hands it back to me.

"You get the friends' discount." He winks.

"What?" Siobhan's tone is sharp. "If you keep giving everyone that discount, you'll go out of business in no time. The Yank's not worth it."

"I didn't open this place to make money," Clive says. "I opened it to inspire people to be themselves. We need that in this town."

"Well, you need *money* to keep it open," she says.

When I walked into the store earlier, Clive instantly went to the used CD bin and took out a Celine Dion album. It's been playing ever since, on full blast. Siobhan hasn't stopped complaining about it.

"You own this place?" I ask Clive.

He nods and says pointedly toward Siobhan, "Though some people act like *they* own it."

"It's for your own protection," she says. "Trust me. Purple People Eater, here, will leave with a free headband, and all you'll get is debt, bills you can't pay, and a load of regret."

"*Some* might call protection avoidance," Clive says.

"Stop talking in undertones, Jane Austen. I get it." Siobhan shakes her head.

Clive laughs. "Jane appreciates my undertones. Don't you, Jane?"

"The Yankee Muppet is using you," Siobhan says, "just like she used Kieran and my bottle of hair dye."

"I have a name," I state.

"Like I care."

Clive puts his finger to his chin and says, "All of these Janes might get confusing. You need a nickname."

I roll my eyes. "Kieran already calls me Bunny. That's bad enough."

Siobhan turns, her arms still full of T-shirts. I can practically see claws come out and spikes along her spine. I should have kept that bit of information to myself. It's clear she doesn't want me getting close with Kieran, though why, I may never know. For the first time since I walked in the store, she eyes me directly.

I qualify the comment. "He said I look like an Easter egg with my hair this color. It wasn't a compliment."

"More like egg-stravaganza," Clive says with a smirk.

In an attempt to smooth over what I've just revealed, I try a new tactic—flattery. "Actually, I could use some fashion advice. All I have are boring white T-shirts. I want something with more pizzazz. What do you recommend to match my hair?"

"Pizzazz? Did you really just use that word?"

"Yes . . ." I hesitate.

Siobhan's expression gets contemplative. I don't think my flattery registered in the slightest. "Kieran said you were mugged. That they took everything. That you were a pathetic little girl he couldn't just walk away from." Her eyes narrow on me.

"He called me pathetic?"

Siobhan counters with her own question. "How is it you have money to buy things?"

I woke up again this morning to one hundred euros on the bedside table. In reality, it wasn't really morning anymore. It was more like early afternoon. At night, I fight with myself. I can feel it, like I'm struggling with the covers, pushing and pulling and trying to stretch them to fit, but they never do. A part of me is always cold. Always uncomfortable.

I'm not proud that Kieran leaves me money, but it's been helpful . . . until now. *Now*, I just feel ashamed.

"Is Kieran giving you money?" Siobhan asks.

A lie would really come in handy right now, but it would only make the gap between Siobhan and me bigger. I have only a split second to weigh my options. The truth won't do me any good, but I decide to go with it.

"Yes." My voice is small.

Siobhan's face turns red. I brace myself for the storm she's about to rain down, the names she's about to call me. Yankee Muppet won't be so bad compared to what's about to come. She has an uncanny ability to state the truth in such a harsh way, I start to dislike myself. She reveals my ugly side and throws it in my face. And she doesn't even know everything. I want to be helpful, but she reminds me how helpless I really am.

But she doesn't yell. She drops the T-shirts on the ground, turns to Clive, and screams at him. "Clive, turn this shit off, or I'll tell everyone about your Jane Austen infatuation!"

Now, inadvertently, I've hurt Clive. I should have stayed in my room.

Clive is in midbite of a cookie, and his mouth falls open. "You wouldn't dare."

"And those cookies are going to make you fat." Siobhan turns away from us, tossing her long pink hair over her shoulder and stomping to the back of the store, leaving the pile of shirts on the ground.

I promptly start picking them up and refolding them, my heart beating wildly.

Clive sets his cookie down.

"I'm sorry," I say, putting some of the shirts on the counter. "This is my fault. I'll fix it."

"It's not your fault. She's been like this ever since I've known her. Her current condition isn't helping, either. She's a bloody basket case of emotion."

Her *condition* . . . Even Clive won't say the word "pregnant." No one seems to be talking about it, and I want to ask a million questions, but I can't. It's a bad idea. Avoidance won't work forever. Pregnancies only last so long. Intuitively, Clive must see the confusion on my face. He hollers to Siobhan at the back of the store.

"I'm taking a break! Don't scare off the customers! And don't eat my cookies!"

Siobhan's voice bellows. "Fuck off! And take the Yankee Muppet with you! She reeks of capitalism and McDonald's!"

Clive takes the remaining T-shirts out of my hands. "Come on. She just needs to cool off."

We walk to the Beachfront Café—a place that serves tea, sandwiches and salads, and pastries lined up in a glass display. There's something vaguely familiar about the place. It's comforting. Or maybe it's just nice to be with only Clive. I can relax with him. My words don't tend to backfire as much.

He wastes no time introducing me to Mary, the owner of the café, who's from Galway but moved down here five years ago for a simpler life. He recites her history as if it were his own. We chat with George, an Englishman who left Birmingham for Waterville after a bad divorce and now has "shagged half the women in town," according to Clive. Maggie, an old widow, was once crowned the Rose of Tralee, which Clive explains is a festival held in the capital of County Kerry every year. I meet Kevin O'Reilly and David Aster and Clara Moore . . .

When Clive has introduced me to nearly everyone except the tourists, we sit at a table outside in the sun, across the street from the ocean, people watching, the sound of the waves in the background. It's a relief to be out of the store and away from Siobhan. I perpetually mess up with her because I'm trying too hard, but with Clive, the conversation is easy and light. I don't feel like I need to explain myself constantly.

His all-black outfit and spiky Mohawk are a wild contrast to the small white teacup in his hand. His pinky finger even points out daintily. He is a walking contradiction, but it suits him perfectly. I can watch Clive, and his truth is revealed on some level. Maybe not all his layers, but some. This is comforting and infuriating at the same time. To see others and know a piece of them feels empowering, but the inability to do it for myself defeats me.

We drink our tea and watch the waves come and go. They are large and angry today, with big whitecaps.

"Do people surf around here?" I ask, recalling the surfboard in Kieran's room.

The teacup lowers from Clive's mouth. "Surf?"

"Yeah, surf."

"Like surfing in the bloody ocean," Clive says.

"Yeah."

"You know the ocean is cold, right?"

"Yes." I giggle.

"Have you ever been surfing before?"

"It's just a question." I shrug, unable to answer him properly, unwilling to lie.

"I'm kind of an indoor person." Clive turns his pale face up to the sun.

And just like that, I realize a truth about myself and wish I had my notebook to write it down. It lifts my mood and returns some of my confidence. "I'd rather be outside."

"That doesn't surprise me. Your skin's not pale enough to be a vampire like myself. I have to work very hard at maintaining this pasty glow."

My color has come back over the past few days, the dark circles under my eyes still there but less prominent. I'm starting to appear healthy again. Even my eyes seem brighter.

The sunshine heats my whole body. I could sit here all afternoon with Clive. It reminds me why I left the hospital in the first place.

"Clive . . ."

"I know what you're going to ask. No, I'm not the father."

I nudge him under the table. "That much is obvious."

"Really? You don't think I could shag a girl like Siobhan?"

"No," I say. "Do you want to shag Siobhan?"

"Siobhan . . . Kieran . . . I'm not picky when it comes to beautiful people."

I laugh. "If that baby was yours, you'd dote on Siobhan even more than you already do."

Clive nods. "I would. I'd spoil her rotten. I've always wanted a child." He turns his face from the sun to me. "But you want to know if I know who the father is."

"Well . . . you seem to know everyone's story."

But he shakes his head. "I do. And I can tell you that the father most definitely is not from Waterville. But that's the extent of what I know. If you haven't noticed, Von's not much of a talker. Never has been."

"I've noticed." I sip my tea. "How long have you known her?"

"Since she was sixteen. She showed up one day, demanding I give her a summer job, but refusing to take any money for her work. Said she was doing it just to piss off her dad and that was payment enough. She had fewer tattoos then. That was the summer she shaved her head. It wasn't a bad look, actually." Clive has a reminiscent expression on his face. "Siobhan didn't need the job. She just needed a place to be . . . accepted."

"Have you ever met her dad?"

"From what I know, he would ship Siobhan and Kieran down here for the summer with some chaperone or another when they weren't at boarding school. But he stays in London or Dublin most of the time. A total workaholic, I think. He owns a trading company or something of the sort. I've never been one for the corporate world." Clive gives me a knowing glance. "If you couldn't tell."

"And their mom?"

"Gone. From what I gather, she up and left when they were little."

"She left?"

Clive nods. It would be easy to keep thinking that Siobhan and I are nothing alike, and never will be, but knowing that her mom left, and that my mom is dead, connects us in a way. I don't remember how it felt to lose my mom, but Siobhan has to live with that memory every day. And leaving is a choice. I get the luxury of forgetting, but Siobhan . . . I can't help but feel a sort of compassion for her. No wonder she believes we all end up alone.

"It was kind of you to take her in."

Clive shrugs it off. "I know what it feels like to not quite fit in properly." He glances around the café, eyeing all the conservatively dressed people, including myself. No one looks like him. "I opened the store, hoping people like Siobhan would have somewhere to go. But in all honesty, I'm a bit worried we're the only people in this town who are like . . . us."

I know that worry. Every morning I wake up and think I'll be different. My skin won't feel foreign anymore. The tattoo that's haunting me will be explained. But that hasn't happened yet. I'm not like anyone, and yet I'm not like myself, either.

"Am I like you, Clive?" I ask.

He sets his tea down and pats my hand. "Definitely. Except better looking."

"Thank you. I needed to hear that," I say. "If it means anything, I think you'd make a great dad."

"Thank you. I needed to hear that," he echoes. Clive leans across the table toward me and whispers, "I can tell you one thing I know about stories like Siobhan's . . . In an Austen novel, it's always the rogue who impregnates the girl. And the girl is always sent into hiding for fear she'll shame the family name. I fear not much has changed."

"You think she was sent here to hide?"

Clive shrugs. "From what I know about their father, I wouldn't put it past him."

"That's awful."

"Siobhan threatened that if I ever asked her about it, she'd kill me in my sleep." Clive smiles. "Can't blame her for that. I've always loved the girl's spunk."

"What about Kieran?"

"He showed up shortly after Siobhan did, a few months ago. Up and left his life in Dublin. I reckon he's here because she is."

"Clive," I say, entering into this topic lightly, "you said you make it your job to know everyone in town . . ."

"I do." He sits up straighter.

"What do you know about Kieran?"

"Ah . . . now we're getting down to it, *Bunny*."

My nerves get the better of me, and I try to back out of the question, but Clive won't let it go.

"Here's what I know. He's a fine-looking creature, that's obvious, but he's no dummy, either. Well bred at boarding school, no doubt, and goes to Trinity. From what Siobhan tells me, he's being groomed to follow in his dad's footsteps and take over the company. Just more fuel added to Siobhan's fire. Dad gives all his attention to Kieran, and she gets ignored. I don't think Kieran appreciates the attention, though. And I don't know too many people who could put up with Siobhan like he does, so he's loyal. Did I mention how good looking he is?"

"You did." I nudge Clive's foot under the table.

"Does that answer your question?"

Kieran sounds as good as I thought, but why does it feel like he's avoiding me? Why bring me here if he doesn't want to see me?

Clive examines his watch. "I need to get back to the store before Siobhan burns it down."

"One more question," I say. "In a Jane Austen story, how does it all end? There's a happily ever after, right?"

Clive gets solemn. "Depends on which character you are."

This story needs to have a happy ending for everyone involved. I haven't let myself conceive of another option. It's too much even to think about—that my memories might never come back. That I might be stuck . . . lost . . . forever. That leaving my dad wasn't temporary. The sadness of these thoughts makes me want to grab Clive and hold on to him until my arms hurt.

"What about you, Jane? What do I need to know? Are you running away from something in Cleveland, Ohio? An ex-lover, maybe? Overprotective parents? A feud with a best friend?"

A blush creeps up my cheeks. I settle on something as close to the truth as possible, because Clive deserves that. "I needed to try on a new life. Some place where my past can't get to me. Ireland seemed friendly enough."

"An ex-lover it is then. I can tell. I've read enough Austen to know." Clive takes a napkin from the table and starts to write on it. He scribbles fast. "Here." He holds it out to me.

"What is it?"

"Shannon Walsh's address."

"Who's Shannon Walsh, and why do I need her address?"

"It's where Kieran is." Clive winks at me. "*Bunny.*"

I try to hand it back to him. "I think I've pried into Kieran's life enough."

But Clive pushes my hand away. "You should go over there. You might just be surprised."

"I think I'm done with surprises."

Clive doesn't back down. "Austen knew that surprises make stories more interesting. You can't be afraid of them, or you might miss out." He's written detailed directions to Shannon's house, complete with a map.

"Embrace the surprises in life, Jane," Clive says. "It'll be worth it. I promise."

CHAPTER 10

Shannon Walsh lives in a small one-story house outside of Waterville, perched up on an emerald-green hill where sheep graze. Bright red flowers line the hedgerow and block the property from the road. The red flowers look like upside-down teardrops and brighten the sidewalks and lanes everywhere in this town.

The entire walk over, I tried to come up with a good reason why I'm inserting myself into Kieran's life . . . again. Nothing comes to mind. This could be a catastrophe, yet my feet keep moving.

Sweat sprinkles my forehead, and my legs are tired when I stop in front of the oddly painted house. Half is bright pink and the other half lemon yellow. Clive's paper with the directions and address confirms that this is, indeed, the right place. As if on cue, Kieran appears at the top of the driveway. My mind wipes totally clean.

Kieran's skin has a kiss of sun, his hair a mess, his clothes ratty and torn. He doesn't have the air of a businessman in the slightest. But Clive is right—he really is quite good looking. My sweating gets worse.

His truck is parked in the driveway, a large ladder sticking out of the back, and I piece together quickly that he's at Shannon Walsh's house to paint it, though I'm still unsure who Shannon Walsh is. She is the variable. She could be shagging Kieran.

The long brush in Kieran's hand is coated in yellow paint when he turns to me, an unreadable expression on his face. The sun has stayed out this afternoon, which I'm starting to realize is an oddity. It may not rain all day, but most days it's going to rain some. Today is the warmest it's been. I wipe tiny beads of sweat from my forehead as Kieran watches me walk up the drive, his eyes bright in the sunlight.

His red T-shirt and jeans are speckled with paint, along with his hands. He even has a yellow streak across his cheek. Kieran squints in the sunlight as he sets down the paintbrush. I give him an uncomfortable grin.

"Found you," I say.

Kieran cocks his head at me. "I wasn't hiding."

"No." I point to the paint. "You're clearly painting a house. How's it going?"

"Very slowly." He wipes his brow with the back of his hand and glances at the sky. "But the nice weather is helping." His eyes come back to me. "You walked all the way here?"

I try to sound nonchalant. "I needed some exercise."

"Is that it?"

The way he says the words is unreadable, like the look on his face. I go quiet, standing in awkward silence. What *am* I doing here in a stranger's driveway? I blame Clive for putting the idea in my head and my feet for not leading me in a better direction. The urge to turn and run hits me hard.

"I just wanted to thank you for the money," I blurt out. "But you don't have to do that." Kieran kicks at the loose gravel with his shoe. His silence is deafening.

I pull the money from my pocket and shove it into his hands. "I'll find a way to pay you back. And I'll return the stuff that I bought. I'm not sure the store will take back underwear, but I'll figure something out. I don't want to be your charity case."

"Charity case?"

"Yeah, charity case." I turn to leave. It was a long walk here, my legs are aching, and my head kind of feels like it's not attached to my body right now, but I can't stay.

Halfway down the driveway, I hear Kieran say, "You're not a charity case."

I pause before turning around, confused. "But you gave me money."

"I know."

"Lots of money."

Kieran rolls his eyes. "I'm aware. But charity assumes that I think you're needy, and I don't think you're needy. Someone shitty mugged you. It's their fault you have nothing. I'm just trying to help."

I avoid his eyes, my lie stinging.

"So you bought underwear with the money . . . Care to expound? Maybe a description or two?" Kieran says. A cocky grin rests on his face.

But I don't deserve his kindness and help. All the bad things I've done are eating at me, the guilt almost too much at times. "I want to pay you back."

"I don't care about the money."

"Well, I do. I want to pay back every penny you've given me."

"We use euros in Ireland," Kieran goads me.

"I mean it. I don't want your money. I want to earn my own. I am an independent woman who doesn't need the help of a man." I say it forcefully, in hopes I might actually believe it down to my core.

"There's that tenacity I like." Kieran holds out his hand. "You've got a deal, Bunny. I'll butt out. From now on, you'll earn your own money." After we shake, he goes to the back of the truck, gets a paintbrush, and hands it to me. "You can start now."

"What?"

"You said you want to work. You're going to help me paint this house so you can get out of this small town and see more of Ireland. You didn't come here to waste away in Waterville all summer."

"Right," I say, though the thought of leaving makes me uncomfortable. That's not what I meant when I said I was an independent woman. But I play along. "I need to see Dublin before I go, right?"

"Yes, you do."

The sun glares as I look at the partially painted exterior. I'm not worried about the work. It's painting. It can't be that hard. And earning my own cash does sound nice. But what about Shannon? "So . . . will the owner mind that I'm here?"

Kieran pulls more supplies from the back of his truck. "She most likely won't even notice." I wait for him to explain, trying to act nonchalant. "She's been legally blind for over ten years now. That's what the bright color is for. So she can tell which house is hers."

"How old *is* Shannon?" I ask.

Kieran pours more yellow paint into a plastic bucket. "I think she just turned eighty-five."

This is the surprise Clive was talking about. I control my laughter.

Kieran hands me the bucket. It's heavier than I expect, and it yanks my arm down with its weight.

Adjusting, I say with gusto, "Where do I start?"

Kieran seems intrigued. "Have you ever painted anything before?"

It already feels like my hand's going to fall off, but I act like I'm not struggling under the weight. "Of course, I have."

Trying not to spill, I lug the bucket over to the house. What did I get myself into? I set it down in front of a section that hasn't been covered in yellow yet. This can't be that hard. Even with no memory of doing it, painting is pretty straightforward—dip the brush in the bucket, wipe the paint on the house, repeat.

"So how'd you get roped into this job?" I ask as I go through the motions.

"Shannon needed help. I offered."

I turn to face Kieran, tucking a few wild pieces of hair behind my ear. "That's sweet." He stifles an unexpected laugh in return. "What?"

"Nothing."

"What?" I ask, pressing harder.

"You have paint on your cheek." When wiping my face makes it worse, Kieran chuckles more. "Just leave it, Bunny."

I groan at him before focusing on painting again, moving the brush up and down and sideways, smearing paint this way and that. When Kieran comes up behind me, I startle. He grasps my arm.

"Not like that." He takes my hand, dipping the brush into the paint and gently wiping the sides of extra yellow paint. "Like this."

His hand moves with my hand, up and down in a rhythmic motion, uniformly, smoothly, and much more effectively, covering the pink with yellow.

"Slow and even," he says into my ear.

His chest presses to my back. I should pay attention to what he's showing me, but all I can do is focus on the heat between us. His arm rests on my arm, his fingers encircle mine, intimately. When he turns his attention from the painting to me, I realize I'm holding my breath.

"Got it?"

I step away from him hurriedly, finding much-needed space and air. Distance is good. It keeps boundaries in place. For a moment, I wasn't focused on my endgame. All I cared about was Kieran and the closeness of his body.

But I have a life I plan to get back to.

"I got it," I say.

Kieran nods and casually goes back to his section of the house, as if something didn't just spark between us. Maybe it didn't for him. It's a bad idea to linger on feelings that shouldn't be there anyway. My life has enough disappointment in it. I'm trying to reduce pain, not add to it.

The goal is to go back to Clementine's life *without* extra pain. To say good-bye to this fake life easily. I'll be an American girl he helped, like he helps everyone else. That's the charade. Without it, this all falls apart.

"So you're a bartender and a painter," I say, smoothing paint just as he showed me. "What else do you do around this town?"

Kieran runs a large roller brush through a tray of paint. "Whatever people need help with."

"So you're a good Samaritan."

Kieran glances at me for a beat before going back to painting. "I'm not that good."

"I'm not sure I believe you. You *seem* that good."

Kieran keeps his eyes on the house. "Believe me, Jane."

When he uses my fake name, it feels formal and detached, and I'm reminded how little we really know about each other. Our connection is inflated because I lack an attachment to everyone else. That doesn't mean Kieran feels the same.

But selfishly, I like that he calls me Bunny instead of Jane. It makes my lies carry less weight.

I dip my brush back in the paint and keep working. The sun is hot on my back, but it feels good to be doing something productive, where I can see progress, results. And I like being outside. The movement of the brush is almost meditative. I forget how tired my legs are, how heavy my head feels. For a while, as I paint, I just settle, letting everything—the plane crash, the ripples that continue to rattle me—disappear. Coming here today was a good idea.

"So what's your favorite dare you've ever done?" I ask.

"I don't know," Kieran says.

"Come on. All of those pictures in your room. You've got to have a favorite."

"I don't."

I blow out an exaggerated breath. "Now you're lying to me. I can tell. Everyone has a favorite." Though I'm unaware of what mine is, I want to hear about Kieran's. A part of me is more desperate than I thought to really *know* him. "There must be some experience that beats out all the rest."

A quiet falls between us as I wipe more sweat from my head and shake out my tired arms. Kieran seems lost in thought, his paintbrush at his side. Then a small smile pulls at the corners of his mouth. "Bungee jumping in New Zealand."

"You've been to New Zealand?"

Kieran nods. "Two years ago, after I did my Leaving Cert."

"Your Leaving Cert?"

"When I graduated from school," Kieran amends. "A group of us went the summer before university. It was a present from my dad—a trip to anywhere in the world." Kieran pauses. "That's what he called it—a present—but it was really a bribe."

"A bribe for what?"

"To force me into business school."

"Why did you say yes if you knew it was a bribe?"

"Because I was young," Kieran says. "And bungee jumping in New Zealand sounded like loads of fun. And because my father would win in the end anyway. Some people earn love. Some people blackmail others into it."

The information Clive gave me seems to match well with what Kieran says, and I almost ask more questions about his father, but remembering my past interactions with Kieran and Siobhan stop me from making that mistake again.

"Well, was it worth it at least?"

"Worth it? I don't know," Kieran says, and then the devilishness returns to his eyes. "But it *was* loads of fun."

"Tell me about it," I say, intrigued.

Kieran looks as though he's still astonished he's bungee jumped in the first place.

"You're in a cable car, hanging over the Nevis River, attached to a really big rubber band. I'd been skydiving before, but this was different."

The thought of falling through the air sends my nerves on a ride.

"You're not alone when you skydive, but bungee jumping . . . nothing is safe about it." Kieran shakes his head in apparent disbelief. "And the truth is I'm not good with heights."

"You don't like heights, but you *chose* bungee jumping? That's insane."

"No, Bunny." Kieran's eyes catch the sunlight. "It isn't a dare unless you're afraid to do it."

"Well, it sounds kind of awful."

"It was in a way. And in another way, it was amazing," he says. "That's the thing with fear—conquer it, and you find freedom."

"Is that why it's your favorite?"

"That's one of the reasons." Kieran goes back to painting. He doesn't offer any more than that. A few days ago, I would have pushed, but now I'm starting to be aware of his sharing limit. It just feels good to know more about him.

We work as the sun travels toward the horizon, almost running into each other awkwardly a few times as we both dip our brushes into the paint tray at the same time. When my arm feels like it might fall off, I stand back, taking in our progress. The house is nowhere near done. It feels like we've barely made a dent. A wave of exhaustion comes over me as the sun hits my eyes, knocking the wind out of my chest. I stagger to the side, my sight blurry, but catch myself quickly and regain my balance.

"Are you OK, Bunny?"

"I'm fine," I say. A thin strip of pink paint lines the top of the house where the roof meets the walls. It's too high to reach with the roller. One of us needs to paint it by hand. "What do we do with that?"

Kieran gestures to the ladder in the back of the truck. "I'm avoiding the inevitable."

"I can do it," I say, happy that I can finally help Kieran, instead of the other way around. And then I say, for an added jab, "I wouldn't want you to get scared or anything. It's pretty high up."

"Bunny, have you ever been up on a ladder before?"

"Sure. Lots of times." Presumably, I have. I'm eighteen years old. I've probably done a lot of stuff.

Kieran gets the ladder out of the back of the truck and rests it against the house, making sure it's secure.

"It's all yours."

He holds my bucket and brush as I step up on the first rung, getting my bearings, a false confidence to my action, knowing my life is just a pile of assumptions—right or wrong. My throat tightens at all the steps it will take to get to the top. I grip the ladder harder. But backing out isn't an option. I've cornered myself in another lie.

Kieran hands over the paint and brush. "I find it best not to look down."

"I'll keep that in mind," I say. I carry the paint bucket and brush with me as I climb to the top—Kieran holding the ladder still—and set the paint down on the tray at the top. Not so bad.

"So what is it that scares you about heights?" I ask, examining the strip of pink paint on the house.

"It's the feeling I get."

"What's the feeling?" I dip the brush.

"The feeling like no matter what I do, I'm going to fall. Something will toss me over the edge. Instead of letting that happen, I make the decision myself. I get to decide when to jump."

"That's actually really beautiful." I remove the brush, forgetting to wipe the excess paint away, and watch as yellow droplets fall to the ground.

Time moves in slow motion then—the falling paint, my body going numb, my hands gripping the side of the ladder until my fingers ache with pain. It's panic in the most pure form—a sensation I'm well acquainted with—but this time, a new feeling emerges as I feel my body lose control.

"The captain has asked that you remain in your seats. We are experiencing some unexpected bumps."

My body starts to shake.

"All bumps are unexpected. If you knew they were coming, you'd avoid them completely."

I hold on to the ladder, but I don't trust it. I can't. Resentment overrides the panic. People walk through life feeling safe, taking risks because they believe everything will be OK. That ability was stolen from me along with my memories. Ripped from my hands. I will never feel safe again. This is all I'm capable of feeling. There is no "getting better" after you realize that everything and everyone can fail you.

"Bunny . . ." Kieran's voice breaks through the veil. "Bunny, why don't you come down?"

"I can't."

"You're just panicking a little. That's OK. Just take it one step at a time. I'm right here at the bottom of the ladder. I won't let anything happen."

I shake my head relentlessly. "You don't know that." If I open my eyes, I'll see how high up I am. My legs will give out.

"You're right," Kieran says gently. "But I know how you feel right now. This happens to me every time."

I swallow, trying to relieve my dry throat.

"What do you do?" My voice is weak. When Kieran doesn't answer for a moment, I plead. *"Kieran."*

"I'm here," he says quickly.

"Tell me what you do."

"You're not going to like this, but . . . remember what I said about fear. If you conquer it, you find freedom."

"Yes."

"I live in the fear. I stop fighting it, and let it wash over me."

"You're right. I don't like that. It sounds horrible."

"It is at first. But then it's not so bad. Fear wants you to stay scared, Bunny. But you don't have to give in. You don't have to let it control you."

I think for a brief instant that I might be strong enough to be OK. I have power over this. One step at a time, and I can get off this ladder. Not everything breaks. Not everything fails. But then the wind blows off the ocean, rattling the top of the ladder, and the panic is back. I grasp even harder.

"Tell me something else," I plead, squeezing my eyes shut. "Just keep talking."

"What do you want me to talk about?"

"*Anything.*"

"OK . . ." Kieran pauses. "There's a moment bungee jumping, when you're free-falling—"

"Maybe not that." Now my knuckles are turning white from gripping the ladder.

"Just listen," Kieran says. "The air actually feels thick. Almost like it's keeping you afloat more than pushing you down. And you forget to be scared. You forget to be anything. You're just . . . still and falling at the same time. At the end, when the bungee catches, you're actually disappointed because it felt so good. It's over too soon."

"Really?"

"It's the upside of falling down," Kieran says. "It's why you jump in the first place . . . for *that* moment."

I feel my hands loosen on the ladder, the blood coming back to my legs. "An upside?" It never occurred to me.

"There's always an upside, Bunny," Kieran says.

When he uses my nickname, I'm able to move again.

"Just take it one step at a time."

Kieran coaches me, telling me which foot to move, and where each step is. I descend slowly, fear still gripping me, and along with the resentment comes added shame. I should be stronger than this—strong enough to do what Kieran says and let my fear go. I should be grateful to be alive. But I can't seem to do that completely.

Pushing the helpless feeling aside, hiding it, like I do everything else—that's my only choice.

Eventually, my foot finds the last rung, and then solid ground.

"You can let go of the ladder," Kieran says.

I feel him next to me, his hand brushing my arm, waiting for me to reach out and grab it. I slowly peel one hand away from the ladder. Kieran's hand wraps around mine, and I let go with my other hand, reaching for him. He finds me, his grip warm and strong. Relief comes at last, and he's the one who offers it. But I couldn't do it on my own, so even though the panic has eased, disappointment lingers.

"You can open your eyes now."

Kieran stands in front of me. He exhales like he was holding his breath, and a warm wave of calm comes over me.

"I guess you're a little afraid of heights, too," he says, his hands still holding mine, fastening me to the ground.

But the relief is short lived. I step back quickly, releasing his hand. Kieran can't be my anchor. He reminds me that my life can get better, that *I* will get better, but what am I giving him? And why can't I do this on my own?

"I thought I was over it," I say, eyes on the ground. "I guess I'm not."

"We all have our flaws."

Clouds now cover the sun, and rain looks inevitable. The wind picks up.

"I think we're done for the day," Kieran says. "Probably for the best."

As we drive back to the cottage, rain falls on the windshield. I lean my head back against the seat and close my eyes, refusing to cry.

I'll just have to get used to the dull ache in my heart, like everything else. Forgetting the warm feeling of Kieran's skin might be hard, but I can be willful when I need to. If I don't . . . I fear I'll get dangerously close to a line that, if crossed, I won't come back from.

I'll be broken no matter how this story ends.

CHAPTER 11

Sleep eludes me. It's dark outside. As I lie in bed, a gloom creeps inside me as well. I feel empty, and my heart aches, but for reasons I can't understand.

When I drifted to sleep earlier, I felt it again. I was reaching for someone. I could feel fingertips inches from mine and then in an instant, they were gone. It would be one thing to be alone in my dream. But to know something is there—something is just out of reach, and I can't grab it—that's torture.

I tiptoe down the hallway to Kieran's room. I raise my hand to the closed door, but I think better than to knock.

Instead, I make a cup of tea in the kitchen, knowing I can't go back to sleep for fear of the nightmare returning.

When the silence in the cottage becomes too much, I find calm outside. The repetitive sound of the ocean blocks out the noise inside me. Waterville is fast asleep as I walk the streets, feeling a familiar loneliness. It's better to walk than to lie in bed waiting to feel normal, and only be discouraged when it doesn't happen.

At the center of town, an ancient phone booth, rusted and seemingly unused, catches my attention. With no technology at the cottage, and Kieran's and Siobhan's cell phones always somewhere near or on them, my ability to contact the world outside of Waterville is extremely limited, which I appreciated . . . until now.

I pick up the receiver and, surprisingly, hear a dial tone. A sign at the top of the phone says, "For directory inquiries, please dial 11850." Before I can think better of it, I punch in the numbers, and soon I'm connected to the hospital in Limerick.

"I'd like to speak with Nurse Stephen," I say.

"Which Stephen?" the hospital operator says.

"Um . . ." I don't even know his last name. "He's Jewish and gay."

The line goes quiet for a second, and then the operator says, "Hold, please."

The phone begins to ring again. A few seconds later, Stephen is on the other end.

"Third-floor nurse's station."

At the sound of his voice, I feel a rush of relief.

"Stephen," I whisper into the phone. "Can you hear me?"

"Clementine? Is that you?" His voice sounds frantic.

When he uses my old name—my real name—the hair on my arms raises, like the ghosts of my past just emerged to haunt me. Is it *really* me?

"I've been worried sick. Where are you?" he asks.

I hug the phone to my ear, tears threatening to spill down my cheeks for a second time today. "You don't need to be worried. I'm OK."

"Why in God's name did you leave the hospital?"

"I just . . . I couldn't do it, Stephen."

"Couldn't do what, love?"

"I couldn't pretend I was *her* when I'm not. It's not coming back to me, Stephen. My memories . . . they're still gone."

I hear him exhale. "Just tell me where you are."

"I'm OK. Really. I don't want you to worry about me." Just hearing Stephen paints a picture in my head. The smell of disinfectant. The clinical, monochrome clothes. But here at the center of town, surrounded by colorful houses and a slight breeze of cool night air, I can hear the waves crashing and smell seawater.

"Clementine?"

"I'm here," I say. "I need to know something."

"What is it, love?"

"Is my dad . . . ?"

"He's here," Stephen says. "He refuses to leave."

A piece of what's weighing on me lightens. "Will you tell him I'm OK? Will you do that for me, Stephen?" But he doesn't respond right away. Even now, after all the help Stephen has offered, I can't give him Clementine back. Going back to Limerick wouldn't solve anything. His loyalty is a gift I don't deserve, but this is important. I beg him. "*Please.* Tell my dad I'm OK."

"OK," he says finally. "Clementine, what's that noise in the background?"

"I'm by the ocean, Stephen."

"That doesn't really help, love. Ireland is an island."

"I'm doing what you said. I'm adding to the list. You're right about food. I know how to bake. And I dyed my hair purple. Purple! I have a friend named Clive, too. I think you'd really like him. He's *lovely.*" I use the word on purpose, to sweeten the anger I'm sure Stephen feels. I wait for him to say something, but he's quiet on the other end of the line, so I ask, "How is my dad?"

Stephen chuckles into the phone. "He's told me all there is to know about Cleveland. Apparently, you have the Rock & Roll Hall of Fame and a river that caught on fire once. Can you imagine? He also said that all good Clevelanders hate two things: the Pittsburg Steelers and Bill Belichick. Does any of that ring a bell?"

"No . . . nothing." I shake my head, not surprised. "Tell my dad that I promise the second I find myself, I'll come back to him. Tell him to wait for me."

"Just come back, and we'll get this sorted out."

"Promise me, Stephen," I say emphatically. "Say the words."

He exhales into the phone. I'll wait all night if I have to, but Stephen doesn't make me do that. Reluctantly he says, "I promise."

"I haven't forgotten how good you were to me." Tears well in my eyes again, and this time a few escape down my cheeks. "Thank you."

I force myself to hang up, even though I wish I could stay on the phone with him all night, wrapped in his familiar voice.

By the time I get back to the cottage, my body feels tired again, relaxed. Sleep seems possible, knowing my dad is still here, knowing Stephen still cares.

I'll give myself two more weeks in Waterville. If my memories don't show up by then, I'll be forced to take drastic measures. After all, the tabloids seem to know a lot about Clementine Haas. There are ways to make her come out of hiding. I just hope it doesn't come to that.

CHAPTER 12

The plane crash becomes second-page news when a British pop icon marries an actor. Then scandal erupts within the British royal family, bumping the marriage to the inside covers, the crash lost somewhere in the back of the tabloids, with no pictures, next to the personal advertisements and weight-loss gimmicks. My fear of being noticed is almost gone. But that's only one fear in the list of many that wake me at night.

Shannon Walsh's house slowly turns from pink to yellow. I deliver treats to Clive at the Secret Book and Record Store, and in return he takes me to the Beachfront Café for tea, mostly to avoid Siobhan. Her attitude toward me hasn't changed.

Kieran and I dance around each other as we paint, and every time we're within close proximity, the dull ache creeps back into my heart. It's become consistent, expected, a sort of comfort, if only it weren't so frustrating. I'm starting to need him, which might be what frightens me most.

The only solution is distance. I paint one side of the house. He works on the other. It's the only way to save myself from the feelings I can't seem to get rid of.

And my memories . . . They aren't coming back.

I wake with nightmares, jostling, grabbing at the air, a scream hurtling toward my lips, with just enough time to stuff a pillow into my mouth so no one hears me. My first instinct is to knock on Kieran's door so he can make me feel better, but I resist the temptation. Going outside is my only reprieve. I don't make my way into town again to call Stephen. That can only happen once. The next time I talk to him, Clementine will be back.

Two weeks have passed with no improvement. My time has expired, and even though I'm dreading this, the truth can't be ignored anymore. The longer I lie, the worse it gets. That's the truth about lies—when they linger, they slowly trick you into believing they're the truth. When it all falls apart, the pain is even worse, because it's now a part of you. And my lies are beginning to feel like the truth. The line I thought was secure in my mind has blurred, along with everything else. Clementine is losing strength as Jane gains a life. But whatever life Jane has is false.

The first tourist buses arrive for the day as I make my way into town. The air smells fresh and clean. Puddles pool on the cement. The sand on the beach is damp with the sudden rainstorm we had this morning, but the clouds have since departed, and the sun is out. It warms my back as I walk, my sunglasses shielding my eyes, but now I'm not so naïve as to think the rain is done for the day.

Waterville's one internet café is down an alley off the main street. A bell announces my arrival at the small shop lined with old computers. An older man with brown hair stands behind the counter, a grin plastered on his face. Only one other person is in the café. He glances over his shoulder at me as I walk up to the counter. I ask the man working how much it costs, and he points to the coin machine next to a computer.

"You put money in," he says. "Five euros. Twenty minutes."

I thank him and take a seat at the computer a few down from the only other patron. His strawberry hair swoops over his forehead. Freckles cover most of his exposed skin.

"It's dial-up," he says in an American accent. "*Dial-up*. It's like I time-traveled back to 1999."

"Were you even alive in 1999?" I ask. He doesn't appear any older than me.

"You're American." He perks up immediately. "You're right. I *was* barely alive in 1999. But I've seen pictures. Awful time. Lots of pleather and crop tops."

Unfortunately, he doesn't read my silence well.

"And boy bands. I think 1999 was the height of the boy band epidemic. Nasty, contagious disease. But I think it's finally worked its way out of American pop culture. Though I cannot say the same for Ireland. Have you listened to the radio here? They're still playing Robbie Williams. *Robbie. Williams.* I can't believe I gave up a summer in the Hamptons for this." The guy gestures at his computer. "And my dad took my phone. Said I needed to experience the charm of Ireland without technology. 'Charm' is another word for 'ancient shithole.' They don't even have sinks with hot and cold water running out of the same tap. That's archaic."

"I think it's charming."

He gives me a flirtatious eyebrow wiggle. "You're kind of charming."

"What?"

"Look, you're the first pretty girl I've met on this gruesome trip my father calls a 'father-son bonding adventure.' I gotta know. What's a beautiful girl like you doing in the middle of Ireland?"

"We're not in the middle of Ireland," I say. "We're in Southwest Ireland."

"Semantics. Seriously, what are you doing in no man's land? You know it rains here all the time, right?"

"Yes."

"Why not go to Italy? It doesn't rain nearly as much in Italy."

"I don't mind the rain." I start to move to a different computer, but before I can, he scoots his chair toward me.

"Are you from Seattle or something?"

"Cleveland," I say.

"A midwesterner. They breed masochists."

I cock my head at him. "Why don't you go home if you don't like it here?"

"I wish I could," he says, "but my father coerced me into taking this trip because he feels guilty for leaving me and my mom for a big house in the Hamptons and an even bigger set of breasts on my stepmom"—he puts up his finger—"who happens to be only five years older than me. My name's Andy, by the way. My therapist says people need to be more honest with each other. So that's my truth."

"Did your therapist also tell you that you're kind of overwhelming?" I ask.

"I already knew that." He stretches back in his seat, resting his hands behind is head. "Now it's your turn."

"My turn for what?"

"Tell me your problems, and your name."

"I don't have any problems," I lie.

"Oh, you have problems. It's written all over your face." I grab my cheeks, and he smiles. "I knew it."

"I'm not telling you my problems."

"A girl with secrets. Even better." He points at me. "The purple hair helps with the mystique."

"Lavender," I say. He cocks his eyebrow at me. "The hair color is Lusty Lavender."

"Lusty Lavender. You just keep getting better." He's charming, in a slightly unpredictable way. "Well, Lusty Lavender, you're the best thing I've seen on this trip. This whole island smells like manure."

"Maybe it's not the island. It's you. I think it's lovely here."

"I think *you're* lovely. Can I buy you a drink?"

"It's eleven in the morning."

"I won't judge you"—he winks at me—"if you don't judge me. Have you noticed how they tell time here? When someone says it's half five, does that mean it's five thirty or four thirty?"

"Five thirty."

"Thanks for clearing that up for me. So how about that drink? Just don't order wine. It comes in mini bottles. Like the shitty kind you get on airplanes, in coach. You really should go to Italy. Ditch this place."

"Thanks for the offer, but I'm OK." I stand up to move to another computer.

"I get it. I get it. My therapist says I need to be more self-aware, but if I can't buy you a drink, can I at least get a picture with you?" I glare at him. "In truth, I just want to brag to my friends that I met a hot girl on this trip."

"You really are messed up," I say.

"I know." Andy shrugs. "I've spent a lot of time in therapy to figure that out. But also, it turns out, we *all* are."

I can't really argue with that. I might be a bigger mess than he is.

"So what do you do . . . to clean up the mess?" I ask.

"My therapist says it all starts with telling the truth." Andy exhales. "So the truth is, if I get a picture with you, it will royally piss off my dad, who made me promise I would take this 'father-son bonding trip' seriously." He holds up a camera. "Just one little photo to help out a messed-up guy?"

"And you promise to leave me alone after that?"

Andy crosses his finger in an *X* over his heart. "You have my word."

"Fine," I say.

Andy puts his arm around my shoulder, hastily snapping a picture of the two of us. He looks at the display screen and says, "Thanks. It's perfect. I'll leave you alone now." He zips his lips closed.

"Thanks."

I move to the other side of the café. I can't have Andy over my shoulder when I search "Clementine Haas." He may be nosier than Clive.

The computer takes a few minutes to come to life, and after a lot of obnoxious noises, it finally connects to the internet. I check one more time to make sure Andy isn't hanging over my shoulder, but he's engrossed in his computer.

I try to settle into my seat, but anxiety keeps my toes tapping against the floor. I bite my nails without trying to stop myself.

I told Kieran I needed to email my parents before going to paint at Shannon's. He apologized for not having a computer and held out his cell phone. "Would you like to call them?"

I politely declined, claiming I didn't want to run up his bill, and he pointed me in the direction of the café. I was partially relieved when he suggested it, but the other side of me wanted Kieran to give me a reason *not* to do this. My stomach sat high in my ribs, jumping and spinning, all morning.

Google pulls up on the home screen. Clementine Haas, Cleveland, Ohio, is bound to bring something up. But my fingers can't seem to type the words. My stomach lurches at the thought of what might appear . . . or what might not. The questions that plague me daily come to the surface again. What if I don't remember? What if all I see are images of my life, but not a single memory surfaces? What if I do remember, and I don't like what I see? What's worse—blindly not remembering, or seeing your life in front of you, only to be disappointed?

But the time for delaying is over. I said two weeks, and it's been that long. My father is waiting for me. I gave myself a deadline because leaving him behind isn't fair when I can take action. I type: *Clementine Haas, Cleveland, Ohio.* Then I change my mind and delete *Clementine.*

Haas, Cleveland, Ohio.

Baby steps. Start small and work my way up. This is a big moment that I need to take in tiny increments. I click on the "Search" button before I can change my mind.

It takes a few seconds for anything to appear. When the screen lights up with links, I lean in closer to the computer, protective, my stomach a mess.

At first glance, every link is about the crash—article after article about what happened to me. The words bring up panic and disbelief, which scream at me that I am not ready to read about the worst moment in my life. I can't even get up on a ladder.

At the bottom of the page, one article gives me pause. It isn't about me. I stare at the words, reading them over and over.

Owner of the Local Bakery, Born and Bread, Killed in Drunk Driving Incident

I click on the article, and seconds later, it appears on the screen.

November 23, 2005. Lakewood, Ohio—Thirty-six-year-old Mary Haas was the victim of a hit and run early Monday morning on the corner of Detroit Road and Riverside Drive in the Cleveland suburb of Lakewood. She was taken to Fairview Hospital and died, due to complications from the incident, late Monday afternoon. Officers found the suspect and have confirmed that Roger Spiegel had been drinking prior to the incident.

Mary Middleton Haas, known to most as Mimi, was the popular owner of the neighborhood bakery, Born and Bread, a Cleveland staple for over fifty years. Haas bought the bakery in 1995 when then owners, Ruth and Rex Benson, threatened to close. Haas reinvigorated Born and Bread, attracting people from all over the city to her popular sugar cookies.

"She will be deeply missed," said Stacy Partridge, a longtime patron. "Everyone who walked through the doors of Born and Bread felt her passion for that place."

Mary Haas leaves behind a husband, Paul, and a six-year-old daughter, Clementine. Funeral services are planned for later this week at St. James Cathedral, just blocks from the bakery and the site of the incident.

After my tenth read, I'm still paralyzed. Numb. Disconnected from my entire body. *My mom died because of a drunk driver. She owned a bakery.* I say it so many times internally that I know I'll never forget it, but . . . what happened next?

Reading the article is like reading a book. I want to turn the page and let the story continue. Does the bakery shut down? Does the driver, Roger Spiegel, go to jail? Do thousands of people show up to the funeral? What happens to her family?

But it's not a book . . . It's my life. Of all the memories, how can I not remember *this* one?

I told Kieran my last name was Middleton. My brain must have picked it because it's my mom's maiden name. But even now as I say it, I don't feel a connection.

I'm filled to the brim with nothing. And nothing feels awful. I shut down the computer and stand up hastily from my seat. The chair squeaks, and Andy glances over at me.

"Leaving, Lusty Lavender? Are you sure you don't want a drink?"

With my sunglasses hiding my tear-filled eyes, I run out of the café.

When the hospital called my dad, he told them about my mom's death. I read it on my chart, so this shouldn't be a surprise. But a small note, scratched in Stephen's handwriting, is different than an article with details—details a girl should know about her mom.

I can't recall the bakery at all. The article said she was known for her sugar cookies. Is that why I have a knack for baking?

A pack of tourists walks toward me in a clump, taking pictures and chatting, laughing—all as my world deteriorates. Surrounded by strangers, I stop on the sidewalk, unable to move. Unable to do anything but watch them pass by as I sob like a scared child. People watch, but I'm so tired of holding myself together. It takes too much energy to keep all the pieces in place.

No amount of grasping, clenching, squeezing, or moving forward can fix this.

"Are you OK, sweetheart?" An older woman carrying an umbrella touches my arm. Her hair is nearly black except for a thick streak of gray. Her hand has a diamond ring on one of the fingers. That ring holds a memory. A teardrop necklace dangles from her neck, and I'm sure she could tell me where she got it, who gave it to her, and the line of recollections she has about that one person.

"Do you look like your mom or dad?" I ask her in between sobs.

With a surprised expression, she answers, "My mum. Why?"

I notice a scar on her chin and point to it. "And how'd you get that?"

"I fell off my bike when I was little." She cocks her head at me. "Can I help you in some way?"

My cheeks are wet, my sunglasses fogged.

"I have a scar on my knee. I noticed it two days ago," I say. "I don't know what it's from."

Her hazel eyes are kind, warm. I can tell she wants to help, but I know how this ends. She may not know it, but she is a walking story. And me . . . I'm full of scars with no stories.

I push away from her, running through the crowd, at a loss for control. For two weeks, I've kept my pain to myself. I've walked around like I'm normal, but I'm not. I barely feel human.

The false reality I've created crumbles, and anger and grief take its place. Pieces of hope don't amount to much right now. They aren't big enough to hold on to, to keep afloat. In all my efforts to shelter people from pain, it's amounted to nothing. All of this—it's useless.

At least now I can let go of my lies. My fantasy of returning to my dad as Clementine is gone. When you have nothing, you'll be anything. What do I have to lose? Clementine or Jane—the hospital is just another box in a plethora of boxes. If I can't escape my mind, why does it matter where my body is?

I can go back to Limerick, back to my dad, and do what I should have done in the beginning. I should have been strong enough to stay. Brave enough to face my life.

Back at the cottage, I collect my clothes, but even they were bought with someone else's money. They aren't mine. They're just fabric in the story I've weaved about a girl who doesn't really exist.

I leave the clothes. The only things I take with me are the clothes I'm wearing, my notebook, and sweatshirt. I am now just as I came.

From the money Kieran has given me, I've taken just enough for the bus ride to Limerick. I said I didn't want any more of his money, but I'm desperate. When it feels hard to leave, I swallow it down. This is final. Besides the hospital, Waterville is the only place in my memory, and I will never forget it. It wasn't all bad here. But it was all just a ruse.

Siobhan walks in the front door, startling me on my way out. She's not the person I want to see right now. My face is painted in tears. Hers is a picture of made-up perfection.

"Are you crying, Muppet?" Her voice holds no caring, and yet even her body, maybe more than others, holds her story. Colorful pictures ink her skin, and the child she's carrying . . . it's an extension of her story. It feels utterly unfair. "Don't tell me Kieran finally came to his senses and kicked you out."

Two weeks of emotions flood out of me in a final, unfiltered burst. "I wanted to like you. I tried to be your friend. But you have no compassion for other people's feelings. You only care about yourself and *your* problems. Did it ever occur to you that other people are hurting, too? That there are bigger problems than what *you're* going through? At least your problem will result in love. You're going to have a baby who will love you unconditionally. And Kieran and Clive, they support you. And you don't deserve any of them."

I don't wait for her to slam the door on me. I do it myself. She can tell Kieran exactly what I said. I'll never see him again.

Clouds roll into town as I walk away from the cottage. Siobhan was right about one thing—try as I might, I was destined to end up alone.

CHAPTER 13

The only way to Limerick is through Killarney, and the Killarney bus only comes once a day. As I wait, the rain begins. The bus stop is merely a bench, uncovered. One hour later, I'm soaked. The hood of my sweatshirt covers my head, but it does me little good. My jeans are heavy on my legs. Drops of water run down my cheeks, mixing with my tears from earlier.

My eyes are the only dry part of my body. I have no tears left. Resentment has been replaced with apathy. Begrudging people their memories doesn't help me, and losing my calm only sets me back. If this is the way I have to live, I better get used to it.

At least I'm done lying. It's time to face my truth.

I focus on the ground, puddles collecting at my feet as I wait. Cars and tour buses pass by. Every few minutes, I look down the street for the bus to Killarney. The woman at the ticket office said to take the 279A to the Killarney Coach Park and get on line 300 straight to Limerick. It sounded easy enough with just one transfer, but the waiting and the rain are wearing on me. There's too much time to think.

I sit back on the bench, wrapping my arms around my waist, my head down. When a car slows in front of the stop, I look up quickly, hoping it's the bus, but soon realize I've made a mistake.

"Bunny, what the hell are you doing?" Kieran yells out the window of his truck.

I turn away from him. "Just keep driving."

"It's pouring. Get in the car."

"No." I can't make eye contact with him. My mind is made up, and Kieran weakens my defenses.

"Get in the car, Bunny."

"I'm leaving. You can't stop me."

"I'm not looking to stop you," he says. "I'm just trying to prevent pneumonia. Now get in the car. The bus won't be here for another hour."

Another hour in the rain . . . Even my bones feel wet.

"You can wait in the truck."

"You're supposed to be painting," I say.

Kieran checks the sky. "Not in this weather. Come on, Bunny, just get in." His voice is so welcoming, and he looks really dry. And just seeing him is comforting.

But I promised myself I would be strong, be brave. Kieran weakens my determination. I'll miss him. Painting Shannon's house with him every day was the best part of my two weeks in Waterville. Even the discomfort was at times a . . . comfort. Something sparked between us. With him so near me now, the ache comes back to my chest.

"No," I say. "I'm fine. Drive on."

"No." Kieran throws the truck into park. "I'm not leaving."

A small line of cars has accumulated behind his truck.

"Yes, you are," I say through clenched teeth.

"You can't boss me around. I'll just have to sit here in this dry truck, waiting for the bus with you."

"You're blocking traffic."

Kieran shrugs. "That will probably delay the bus even more." He rests back in his seat and puts his hands behind his head. "I don't think the rain is supposed to let up until later this afternoon, but no matter."

Someone lays on a horn.

"People are getting mad," I say.

"You could spare them all that anger if you just got in the car."

Another horn honks. The sound is rattling. I can't put up with this for another hour.

I get in the front seat of Kieran's truck and slam the door with all my might. My anger only makes him smirk more.

"One hour and I'm getting on that bus," I say.

"Grand."

"*Grand*," I snark at him.

Kieran pulls away from the bus stop, allowing traffic to move again. He parks along a side street but keeps the truck running with the heat turned up. I warm my fingers over the vent. For a while, he and I are quiet, eyes trained out the windshield.

"What happened?" Kieran eventually asks.

"Nothing. It's just time I leave and do this on my own. I can't stay here all summer."

"Is that it? Siobhan didn't—"

"No," I state firmly. "I'm leaving because *I* want to."

"You want to leave?" Kieran sounds hurt, which I didn't expect.

"No," I say hastily, turning to face him. "You've been wonderful." When our eyes connect, I can feel the pull between us. But I need to let this go. "I just think it's for the best."

"For you or for me?" Kieran asks. "Because if you're leaving for me, don't. If you're leaving because it's the best decision for *you*, then go. I won't try and convince you otherwise."

I'm leaving because I don't want to hurt anyone. I'm leaving because I'm alone, and nothing can change that until I remember who I was. But with Kieran next to me, the loneliness seems to evaporate. Even now, I'm dreading getting out of this truck and boarding the bus—pulling away from this town, leaving Kieran behind. It will feel awful.

"I lied to you!" I blurt it out.

Silence hangs heavily between us. I've wanted to speak those words for two weeks, but even after they're out, the relief I thought I'd feel doesn't come. Even when I claim Clementine's life, what is there? Other than a trail to the past with no feelings attached to it—the story is there, but the sentiment isn't. But Kieran . . . I feel our connection as real as I feel my body. Why would I want to give that up?

"OK . . . ," Kieran finally says with a puzzled expression.

"I didn't come to Ireland for the summer to prove to my parents I could survive on my own. I ran away from my life. I just needed to get out. I felt boxed in, like my life was laid out for me—college, job, marriage, kids—one domino after another. But I had no say in any of it. So I cleared out my bank account and bought a one-way ticket to Ireland." The story flows easily, the truth on some level, though laced with falsehoods, too. "Haven't you ever just wanted to abandon everything and start over?"

"Yes," Kieran says seriously.

"You have?"

"But I'm not as strong as you."

"I'm not strong. I'm weak. I ran away."

"Ran away? Or ran toward?" Kieran says. "It's subjective."

The rain has stopped. Breaks in the clouds allow the sun to peek through, and my clothes are starting to dry. The chill in my bones has warmed, along with the anger.

We sit for a while, no words. Today has been a mess, but somehow Kieran has managed to fix it, to make me feel capable again. Can I really leave him behind?

"The bus should be here in just a few minutes," Kieran says, his eyes trained in front of him.

Run from or run toward . . . He's right. It is subjective. This is my opportunity to decide how I want to live. And tomorrow is, too. Each day, another decision. There is no running from that.

"Truth or dare?" I say.

Kieran looks at me more with curiosity than surprise. "Interesting question."

"Truth or dare?" I repeat.

"You know my answer, Bunny."

My decision is made. Forward I go. "I want to have some fun today."

"*Fun.*" He says the word with a hint of mischief. "And what is your idea of fun?"

"I dare you to take me surfing."

CHAPTER 14

After a brief stop at the cottage—luckily Siobhan is gone—to swap out paint supplies for surfing gear, we drive with the windows down, the sun out now, warm air blowing over my skin.

"So where are we going?" I ask. Out the window, my arm floats in the wind, the smell of ocean replaced, as we leave Waterville, with grass and manure.

"Inch Beach," he says, his eyes on the narrow, windy road ahead, lined on both sides with green hedgerows.

"Is that close?"

Kieran glances at me with a smirk. "Close enough."

It takes almost two hours. We drive through small towns, similar to Waterville, though not along the coast, and at one point get stuck in a traffic jam caused by sheep crossing the road. I don't mind. The weight of the morning is gone, and when we finally pull into Inch Beach, where cars are allowed to park directly on the sand and surfboards pepper the ocean, I'm practically weightless.

A wide stretch of sand surrounds us, enclosed by rolling patchwork hills that gradually build into low mountains. Like in Waterville, the land here is bright green, the ocean a striking blue next to it. Surfers coast through the waves or lie on the beach, half-covered in wet suits and lounging on towels. A few pop-up stands advertise board rentals and food.

Kieran gets his surfboard out of the back of the truck and digs it into the sand.

"You need to change," he says, casually.

"Into what?"

Kieran searches through his bag. He pulls out a bathing suit and holds it up. "This."

"No," I say emphatically. He holds the suit by its strings, because that's all it's made of. A string bikini.

He shrugs. "It's all Siobhan had."

"Didn't she have something more . . . conservative?"

Kieran laughs. "I'm pretty sure Siobhan has never used that word before." He gives me a taunting grin. "You're not getting bashful on me, are you, Bunny? You proposed the dare. You can't wimp out now."

I snag the suit from him. "Where do I change?"

"Here." Kieran gestures like we're standing in a dressing room, with walls and doors and privacy, not on an open beach. He pats the truck. "You can change in here if that's more comfortable."

It's not the bathing suit that makes me nervous. It's being in a bikini in front of *him*. If it were Clive or Stephen, this wouldn't be a big deal. Stephen's seen all of me. He knows my bra size. But I need to keep control of myself around Kieran. To keep our boundaries in place. Yet there is no getting out of wearing this suit. I chose the dare after all.

I groan and climb into the truck to change as Kieran goes to the rental shop. With the suit on, the last item of clothing I need to part with gives me pause—my socks. Exposing my tattoo might lead to questions—questions I have no answers to.

He's back with another surfboard and knocks on the truck. "Need help tying anything? You know me—always happy to help."

I rip off my socks, knowing it's better to do it swiftly, like a Band-Aid, than linger on the what-ifs. I step out of the car.

"I'm ready." I put my hands on my hips, displaying myself proudly.

Kieran turns around, and we make eye contact. Time seems to move slowly, the heat in my cheeks betraying me, but he doesn't give my body a glance. He hands me the surfboard. "Grand. Follow me."

We approach the water's edge, where Kieran sets down a bag filled with towels and wet suits. We prop our boards upright in the sand. Surfers ride the waves just off shore, gracefully turning back and forth, becoming one with the water. Occasionally they fall, and I hold my breath until they reappear on the surface.

"You need a suit, too," I say.

Kieran pulls a towel from the bag and hands it to me. "Who said I wear a suit when I surf."

"Pardon?"

"Too much bunching under the wet suit." Kieran starts to undress—first his shirt, his chest exposed before I've had time to process what he's doing. He has tan lines, and his chest is pale. It's also just as defined as I remember. He goes to unbutton his pants.

"You're just going to strip down right here?"

"I'm not the bashful one." He winks.

"Clearly." I swallow the dryness in my throat.

He laughs. "No one will see me if you hold up the towel, Bunny. Or should I just expose myself to the entire beach? I'm fine with either."

Kieran's pants are coming off quickly. I grab the towel and wrap it around his waist.

"Just in time." He wiggles out of his jeans and kicks them away. His boxers come next. When he bends to slip into the wet suit, I worry I might drop the towel or faint.

When he's done, Kieran takes the towel and casually says thanks, like it was no big deal. Like I didn't just see him take off his clothes. Like he's not now in a tight black wet suit that accentuates . . . everything.

I focus on the ocean. The waves are large, angry from the bad weather earlier.

"Bunny."

"What?" I still can't look at him.

"Your wet suit," he says.

"Maybe this was a bad idea. I don't even know how to surf."

"I'll teach you."

"What if I can't do it? What if I fall? What if . . ."

Kieran turns me toward him. He holds me and leans his face closer to mine. "I won't let anything happen." His blue eyes match the clear sky. Our faces are so close I can practically feel the heat coming off him. "You can't be overwhelmed by the what-ifs, or you'll miss out on the best part." The rush he gets from a dare is evident. It's practically tangible. "You didn't leave your life behind just to come to Ireland to paint a house, did you?"

I've spent too much time thinking about a life that doesn't exist. This is my chance to *live*. I work my way into the awkward wet suit without another thought.

We take our boards to the water, where the waves are just coming on shore. Kieran lays them both in the wet sand.

"We're going to practice pop-ups. It's how you go from lying down on your board to standing." Kieran is all business, his demeanor cool. I try to reciprocate as he demonstrates pop-ups, lying on his stomach on the board and then pushing himself onto his feet in one smooth move. He makes it seem easy, even graceful, and I find myself mesmerized. "Now you try."

Pop-ups are harder than they appear. I do it a few times, trying to be as effortless as Kieran and failing miserably. He critiques my technique. "Don't look down . . . Keep your eyes forward . . . Try to land in the middle of the board."

At one point, I fall off, rolling my ankle. It hurts my pride more than my foot. I'm exhausted before we've even been in the water.

"You see those tiny waves right there?" Kieran points just off shore. "That's where we start. When you paddle out, try to stay centered on the board."

"Paddle out?" I say. "But we just started. I fell off the board and it's *on the sand*. I can't be ready yet."

"Some things have to be learned by experience, Bunny. You just need to do it." My breath hitches. I'm not sure I'm wired the same way Kieran is, acting without thinking. "I'll be right next to you. I promise."

He picks up his board, and I try to shake off my nerves. Backing out of this dare isn't an option, though. Worse comes to worst, I won't stand up. I'll stay on my stomach and just roll into shore.

"Hook the strap around your ankle," Kieran instructs me. "That way you won't lose your board."

The cold water hits my feet, shivers covering my arms and legs. We walk out to the waist-deep waves.

"I'll point at you when I see a good wave. You need to paddle quickly and try to catch it as it breaks. Go for it head on. If you catch it on the side, you'll roll the board."

I acknowledge what Kieran's said, without really digesting everything. My ears are fuzzy with the sound of the ocean. I remind myself that this sound makes me calm at night.

Kieran hops onto his board and paddles out. I follow his lead, imitating his movements, pushing my hands through the small waves, trying to blink salt water from my eyes. When we're out a bit farther, Kieran sits up and straddles his board. His legs hang in the water on either side. My arms are tired, my teeth are chattering, and I worry that if I make a sudden move, I'll tip over.

"Don't be afraid of the water, Bunny. If you feel like you're going to fall, fall backward, not forward. Butt first, not head first. Got it?"

His words seem to go right through me, but I nod anyway.

"You can do this," he says.

We've come this far. The only way I'm getting back to shore is on this board. The water will move me in that direction naturally.

A group of kids on the beach practices pop-ups. They don't look scared. They seem excited, laughing, having fun. If they can do it, I can do it.

"Ready, Bunny?" Kieran yells. He points at a wave. "Remember, paddle fast and hit the wave head on!"

We take off. I push my arms speedily through the waves. I spit salt water and try to breathe evenly, my eyes on the shore. The current pushes my board, helping it to roll with the waves. When I feel one start to crest under me, it lifts me up, and the board gains speed. I grip the sides, trying to remember how to stand up.

Eyes forward.

Don't look down.

With my chest lifted, my knees bent, the board teeters underneath me, but I stay in control and plant my feet. I hold myself in a squat and realize what I've done—I managed to pop up. It brings a wave of euphoria. The board rattles from side to side, but my feet control it, and it glides along the wave. With more confidence, I extend my arms out for balance.

The water that scared me is no longer angry. The sun plays on its surface, accentuating the blue. It's mesmerizing. Even the cold doesn't affect me. My day has turned around entirely. I could be on a bus headed for Limerick, but my decision to stay feels so right. I am more alive now than I have been in weeks. No more letting go, no more walking away when fear threatens to consume me. I'm stronger than I think.

The wave begins to slow, my board coasts, and I turn to find Kieran. My whole body is zinging.

"I did it!" I yell over my shoulder. "I did it!"

But Kieran isn't there. Something unexpected is instead.

I forgot that waves keep coming. The whitecap of the next one is large. The roll of the crest rushes at me with a sound that consumes the moment. Did Kieran say to go into the wave or ride on the side of it? But waves don't wait for answers.

It pummels me, tossing me off my board. I don't know which way I fall—front, back, sideways. The water pulls me under, carelessly tossing, grabbing, pushing me down, suffocating me.

It's now when an important question occurs to me—do I even know how to swim?

CHAPTER 15

"See the sand swirling and being pulled out with the waves? That's the rip current."

"What happens if I get caught in it, Dad?" The sand under my feet is coarse and rocky. Sailboats with colorful sails glide far off shore. The hum of a powerful engine sings in the background.

"It will pull you away from me. You'll be so far from shore I won't be able to get to you. And I can't lose you, too. If you're going to play in Lake Erie, promise me you'll never forget the rip current."

I reach as if I'm trying to grasp the memory, but it's as fluid as water through my fingertips. When I think I have it, the memory slips through my grasp.

The water pulls me down, yanking at my body like I'm a ragdoll. The surface eludes me. I can't tell which way is up and which is down, my body kicking and pulling, unable to find a break from the water. The salt stings my eyes and burns my nose. This isn't a lake. The ocean makes itself known, where daring to trespass means risking being made a plaything by its waves.

Kieran told me to let fear have its way. Let it wash over you, like an uncontrollable current. Only then can you realize that fear has no power. You can be free.

"It's not the current that will drown you. It's the exhaustion from fighting it."

Through the water, I can practically see the memory play in front of me before it dissolves in the sea.

My only option is to surrender. Stop fighting. It's actually quite peaceful. To untangle fear and let it drift away. I begin just to float. The water only fights back when threatened, and I'm too tired to fight. I have to let go.

Is this the upside of falling down?

A solid object connects with my feet. Sand and rock. The bottom. Instinct has me pushing off the ground, my arms pulling at the water. I swim, my body moving as if it's done this a million times before.

My lungs burn and tighten, but as I coast up toward the surface, I know I'll make it. This is not the end. I won't let that happen. Within me appears strength like I haven't experienced before.

My head breaks the surface. Ragged, uneven breaths come one after the other. Salt water stings my eyes as they adjust to the sunlight. Before I even have a second to search for the shore, someone grabs me around the waist, pulling me.

"I've got you. Hold on to me." Kieran hugs me close, pulling me through the waves. I wrap my arms around his neck as tightly as I can, and we kick toward shore.

When Kieran can finally touch the bottom, he scoops me up, detaching the cord that holds my ankle to my board. We collapse on the sand, Kieran still cradling me. He presses his face into my neck and breathes heavily. His hair is wet on my cheek. His arms hold me tightly. The weight of his body—the feel of his chest rising and falling with mine, the proximity, the contact—makes everything disappear. I forget almost drowning. The cold of the ocean has no effect on me. All there is right now is Kieran, covering me like a blanket.

He pulls back slightly, scanning my face. But I want him closer. Always closer. "Are you hurt?"

I shake my head, unable to find words. Kieran moves the hair from my face, his eyes taking me in like he can't believe I'm alive. We are electric together. The world falls away when he's with me—the questions and uncertainty—and all I want to know is *him*. Every inch. His lips aren't far from mine, and I wonder if people are like food. Do I need to taste him to know him fully? If we kissed, all that he's made of would be exposed.

"I shouldn't have made you do it." Kieran creates more space between us, but that's not what I need. I feel more alive right now than I've felt since I woke up in the hospital.

My hand connects with his cheek. I turn his face toward mine.

"I felt it. I did what you said. I didn't let fear control me. I was free."

He looks at me in disbelief, guilt still in his eyes. "Bunny, I thought you drowned."

"But I didn't."

He presses a cold finger to my bottom lip, pausing my breath. He focuses on my mouth, and in Kieran's eyes, I see what I feel in my heart. We are connected.

"I saw courage," he says. "That night in the pub when you asked me what I saw in you? It was courage."

I can't resist the urge to move closer. This is all I want. Him. Kieran is right—courage is in me. I need to use it. My mouth reaches for his, as if he holds my next breath between his lips, and I need to take it.

But he stops me. He sits back, his cool demeanor in place, leaving me to wonder if I imagined it all.

"You're turning purple, Bunny. We need to get you dry."

"Does it match my hair?" I say awkwardly. Kieran lets out a small laugh, and he helps me off the sand.

Our surfboards have washed up on the beach. Kieran wraps me in a towel before going to collect them. As I sit on the sand, he busies himself with returning my board to the rental stand and loading the rest of our gear into the truck. Distance settles between us once again.

When the strength has returned to my legs, I change into my dry clothes. Kieran stands with his back to me, resting against the truck, his attention on the ocean. We switch spots, the carefree guy who only needed a towel now gone. I lean on the hood of the truck, watching the sun dance on the water. Every cloud has disappeared. The day has wholly shifted. What I thought today would be has changed. And I don't want it to end. For the first time, the veil of fear has lifted, and I'm seeing clearly.

Kieran rolls down the window of the truck. "Hop in, Bunny."

"How apropos." I smile and hop like a rabbit to the window. It perks Kieran up, but too quickly that fades.

A restaurant sits a ways down the beach, and I ask if we can get a bite to eat before leaving. Kieran agrees, and we leave the truck parked on the sand.

The restaurant's picnic tables overlook the beach. I hug my knees to my chest and turn my face up to the sun, letting it warm me to my core. My hair is half-dry, the ends clumping together with salt water.

"You have a tattoo," Kieran says, drawing my attention back. My bare feet are covered in sand. For the first time, I'd forgotten about it, forgotten to cover it up, forgotten even to care it was there.

I cross my ankles and tuck them under my body. "It was a stupid mistake." And when I say that, it feels *so* true. Kieran doesn't ask me any more about it.

We each get an order of fish-and-chips and a Guinness. The place is quaint and casual. People sit in swimsuits, covered in sand, most of them sun kissed from a day at the beach.

We don't say much as we sip on our beers. At one point, I purposefully cover my top lip with foam and smile at Kieran. He returns the gesture, but only briefly. A weight is back on his shoulders, his eyes pensive.

"Will you miss it?" he asks eventually.

"Miss what?"

Kieran gestures to my beer. "I hear the Guinness in America doesn't compare to here. When you go home, do you think you'll miss it?"

I can't look at him. "I don't want to talk about going home."

"You can't run away from your life forever, Bunny."

"Run away or run toward? You said so yourself." I straighten my posture. "I haven't even seen Dublin yet."

We eat in silence. Kieran pokes at his food, only briefly looking at me when I say something, but then returns to dissecting his fish and fries. By the end of the meal, his food is more mutilated than eaten.

When the plates have been cleared, and our pints drained, I ask if we can take a walk on the beach.

"This may be the only time I come to Inch Beach. I want to take it all in." But I'm just stalling. I want this day to go on forever. Daylight lasts so long here. To sacrifice it driving is unacceptable, not when the ocean sounds so calming, and the sun feels so warm on my skin. Kieran obliges, and after he insists on paying, his penance for almost getting me killed, we walk barefoot down the beach. A distance is kept between us that I can feel. Maybe it's my fault. I'm the one who's pulled away to this point. But after today that feels almost impossible.

I purposefully move closer as we walk.

"So you told me about your favorite dare. What's the one that made you the most afraid?"

Kieran stops and picks up a rock. He examines it.

"Skydiving?" I ask.

Kieran shakes his head, his eyes not meeting mine.

"Spelunking?"

He glances at me sideways now. "You know about spelunking?"

"Doesn't everyone?" I give him a cocky grin.

Kieran shakes his head. "Not spelunking."

"Something else with heights?" I prod, but he just keeps his eyes on the rock, turning it around in his hands.

When he finally throws it into the ocean, it lands with a splash. "I haven't actually done the dare I'm most afraid of."

"Well, what is it?"

He dusts the sand off his hands, and we walk farther down the beach.

"I promise I won't tell anyone." I trail after him, but Kieran doesn't budge. He picks up the pace. I take two steps to one of his. He doesn't stop until I touch his arm. My hand stays on his bare skin. "You can trust me."

It's not fair of me to say, and the instant it's out, I regret it. How can Kieran trust me when all I'm feeding him are lies, as justified as I think they are? Lies are a betrayal, no matter how well intended they seem.

Kieran and I notice at the same time that I'm still holding his arm. I pull back, clasping my hands behind my back. How can I ask him to reveal his secrets when I won't reveal mine?

But he speaks before I have the chance to rescind the question. "Refusing the life that my father insists on. Telling him I don't want it. That I'm done being blackmailed into loving him. That I want nothing to do with his life or his money. That I'm leaving him behind, just like my mother did, to start a new life. That's the dare I'm most afraid of—to live the life I choose." Kieran finally looks at me. "I'm not as strong as you, Bunny. You wanted a different life, and here you are, chasing it. I can't seem to do that."

Any thoughts of confessing disappear, pulled out to sea with the sand at our feet.

"I'm not that strong," I say.

Kieran starts walking again. "You don't give yourself enough credit."

We stay silent, my thoughts juggling between guilt and intrigue. "If you could choose, what would your life be like?"

A wisp of a smirk comes to Kieran's face. "You're going to think I'm crazy."

"I already know you're crazy. I've seen the pictures in your room."

"If I could do anything"—Kieran turns his attention up to the sky—"I'd fly planes for a living."

A sinking feeling drops in my stomach. "But you're afraid of heights."

"But every day would be a rush. I'd never have to bungee jump again." Kieran speaks with the excited tone I've come to recognize.

"You *are* crazy."

Kieran laughs lightly. "It's only during liftoff that I get nervous. Once I'm in the air, the fear goes away."

The blissful expression on his face draws me into him more, and I understand. "Freedom," I say.

"It'll never happen. My father wants me to go into business. Move to London when I'm done with school. Start at his company so one day I can take over, like a good son should."

"But they're *your* plans. You get to choose."

Kieran shakes his head. "It's not that simple. My life is tied to him. I'm a spoiled rich kid, Bunny. Letting that go . . . it's complicated."

Kieran's eyes grow stormy.

"What's your father like?" I ask.

"He's exactly what you'd expect—charming, entitled, power hungry." Kieran glances at me. "He gave Von and me anything we wanted when we were little and then shipped us off to boarding school so we couldn't see how miserable he made my mum . . ." Kieran pauses, taking a deep breath. "For a long time, I blamed her for leaving us behind without a word. Blamed her for not loving us enough. But now . . . When she left, she knew she'd have nothing. No money. No job. Both her parents were dead, and she had no siblings. I don't think she wanted that kind of life for Von and me. We had everything. How could she take that away? But she must have been miserable to choose a life with nothing over the life she had." Kieran shakes his head. "I think she thought we'd be OK. That our dad would change."

"But that didn't happen."

Kieran shakes his head. "You can't change someone like him." He stops, the waves lapping at his feet. "In truth, some days I'm afraid I'm like him. We both need a rush to feel alive. His is just a different kind of rush."

I pull on Kieran's arm to make him face me. "You are *nothing* like him. He manipulates people to get what he wants. You help them."

Kieran's eyes are unreadable. It's as if he wants to believe me, but can't.

"You should tell him," I say.

"It's not that simple."

"It sounds that simple."

Kieran pulls away and turns back toward the ocean. "The truth is never that simple, Jane."

A piece of my heart breaks free when he says *Jane*. He's only done it a few times, but each instance has reminded me of all the lies I've placed on him. He's right—the truth is never simple.

Kieran's eyes match the blue of the sparkling water. "I can't be selfish with my life. I need to think about Siobhan. About her future."

Kieran doesn't say the word "baby." We've never talked about it. It's almost as if Kieran and Siobhan are pretending the baby doesn't exist, moving through their daily lives like nothing is different. But that can't last forever. Her belly is growing. Time stops for no one, no matter how unsure we are of the future.

"If agreeing to this life means protecting Siobhan and her future . . . I'll do it." There's intensity, a fortitude, in Kieran's eyes when he says this, but more is hidden beneath the surface. Why can't Siobhan take care of herself? Why does he feel obligated to sacrifice his life for her? I'm not sure she would do the same. Whatever has transpired between them is complicated, layered. What he's revealed to me so far has taken time, and when I push too much, that part of him locks up. I have to be cautious for fear Kieran will shut me out completely.

"What about you, Bunny?" Kieran asks with what feels like a purposeful change of subject. "What do you want to do with your life when you go back to America? Professional surfer, maybe?"

A radiant hue paints Kieran's skin, like the setting sun is literally kissing his cheeks, and I find I'm jealous of it.

"I don't know," I say honestly. "I'm not even sure I want to go back to America."

"Where do you want to go then?"

"Paris, maybe?" I smile at Kieran. "Open a bakery. Have macaroons all lined up and color coordinated."

"On Île Saint-Louis, tucked next to an ice cream shop?"

"You've been to Paris?"

Kieran nods. "It's one of my favorite cities."

"Maybe we should go there."

He looks out at the ocean. "You'll leave the rain of Ireland for the wonders of Paris. I can already tell."

For a time we stand in the sand, our feet covered as the waves wash up on shore. Kieran watches the sun, but I can't take my eyes off him. Forget Paris. No place could be more wonderful than this.

"Kieran?"

"Yeah, Bunny?"

"I'm not sure what I want, but I think I need more adventure in my life."

"Need I remind you that today's adventure almost killed you?"

"But it didn't."

Kieran shakes his head. "Just because you ran away for the summer doesn't mean you shouldn't go back to your life. This won't last forever. Ireland gets dreadfully cold and dark in the winter."

A chill blows off the ocean as the sun starts to disappear on the horizon, sending shivers up my arms. I want to counter Kieran. I don't know the life I had, but I can't let go of the way I feel right now.

"You're cold," Kieran says. I'm not . . . not when he's close by. I feel warmth in my chest, like I'm wrapped in contentment. In calm. But my body betrays my heart, and my teeth chatter. "I think it's time to head back."

We ride in silence most of the way home. The sky changes color out the window of the truck. I don't remember what the sunset looks like in Cleveland, but I know I'll never forget the colors off the coast of Ireland.

When we pull into the driveway of the cottage, the night has turned dark, but Siobhan's bedroom light is on. I'd forgotten about our run-in earlier today, the sharp words I threw at her. She won't be happy I'm back, but her concern isn't mine. Siobhan will have to deal with me, just like I have to deal with her. I stride into the house with more confidence, prepared for a storm, only to find a pile of clothes sitting on my bed with a note on top.

I'm sick of your boring clothes. These don't fit anyway.
You're welcome.

The sea glass I tried to give her weeks ago is gone from my night-stand. Maybe she has more compassion than I give her credit for. Today has surprised me on multiple levels. This morning, all I thought I had was a sweatshirt and a notebook. But I was wrong. I have so much more than that. Leaving this life is beginning to verge on impossible. I'd set out to find a way home, but what I'm finding is that maybe home isn't where I thought it was.

CHAPTER 16

We finish painting Shannon Walsh's house later that week, Kieran braving the ladder in the end. I bake her sugar cookies, and she invites us in for tea. Her house is cozy and slightly cluttered, with wool blankets draped on every seat and old pictures displayed on every open surface. She plods around the house, dodging furniture, but clearly hard of seeing, squinting through thick glasses, leaning into my face.

"To be young and beautiful again." Shannon shakes her head. "Don't squander it. Soon you'll be old and wrinkled like me. It all goes by so fast."

Kieran is intently examining Shannon's rickety old kitchen table, seemingly unaware of her comment. "This is a bit wobbly. Can I fix it for you?" he asks.

"Good lad." She pats him on the cheek. Before we leave that day, Kieran fixes her kitchen table, leaky bathroom sink, and a sticky doorknob, and he changes five light bulbs.

I hug Shannon before we leave, embracing her small round body like a big pillow. Painting her house was a joy and offered me more than she'll ever know.

As we're leaving, she says to Kieran, "Michael Flynn's dishwasher is out. I told him you could fix it. Would you mind?"

"Not at all."

Shannon winks at me subtly. "It's probably a two-person job. Why don't you take your friend? You know how Michael likes a pretty girl."

Kieran agrees, and I blush at the compliment. But when we climb into his truck and drive away, he's quiet. He's been silently contemplative ever since Inch Beach, and it's verging on maddening. I'd take Siobhan's yelling over Kieran's silence any day. But even Siobhan's temper has diminished lately. I can't find the courage to apologize for what I said, so we just continue to dodge each other. Even at the Secret Book and Record Store, Siobhan keeps to herself. I've noticed Clive watching her carefully.

"Something's not right," he said yesterday during tea at the Beachfront Café. "She actually said to a customer, 'I'm always happy to help.' Siobhan is *never* happy to help."

"What do you think it is?"

"I don't know." Clive's tone was worrisome. "But I've been playing Celine Dion all morning, and she hasn't said a bloody word."

The truck bounces over the road. Kieran and I sit in silence. I consider bringing up the weather . . . anything to fill the space, but I'm worried that one wrong move will push him further away.

I point out the window at the passing hedgerow. "The red flowers I see everywhere. What are they?"

"Fuchsias," Kieran says. "People down here call them the tears of God."

"Why?"

"As Ireland was dying of famine, those flowers were blooming. They survived when so many people didn't."

"That's incredibly sad."

Without warning, Kieran jerks the wheel, jostling me in my seat, and pulls to the side of the road. He throws the car into park and turns to face me.

"I need to tell you something," he says adamantly.

His serious appearance and his stiff posture aren't a good sign. My stomach sinks to my toes as a million possibilities race through my head. This might be when Kieran finally kicks me out of his house. I've been here for almost three weeks. I thought my memories would be back by now, but other than the few wisps, I have nothing of Clementine's life to hold on to. All I have is this. And I can't lose it.

"Yes?" I say hesitantly.

Kieran is too quiet for too long. Finally he says, "I lied to you."

"What?"

Kieran runs his hands through his messy hair. "I . . ." He fumbles with his words, his cool exterior cracking. "I promised I'd butt out and let you earn your own money. But it was really *my* money you've been earning."

"What?"

"I don't charge people for the work I do. It wouldn't be right. I don't need it. But I want to pay you for your work, Bunny. You've earned it."

"I don't want money," I say. I didn't help to get paid. It was an excuse to spend time with him, though I didn't want to admit that at the start. Kieran looks at me for what feels like the first time in days.

"But what about the whole 'I'm an independent woman. I want to earn my own' money?"

"I *am* an independent woman," I say, and truly feel it this time. "And I don't want *your* money."

"But you should get out of Waterville and see Dublin."

"And I'll get there. Someday." I square myself forward in the seat. "Now, are we going to fix that dishwasher or what?"

"Are you sure, Bunny? You don't have to do this."

"Yes. Now, drive."

The hint of a grin pulls on Kieran's face. "Never mess with an independent woman."

Fixing Michael Flynn's dishwasher leads to helping Martin Blake clean up his yard, which leads to painting and rehanging Molly Barry's

"Seaside Bed and Breakfast" sign. Kieran and I have a new job every day. He admits to me that part of the reason he helps is to prove that he's not like his father—that there are people who take and people who give, and his genes won't determine that, Kieran will. The space between us lessens as the week passes. Kieran laughs more. It's no longer a question of whether *I'll* help him, but who *we're* helping next.

~

I wake up one morning later that week, heavy from sleep after the first night I haven't been wracked with nightmares. My body feels fully rested. Inside my notebook, I add a tally mark to the long line of them at the top of the page.

It's been twenty-one days since I woke up and became Jane. I count them one more time just to make sure.

Twenty-one days.

That first day in Waterville feels distant. Lately, I've almost stopped searching for my memories. Some days, I'm so involved in my life here that I forget I had a life elsewhere. But then an uncomfortable feeling creeps up on me, like Clementine is hiding but not gone. As if every turn I take might be the one that leads me to her. But I'm no longer sure I want to find her. Three weeks ago, the anticipation of remembering was all I could think about. My happiness was dependent on it. But now . . . I almost fear the memories' return.

Saying good-bye to Kieran might be the hardest thing I have to do.

The picture I tucked in my notebook three weeks ago is still there—Kieran and his friends at boarding school, laughing and happy. I've kept it for him, but I'm starting to understand that it might be best to let some memories go. It's easier when it's a single memory like this one, compared to a lifetime of them—that fact keeps me attached to Clementine, even when I'm tempted to let her go completely.

For now, the picture stays where it is. So does my list, which hasn't grown all week. Slowly, my life has become less about knowing Clementine and more about living as Jane. Now, when I think of my dad and Stephen waiting for me, the desperation to return to them is gone. I'll be upset when I have to leave Jane's life, and no matter how this ends, I'll be hurt. That is the only inevitability in my life right now.

But today has the potential to be different. Today is significant to Clementine's life and Jane's. Today is notable.

I get dressed in a pair of Siobhan's old tight jeans with intentional holes in the thighs and knees, a red-and-black striped T-shirt, and the Converse Stephen gave me. I am sure Siobhan wore these clothes better than I do, but having the added wardrobe options has been nice.

I walk out of my bedroom, notebook in my back pocket, and hear Kieran and Siobhan talking in the kitchen. I stop my approach.

"I need to tell you something," Siobhan says, her voice lacking the edge it normally does. I hug the wall and eavesdrop on their conversation.

"You're pregnant," Kieran says sarcastically.

"You're such a git." The bite comes back to Siobhan's voice for a second.

Kieran's tone is softer when he says, "What is it, Von? You look tired."

"It's a girl, Kieran."

A palpable silence lingers. I hold my breath, not daring to move.

Siobhan eventually speaks. "Say something."

Kieran's voice comes fast. "Does Dad know?"

Siobhan groans, and I hear her shuffle around the kitchen. "Of course not. He said the baby was bad for business, Kieran. Called me a slut and told me to get rid of it, or he'd cut me off forever. And when I didn't, he banished me here so people in Dublin wouldn't know. He still thinks I'm going to give it up for adoption, and we can all just go back to our lives like this never happened. But I'm not doing it. I'm not giving *her* up. I've made up my mind."

"What will you do then?"

"I don't know," Siobhan says. "But I'll figure it out. I don't need him."

Another pause. "You could tell—"

"No. They're not to know. You promised me."

"But they could help you."

"No. I'll find another way. I'm not telling them."

"Think of what they've been through. It's not right."

"Not right?" Siobhan bites back. "You're not in any position to tell me what's right."

When silence follows, I bite my nails, holding my breath.

"This is my fault," Kieran says. "If I would have—"

"Stop it," Siobhan snaps. "Stop blaming yourself. My problem is ruining *your* life. I won't let that happen."

"You're not ruining my life, Von. I made my choices."

"You came down here because I needed you, and I let you do it because I'm selfish," Siobhan says. "You always come to my rescue. But now *you're* the one doing the hiding. And who's gonna rescue you? You're avoiding your life, Kieran."

"I can't go back to Dublin. Not yet. I can't face . . . everything."

"Well, you can't stay here forever. At some point, we all need to move on. That's what I'm trying to do. I'm taking control of my life, Kieran. You need to do the same."

The house goes quiet for a while. I almost think it's safe to approach the kitchen until I hear Siobhan say, "She was right, you know . . . the Yank."

"Don't start," Kieran says.

"She told me I don't deserve you. That I only care about my problems." Siobhan chuckles. "You were right. The Yank's got spunk, no doubt. She's relentless."

"Reckless at times."

"Kieran . . ." Siobhan's voice is warm. "She was right. Now it's my turn to help *you*. Something I should have done a while ago."

"I'm fine."

"No, you're not. You're hiding."

I try to process all that I'm hearing. It's confirmation of what I've thought this whole time, but what Kieran's hiding from is still a mystery, one he won't let go of easily.

"A girl," he says.

"A girl," Siobhan echoes. "Do you think he would have been happy with a girl?"

I hear Kieran exhale. "I think . . . in the end . . . he would have left no matter if the baby was a boy or a girl. Nothing would have changed that."

My heart breaks for Siobhan and the baby.

"I'm sorry," Kieran says.

Siobhan pauses for a long while. "Are you happy, Kieran?"

"Happy?"

"I'm not naïve," she scoffs. "I have eyes." My breath hangs on his answer, but I don't get it. "He would have wanted you to be happy," she adds. "And to stop hiding from your life."

"It's not that simple."

"You're the one who's made it complicated," she says. "You can set it right."

I wish I knew who they were talking about. I wish Kieran would just open up and tell me the details of his life. I wish I wasn't so drowned in lies that I could do the same for him.

"You're really going to give it all up?" Kieran asks.

"Yes," Siobhan replies. "*Someone* with an annoying American accent pointed out that I can't just think about myself anymore. You could do it, too. You could be happy, Kieran."

144

I wait for him to agree with Siobhan. To take control, like he wants to, like I want him to. But instead he says, "I don't think so."

"Then you have no one to blame but yourself."

A few seconds later, the front door slams. I slink back against the wall, letting the conversation sink in.

A few minutes pass before I walk into the kitchen, fake yawning. Kieran is rinsing dishes in the sink. He's already dressed.

"So what are we fixing today?" I say in a bright tone, but it doesn't change Kieran's serious stance.

"It's Saturday, Bunny."

"Does that mean we get to do something fun instead? Not that trimming David Cromie's hedgerow isn't fun, but . . ." I smile, hoping it's contagious.

"The last time we had *fun*, you almost died."

"I guess the bar is pretty high." My joke doesn't work.

Kieran stays focused on the kitchen sink. "As temping as that sounds, I can't today."

I sit down at the table and try not to sound disappointed. "You can't?"

Kieran turns from the sink and says, "There's a party at Paudie's Pub for the annual Waterville Links golf tournament. It's always a raucous madhouse. Loads of rich wankers looking to drink themselves into a stupor. I told Paudie I'd help behind the bar."

I perk up. "I can help, too."

"Not today," Kieran says, turning back to the sink. "Can you manage on your own?"

"Sure." I nod.

"It's a day off. Relax."

"OK," I say, feeling uneasy.

Kieran dries his hands on a towel. "Just promise me you won't try anything too *fun* while I'm gone."

"I can't promise anything." I force my voice to sound positive.

"No," Kieran says, as if he's not talking to me now, but more to himself. "We can't promise anything, can we?"

He leaves, and I sit at the kitchen table, drinking a cup of tea, my notebook open in front of me. I count the dash marks at the top of the page. Twenty-one.

I guess I'll just have to spend my birthday alone.

CHAPTER 17

Stephen pointed it out when he looked at my chart three weeks ago.

"It's almost your birthday, Clementine. You'll be nineteen on July 9. That's only three weeks away." Stephen was enthused. "You'll have a mad party back in the States. I bet the whole of Cleveland will come out to celebrate you."

The empty cottage echoes. Stephen assumed that I would be home by now. That my memories would be back. That Clementine would have returned to her life and that today would be a day when memories stacked on top of past memories—this one with a special note because I had lived through the worst ordeal a person can, and survived.

Nothing is what Stephen expected it to be. Home isn't Cleveland. I am not Clementine. And that stack of memories is as apparent as evaporated water on hot pavement.

But it's still my birthday. Today I am nineteen. I don't feel any different. My face is the same face I saw in the mirror yesterday. My purple hair is more muted and slightly grown out. My skin has a glow from being outside, and the chronic fatigue that rocked me when I first left the hospital is gone. But I feel an extra energy in the air, like something needs to happen.

I sit alone in the kitchen, mulling over my options. I could spend the day relaxing like Kieran said. Get out my Ireland book and read up on more places to visit. Maybe go see the golf course in Waterville. Catch a boat tour out to the Skellig Islands. But doing this by myself feels awfully lonely. I hate being lonely. And with my strength finally coming back, I never want to be bed bound again, relaxing or not. That's no way to spend a birthday.

And while baking usually makes me feel better, it seems desperately lame to bake my own birthday cake.

Fun won't be found in the cottage, I'm sure of that. With my notebook in my pocket, I head out to find some, hoping this time Kieran is right—it won't end in a near-death experience.

∾

At the Secret Book and Record Store, Clive and I watch Siobhan organize a rack of vintage dresses for the third time. This isn't exactly what I had in mind, but when I walked down the stairs, into the familiar scent of cardboard boxes and plastic wigs, and saw Clive chewing on his lower lip, concern written on his face, my quest for fun shifted.

"She's wearing bloody runners," Clive whispers to me, discreetly pointing at Siobhan's feet. She's wearing a pair of dark-blue sneakers that look like they've never been worn. The place is empty on this Saturday afternoon. In all honesty, I've never really seen the place very busy. I'm not sure how Clive stays in business. Most people who come to this part of Ireland want shops with wool sweaters and Celtic crosses to hang on their walls, not fishnet stockings and spike-studded bras with matching garter belts. "I've never seen her in a pair before," he says.

"Never?" I ask. Clive shakes his head.

"They're too bloody ordinary for her. The closest I've seen was when she came in wearing four-inch platform pleather boots that came up to her midthigh. That's casual for Siobhan."

Her makeup is even muted today, and her pink hair is pulled into a loose ponytail at the nape of her neck.

"Look at her hair," Clive whispers. "Not a speck of product in it. She looks like a buggy-pushing mum who hasn't opened a glamour mag since uni."

"Maybe she's practicing for when she has the baby," I offer. "Trying on a more sensible look."

Clive shakes his head. "Von has never used the word 'sensible' in her life."

It's not my place to share the conversation I overheard between Siobhan and Kieran. Clive may pride himself on knowing everyone in town, but some secrets should remain so.

"Something is definitely off," Clive says. "Siobhan would never wear runners. It's just not like her."

"Why don't you just ask her?"

Clive gives me a sarcastic face. "When has asking Siobhan a question ever ended well for you?"

"Good point." I start to bite my nails. What Clive is saying makes sense when put together with what I overheard this morning. Siobhan's dad wanted her to get an abortion or give the baby away. And now that she hasn't done either, her whole life is about to change. "What would Jane Austen say?"

Clive shakes his head. "This is so Marianne and Willoughby from _Sense and Sensibility_." He leans in close. "Marianne falls madly in love with the dashing young rogue, Willoughby, only to have her heart broken when he marries another woman for money."

"What happens to Marianne?"

"She falls into a deep depression and almost dies." Clive puts his hand to his mouth. "This isn't good."

"But it's just a pair of sneakers, or runners, or whatever you call them."

Clive gives me a hard glare. "It's never just a pair of runners. People are defined by what they wear. It's a walking mantra. Von's clothes usually say, 'Go fuck yourself.' That outfit says, 'I've given up. Pass me a bonbon.' Go talk to her."

"Me? She doesn't like me."

"So it can't get any worse!" Clive shoves me in Siobhan's direction. I stumble and glare back at him, but he waves me toward her. She's reorganizing the rack of dresses for the fourth time as I approach.

"Hi," I say quietly. Siobhan doesn't respond. I shoot Clive a skeptical look, but he gives me a visual nudge to keep going. "I found this on my walk over here. Not very unique, but I thought you might like it anyway." I offer Siobhan another piece of blue sea glass.

She takes it from me and puts it in her pocket without examining it. "Thanks."

"So how are you today?"

"Grand."

This isn't going anywhere.

"So . . . ," I say. "I never properly thanked you for the clothes."

"Don't bother."

"And what I said the other day . . . I was upset—"

"No need to explain." Siobhan moves to another rack of dresses.

Another dead end. I'm running out of options.

"I was hoping you could help me with something," I say.

"What, Yank?"

The first idea that comes to mind slips from my mouth. "Well, it's my birthday, and I thought I'd buy a new outfit. Since you're the most fashionable person I know, I thought maybe you could help me pick something out?" Then I add quietly, so Clive can't hear, "Plus, I haven't seen a customer in here all day. I'm a little worried about this place. I'd like to help Clive out."

From across the store, Clive yells, "It's your bloody birthday! Why didn't you say something!" He crosses the room and grabs me in a hug, squishing me in his arms.

"It's just a day," I say, pinched in his grasp.

"It is *not* just a day." Clive sets me down. "We need to do something special."

"You really don't need to do that."

"Yes. We. Do." Clive is emphatic. He thinks for a second, and then his whole face brightens. "Let's play dress-up."

"Pardon?" I say.

Clive pulls a red pleather halter-top dress from the rack. "Von and I used to do this all the time when the place was dead."

"When is this place not dead?" Siobhan says, a little more pep to her voice.

"Thank goodness you work for free." He smiles at her and continues. "We'd dress each other up to pass the time. Now it's your turn. Let us dress you up for your birthday!"

"I don't know." I back away.

"Come on. It'll be fun," Clive pleads. He turns to Siobhan. "Von, I need your help."

It's right now that I realize this isn't just about my birthday. Clive is doing this for Siobhan, too.

I take the dress from Clive's hands. "Please. I don't trust Clive. I'll end up in that." I point to a pair of assless pants hanging on the wall.

"You'd look damn good in those," Clive says.

I beg Siobhan. "Save me?"

Dark circles hang under her eyes, but a hint of a spark returns to them.

"I think you've proven you're not a girl who needs saving," she says. "You do fine on your own."

It's the first compliment Siobhan has ever given me, and possibly the best birthday gift I could ask for.

"OK," she says. "And no assless pants."

Clive rolls his eyes. "You're such a fucking prude."

Siobhan grabs a stack of dresses, her posture straighter as she walks toward the dressing room. "That word hasn't been used to describe me in a long time."

~

After twenty dresses, ten pairs of shoes, and more jewelry options than I can count, Clive and Siobhan finally agree on my birthday outfit. The dress is white with cherries decorating it. The neckline is heart shaped with capped sleeves, which Clive says accentuate my "perfectly voluptuous" chest. A red belt cinches my waist. The bottom of the dress flares at an A-line from waist to knee. Siobhan adds a pair of lavender T-strap shoes, saying they give the outfit the perfect muted accent.

"It's a refined pinup look," she says, examining me from head to toe.

My reflection barely resembles the girl who walked in the door. "You should do something in fashion one day," I say, but Siobhan waves me off. I've spent every day in jeans and T-shirts that can get covered in paint or stand up to whatever task Kieran and I have set out to do. But not since I've been here have I dressed nicely. It makes me stand up straighter. I actually feel pretty and girlie—a feeling I didn't know I liked until now.

I spin to make the dress flare. "Clive, if clothes speak, what does this dress say?"

"Fuck me."

I stop twirling. "I'm taking it off."

But Clive grabs my arm as I turn for the changing room. "No, you will not. You look brilliant. What's wrong with a little sex appeal? Right, Von?"

Siobhan just glares.

"It's not right," she says. "It's just not right."

Clive seems worried again. "What's not right?" I ask.

"The picture's not complete." She grabs me by the hand, drags me over to a chair behind the counter, and pushes me down in it. "Stay there."

Siobhan disappears into the back room, only to return moments later with her large purse. She dumps the contents on the counter—makeup, a curling iron, gum, money, and more makeup.

"You can't wear that dress without black eyeliner and red lipstick." Siobhan searches through her makeup bags.

Clive gives me two thumbs up, and when Siobhan grabs my chin to turn my face toward her, I say with all the sincerity I have in me, "Thank you, Siobhan. For everything."

She remains callous. "It's your fucking birthday. Don't get used to it. Now close your eyes . . . Muppet."

Three weeks ago, I would have been hurt by her words, but today, nothing could feel better.

Siobhan works on my face and hair for a while, without letting me see what she's doing. She curls and pins my hair back, taking her time. Clive watches us, his reactions varying from surprise to amusement to awe. Occasionally, a customer comes down the stairs, and Clive yells, "We're closed! Special occasion."

This isn't what Stephen or I had envisioned for my birthday, but what has been? I'm beginning to think it's a waste of time trying to predict the future. Life takes too many turns.

"Final touch," Siobhan says, standing in front of me. "Act like you're going to kiss someone." My stomach jolts.

"If you could kiss anyone on your birthday," Clive asks, "who would it be?"

"I don't know," I lie nervously.

"Someone famous, maybe?"

"Stop asking her stupid questions, and let me work," Siobhan says. "Now pout your lips, Yank."

Siobhan smooths on red lipstick and then stands back as I sit, my mouth still holding the shape. She says, so that I can hear, "I can see how someone would fall for you."

"What?" I whisper back.

She turns and says to Clive, "She's done."

"Let's see," Clive says, clapping his hands.

He makes me model my new look, his face bursting with excitement, before I check myself out in the mirror. Siobhan has transformed me into a true pinup girl—black eyeliner rims my eyes, my lips as red as the cherries on my dress. My hair curls back from my face in an old-fashioned style only Siobhan could replicate. I barely recognize myself, but at the same time, I'm not sure I've ever felt more like . . . me.

Clive wears a goofy grin. "Sex, sex, and more sex," he says. "This was a great idea."

Siobhan stands next to him, her hand holding the bottom of her belly, her face pinched. She takes a deep breath.

"Are you OK?" I ask.

She waves me off. "Stop asking so many damn questions."

The three of us stand in the empty store, me dressed to the nines, Clive and Siobhan watching me.

"So . . . ," I say. "What do I do now?"

The store is quiet. All three of us wait as if an idea is just seconds away from presenting itself. But it never does.

"This is an opportune time for a ball," Clive says. "I wish people still threw balls."

"You're having Jane Austen delusions again." Siobhan rolls her eyes. "It's becoming a problem."

"Well, she can't go home. She looks too good. We need to show her off."

"In Waterville?" Siobhan says. "Nothing ever happens in this town."

"Actually . . ." My beautiful lavender shoes have my feet aching to celebrate the day. And my dress . . . Suddenly, I want to dance and twirl. Clive is right. "Would a party work?"

CHAPTER 18

Paudie's Pub is crowded and loud. Kieran said it would be a rowdy party, and he was right. A band plays in the corner, its boisterous tempo intensifying the noise. People crowd around the players, singing at the top of their lungs and clinking pint glasses together. Men talk loudly with slurred speech and belly laughs. It's exactly what Siobhan said it would be like when she refused to come with us, claiming she'd never be caught dead at an event like this, with men congratulating themselves for a day of whacking a ball with a stick into a hole.

"All men want is to beat other men to the hole," she said. "If they had any brains about them, they'd realize how metaphorical that is."

As far as I can tell, I'm the only female in the place.

It's perfect for a birthday celebration.

The music changes to a more melancholy melody while I survey the crowd. Clive and I are out of place here, him in his black skinny jeans and matching tight T-shirt, his hair pointing toward the ceiling, and me, all dolled up and looking like I'm from another time. Clive even made Siobhan add smoky-black eyeliner to his eyes before we left.

Kieran is nowhere to be seen.

"You know this song?" Clive asks me. "'The Fields of Athenry'?"

"Pardon?"

"You were humming along. I thought the only Irish song Americans know is 'Danny Boy.'"

I was? I listen, concentrating on the tune, but it's as if the second Clive pointed it out, the notes are no longer familiar to me. These moments are getting easier to let go of—the result expected, the disappointment tame.

"Of course, I know it," I say, trying to act nonchalant. "You underestimate Americans."

Clive gestures to all the conservatively dressed men in the pub. "That's a lot of sweater-vests."

"What do sweater-vests say about a person?"

Clive cringes. "Never trust a man in a sweater-vest."

Even if Clive and I wanted to blend in, we couldn't. I lean over and whisper, "Everyone's staring at us."

"No, love. Everyone is staring at you. Come on. We need a drink." He pulls me through the crowd, clearing a path toward the bar, pushing people back as we shimmy through. Loud men brag about their day on the golf course. "Did you see my putt on the fifteenth hole? Bloody brilliant." "I birdied that hole. How'd you do?" "I never met a sand trap I couldn't conquer."

Siobhan was right about men and golf.

As we approach the bar, Kieran comes into view. Butterflies flutter uncontrollably in my stomach, while at the same time, my chest pounds. My heart-shaped neckline feels wildly low all of a sudden.

The dress and shoes and makeup gave me false confidence in the Secret Book and Record Store, but here in Paudie's Pub, with drunk men all around me, I'm not so sure getting dressed up like this was a good idea.

"I take it back. This was a bad idea. Let's leave." I pull on Clive's hand.

But Clive counters my pull with a tug. "No, lass. It's your birthday. You're having a good time tonight whether you like it or not."

"I look ridiculous."

Clive leans into me, kissing me on the cheek. "You look fucking gorgeous. Now, stand up straight. Be that confident American girl I loved from the start."

"Confident? More like desperate."

Clive nods. "Confident."

Kieran is tending to the other side of the bar when we sit down, and he doesn't notice us right away. My stomach ties in and out of knots as I wait for him to see me. Clive is talking, but I barely hear what he's saying, my concentration elsewhere.

When Clive notices my lack of attention, he grabs my face and turns me away from looking at Kieran.

"What—" I can barely get the word out before Clive is smoothing another layer of red lipstick on my lips.

"Now," he says, glancing over my shoulder. "I'm going to the toilet. I'll be back in a bit . . . Bunny." He gives my bar stool a spin as he walks away, and I turn to find Kieran looking directly at me.

Time moves in slow motion—Kieran's eyes meeting mine, his pause, his measured pace as he approaches. His expression is unreadable, and I find myself wanting to turn away, but I'm unable to. There's nowhere to go. And the truth is—all I want is to be here. For Kieran to come closer to me until there's no space separating us.

The band plays on loudly, but all I hear is my heartbeat in my ears. I sit up straighter, faking confidence when I really feel unsteady, and count the beats in my head. One . . . two . . . three . . . Kieran gets closer. My eyes can't move from his. I'm pulled in, drawn like a magnet to my other half.

"Bunny . . . ," Kieran says as he approaches. My mouth pulls up in a smile at the sound of his voice, my face beaming, but our connectedness comes to a screeching halt as another figure steps between us.

"Lusty Lavender, is that you?" Andy from the internet café stands in front of me, beer in hand, blocking Kieran from my view. I startle in my seat. "Holy shit, you look hot. What are you doing here?"

Words fail me. The shock of seeing him doesn't let up as I try to find Kieran over Andy's shoulder, but every time I move, Andy moves with me, his eyes alight.

"This day was a total shit show until now. First, I'm forced to play golf with a bunch of dudes, then I'm forced to drink with them afterward. Too many dicks in one place if you ask me. And then you show up, like an angel. How about that drink I said I'd buy you?" And then Andy hollers at Kieran, who's back at the other end of the bar. "No one understands good service on this island."

Kieran's expression is blank as he walks back toward us.

"Yes." His jaw is tight.

Andy smacks the bar with one hand and puts his arm around me. "I promised this beautiful girl a drink, and now you need to get it for her. Anything she wants. I'm buying."

Kieran looks at me, utterly confused. "You know him?"

Andy hugs me in closer, keeping his body between Kieran and me, and says curtly, before I can get a word out, "Of course, she knows me. Now, how about that drink?"

The words to explain all of this to Kieran sit in my mouth, waiting to come out, but I can't find my voice. He turns too quickly to fill me a pint, and I shake Andy's arm off.

"Don't talk to him like that," I say.

But my words go right over Andy's head. "Damn, am I glad to see you. Do you know what my friends are doing right now?"

"No," I say, annoyed.

"*Girls.* They're all doing girls. In the Hamptons. While I'm getting acquainted with different patterns of plaid." Andy gives me an exaggerated eye roll. "But then you walked in, looking like that. You might just be my soul mate."

"I doubt it," I groan.

"This is fate, Lusty Lavender."

Kieran sets a pint down heavily on the bar. "Her drink."

Andy casually hands Kieran twenty euros. "Keep the change, bro."

"What did you call me?"

"Bro," Andy says more emphatically.

"I'm not your bro." Kieran's voice is flat and unforgiving.

Andy ignores the comment and says to me, "See what I'm saying about the service here. God, I can't wait to be back in America where people understand their place in life." Then he waves his hand at Kieran. "You can go away now." Andy turns to me, his mouth still moving, words still coming in a waterfall directed at me. I barely have time to digest what's happening. "You know what I've done all week? Nothing. Absolutely nothing. There isn't an entertaining thing to do on this whole island." Then Andy surveys my body. "Until now."

He grabs my hands and yanks me off the bar stool. "Let's dance, Lusty Lavender."

And before I can protest, before I can stop the train wreck that this night is becoming, Andy pulls me away from the bar, his hand so tight on mine I can't let go. Kieran doesn't help. He doesn't even turn in my direction. It's as if I'm a stranger to him. It feels like my heart could just break into pieces and scatter onto the dirty pub floor. This wasn't supposed to happen. Why isn't he coming to my rescue? That's what Kieran does. Can't he see I need his help?

Andy pulls me into him, grabbing me around the waist. I press his chest back and adjust his hand that's creeping too close to my butt, with an eye on Kieran the whole time. When he still doesn't look my way, my feeling is of more than disappointment. I feel helpless again. Weak. Kieran gives me strength and takes away my fear. I can trust him, but right now, he's pulling all that away.

"Seriously, I'm going to have dreams about that dress," Andy says. "I'm just being honest. You look hot."

He spins me out and then pulls me back in, trying to hug me closer. Even when I resist him, it's useless.

"I know people think this music is enchanting or whatever, but let's be real—it's fucking depressing," Andy says. "Like I want to constantly hear about all the people who died in a famine."

"That's horribly insensitive."

Andy continues without listening to me. "Now, St. Patrick's Day in Manhattan—that's a real party."

The need to cry tightens my throat. I do *not* want to cry. Crying is weak. I didn't shed a tear when I woke up in a hospital without my life intact. But Kieran . . . he has the power to reduce me to a weeping teenager. This was a mistake. I've been transformed into a helpless person again, being led around by Andy, whose own interests mean more to him than anything else.

I push myself away from him, peeling his hands off me.

"Lusty Lavender?"

"You want to know something?" I say. "You're an ungrateful, arrogant American asshole with no appreciation for . . . anything."

"I know that," he says with a shrug. "Now, come on. Let's dance."

I groan. "Don't follow me. Don't talk to me. Don't even look in my direction." I turn with a huff and walk away from him. I will not be reduced to feeling less than feeble and powerless. I've come too far, survived too much. If Kieran won't help me, it's time I help myself. Time I trusted myself.

I push my way through the crowd of men, ignoring their catcalls and whistles. My hair comes down when I pull free the pins Siobhan so expertly placed. I wipe clean the red lipstick with the back of my hand. This was all dress-up. It's not me. If I could magically change back into my jeans and T-shirt, I would. Now I understand Siobhan even more—the way she dresses, the tattoos—she takes power in being wholly and truly herself. I can do that, too, even without knowing who I was before. And right now, I need to get out of here.

I try to find Clive in a sea of clones, shoving sweater-vest after sweater-vest to the side, when someone grabs my wrists.

"I said don't follow me!" I pull away furiously, only barely glancing up in time to see Kieran with his hands up in the air, surrendering.

"OK. I'll let you go."

Kieran backs away, but I yell at him. "Why didn't you help me?" He starts to respond, but no answer will suffice. "No. I don't need your help. I don't need anyone's help. I'm leaving." When I try to stomp away again, Kieran grasps my arm and holds me back.

"Stop being so stubborn, Bunny," he says.

"I'm not being stubborn. I'm being strong. *I am a mighty creature!*"

"I know that." He says it so casually it gives me pause.

"You know that?"

"I knew it from the second I met you. I just came to warn you. That American guy . . . I know his type. I *am* his type. He's got a raging Superman complex because he has more money than he knows what to do with, but he'll get you in trouble."

"I don't need you to warn me. I can take care of myself."

"I'm well aware of that." Kieran's face is unreadable.

My tough exterior breaks. "Is that what you think of me? That I would want someone like him?" A sinking, aching feeling overtakes my chest. "You're not like him at all. He's an ass. You're . . . you're . . ."

A flutter of a smile pulls at Kieran's lips, like he bested me again. Like me breaking down in front of him is amusing. "I'm what?"

"You're an ass, too!" This time I really mean to stomp away, but Kieran doesn't let it happen. One second he's serious, the next he's laughing at me. I have whiplash from his change in emotions. But before I can get anywhere, Kieran wraps his arm around my waist, his other hand lacing between mine. He presses me to his chest with conviction.

I struggle to wiggle out of his grasp. "What are you doing?"

"I'm trying to dance with you. Would you stop fighting me?"

Stillness. I can't move my feet. "You want to dance with me?"

"If you would just stop trying to run away."

Kieran's hand presses into my lower back. A warm feeling cascades down my spine. Resisting him isn't an option. My heart overrules my stubborn mind.

"That's better," he says. "Now we move our feet."

We sway, keeping beat with the band, the tune they're playing a sweet melody that gives me pause again. For a breath, it's familiar. But with Kieran so close, the song fades into the background. His blue eyes run their way from my toes to my head, lingering in places, making my heart flip in circles. This is when I should back away and save myself heartache, but logic has no sway over me tonight.

Instead, I say, "What do you think about my dress?"

Kieran pauses, releases me, and scans me again. "Can I be honest?"

"It seems to be the theme of the night."

Kieran grins. "I like you better in a worn-out T-shirt with paint on your face. This dress . . . it isn't you."

Knowing that Kieran sees the true me only makes me want to move closer to him. My entire being, inside and out, calms.

"So what prompted this . . . whatever it is?" he asks.

"It was a birthday gift from Siobhan and Clive."

Kieran stills. "It's your birthday?"

"Nineteen, today."

Kieran's eyes hold my gaze. "Happy birthday, Bunny."

The intensity in his eyes makes me electric. He wraps his arms around me again, and we dance more, the song shifting to another.

"I'm sorry I don't have anything to give you," he whispers in my ear.

The closer Kieran is to me, the more delirious I am, floating, never wanting this to end. *This* is what I wanted for my birthday. Take away the stupid dress and the makeup and just give me Kieran.

"You've given me enough already."

"Have I?" Kieran sounds unsure. He's cautious still. I can see it. But he doesn't need to be anymore. I'm not helpless. I've made a life for myself from literally nothing.

Clive asked me earlier who I wanted a birthday kiss from. I muster a level of courage I haven't felt before. Call it confidence or tenacity or the determination not to be weak, no matter the circumstances, even when life turns upside down. Stephen said I was a mighty creature. I didn't believe him then, but I do now. I don't need Kieran to save me. Control has been in my grasp this entire time. I'm done waiting for a life that may never exist again. Clementine may never come back. Sometimes letting go is braver than holding on until you break.

"You could give me *something* for my birthday," I say.

"What would that be?"

I pause, but only for a second, not out of hesitancy, but out of the need to remember this exact moment for the rest of my life. "A birthday kiss," I say, and then tap my left cheek. Kieran's eyes follow my finger. "Right here."

"Are you sure?" he asks. I nod, and almost instantly, Kieran's lips lightly touch my cheek, the feeling of his warm skin sending heat all the way to my toes.

"And maybe one here?" I tap my other cheek.

He does the same on my right side, his lips lingering for a breathtaking moment. He inches away from me slowly, our faces close, his eyes intensely focused on mine. I can feel the pulse between us.

"And the last one . . . ," I whisper.

"Where?"

"Here?" I tap my lips. Kieran's eyes follow my finger. The space between us closes, my own doing. It's my birthday after all. I'm one year older. I'm leaving Clementine and her past behind. No more distance. No more dancing around my feelings, worrying what might have been. I'm jumping into my future. Letting myself go. If one *must* fall into love, to give up and dive headfirst, knowing that everything can change in a heartbeat—there must be an upside.

"If that's what you want," Kieran says.

This is what I want. My heart races, my skin electric, the uncertainty of life is washed away in an instant—this is the upside. This is the upside to crashing: madly letting go and giving yourself to someone else. This is the freedom beyond the fear.

As Kieran's lips edge closer to mine, I soak in his warm breath, the clean scent of him, the intimacy of our bodies at last. I won't let go. Not now. Not when we've come this far.

Kieran whispers, "Bunny . . ." The word floats out of his mouth and into mine, as if he's planting a seed that will forever be locked in my body. His hands knot behind my back as he grabs my dress. The tips of his lips touch mine. Time seems to stretch, infinity in a second . . . and then it suddenly ends, quicker than an exhale.

I open my eyes, lightheaded, to see who pulled us apart.

Clive is next to us, his words frantic.

"It's Siobhan," he says through tight breaths. "Something is wrong with the baby."

CHAPTER 19

Waterville doesn't have a hospital, which Kieran is absolutely sure his dad knew when he banished Siobhan from Dublin to Southwest Ireland.

Clive and I make a brief stop at the Secret Book and Record Store so I can change back into the clothes I was wearing earlier. The dress stays behind, along with my moment with Kieran, but the memories remain.

In the fading light, we drive from Waterville to Tralee, a larger city with a hospital an hour and a half north. Kieran and Siobhan left Paudie's Pub immediately in Kieran's truck. In an instant, the dutiful, caring, worried brother was back and ready to help his sister.

Clive and I trail a few minutes behind in Clive's sensible sedan that contrasts with his outward appearance. We ride in silence.

"He was scared," I finally say. Fear is not an emotion I've seen Kieran wear much. I saw it when he pulled me from the water at Inch Beach. But tonight . . . he was petrified. "She said she's only thirty-two weeks. It's too soon."

"It's going to be fine."

But the longer we sit quietly, green pastures passing, the road narrow and windy, the less confident I become.

I place my hand on Clive's. "You're right. She'll be OK."

He glances at me. "I know she'll be OK. She always is. But the little one . . . Sometimes what we thought we'd never want becomes the only thing we desperately need."

I keep my hand interlaced with Clive's the rest of the drive. We say nothing else.

Houses are packed side by side, one right after the other, as we drive into Tralee. There are fast-food chains, large department stores, hotels, hostels, and bed and breakfasts. The streets are lined with cars. I roll down the window, but the calming sound of the ocean is long gone. The air smells like cement and gasoline. Beyond the seclusion of Waterville, I don't know if I feel exposed or invisible.

The hospital is lit up. Clive and I insisted on coming, but now that I'm miles away from the comfort of the cottage and the ocean, standing here in a cold parking lot, the ominous building looming over me, I wonder if it was such a good idea. I can't seem to move my feet, as if I'm frozen in place.

"Blood pressure is ninety over sixty. Pulse is weak but there. I can't believe she's alive."

There's pain pinching behind my eyes. My hands go numb.

"Whatever happens, I'm not going to let you die."

"You can't promise that. You can't promise anything."

My bones ache with the memory of a fading voice. My head pounds.

"I'll make it my dying wish. You will survive this."

Who said that? Why can't I see a face? Does it even matter now? I'm no longer worried about remembering. Instead, I'm terrified that remembering will make all of this disappear. It's my future I'm desperate to keep now.

"Jane . . ."

My hands are sweaty when I press them to my cheeks. I force my eyes open. Clive stands in front of me with his arm outstretched, his palm open.

"Come on, love. I'll buy you a tea. It's going to be a long night."

Clive wraps his arm around my shoulder, guiding me toward the entrance. He doesn't know my history in Limerick. Doesn't know how I cringe at the thought of being locked in a hospital room, or that I ran away from a place just like this.

I will my body forward, because it's Siobhan who's breaking right now. A rush of cool air hits us as the automatic doors open. The clinical smell of alcohol overwhelms me, turning my stomach. But there's no stopping.

While Kieran is allowed to stay with his sister, Clive and I are restricted to the waiting room. Uncomfortable chairs are our beds tonight. A muted TV sits in the corner.

"Do you mind if I turn this off?" I don't wait for an answer. I'm not sure if Clive would notice anything on the TV, me, or anyone else.

Tea and biscuits keep us sane.

"They're not sugar cookies, but my options were limited," Clive says, returning from the cafeteria.

We share the food. I lean my head on Clive's shoulder, letting the tea warm my body. It works, but only partially. My fingers and toes are cold.

"I'm glad you came to our small town this summer, Jane," Clive says. His black eyeliner is smudged.

"Me, too."

"You don't talk much about home. Do you miss it?"

"The truth?"

Clive gives me an encouraging look.

"It doesn't feel like home anymore."

"Can I make a confession now?" Clive focuses on his almost-empty cup. His hair has fallen and hangs long over his forehead. "The store isn't doing well. I thought people would embrace it in Waterville. But like with so many things, I'm a bit ahead of my time."

"What are you going to do?"

"I don't know." He shakes his head. "But I can't bear the thought of Siobhan losing the baby *and* the store. She needs us both. And in truth . . . I need her. I'd be lying if I said I didn't fantasize about us raising that baby together."

"Really?"

"It would be the best-dressed kid in all of Ireland, with a fine taste in music."

"That sounds like a great ending to this story," I say.

Clive laughs. "Too bad we live in reality."

I nuzzle into his side. "We'll figure something out."

"How can you be so positive?"

"You know how stories go," I say. "There's always a point where everything seems lost, but trust me . . ." My foot carries a tattoo from my past, but the pressure I felt to hide it is gone. That past no longer belongs to me. "It's never the end. Even when you think your life is over, a new story line appears."

Clive leans back in his seat. We yawn in unison. The doors to the restricted area haven't opened in hours. I fear the longer we sit here, the worse the news will be.

"I don't care about the store. It can be replaced," Clive whispers. "But her . . . I love her in a weird way."

I snuggle in closer. "You and I both know being conventional is overrated."

∾

"You're not from around here, are you?" I ask.

"Why do you say that?"

The smell of hot dogs, fried food, and beer. Yelling echoes in the background. I'm in a stadium. It's not a concrete image, more of a knowing—I've spent a lot of time in this place.

"Your shirt's a dead giveaway."

"*What's wrong with my shirt? My cousin gave it to me.*" *A man speaks to me, his face unclear.*

"*Your cousin must hate you.*"

"*Why is that?*"

"*'Cleveland Browns Undefeated 1996–1998,'*" *I say, reading the shirt that any Clevelander would consider a horrible joke. "That's when the Browns moved to Baltimore. My father still resents the move to this day. All good Clevelanders do. I wasn't even alive when it happened, and I hate Baltimore. You're going to get your ass kicked if you go into the Dawg Pound wearing that.*"

"*Bloody hell,*" *he says with a laugh, light and warm, like his voice. I lean into the memory, searching his face, haloed with blond hair. "I knew it couldn't be that easy. Dares never are.*"

~

I wake up, startled, my neck sore from craning it awkwardly in the chair. The waiting room is lit by early morning light. The voice in my dream mixes with the voices of the man behind the reception desk and the doctor talking on his cell phone in the hallway.

Yesterday replays vividly in my mind, and any attention I was paying to the dream turns toward reality. Clive sits across from me, awake, fixated on something over my shoulder.

"Any news?" I say in a raspy voice.

Clive gives me a puzzled expression. "News?"

"About Siobhan."

"No." Clive turns off the TV. "Couldn't sleep. Been watching episodes of *Shortland Street* on mute for hours."

"What time is it?" I stretch my arms.

"Nearly six in the morning."

My birthday is officially over. And I can remember it: Kieran dancing with me, his hand grasping at my dress, the heat between us alive.

We were so close in that moment. But until we know what's happened with Siobhan, I have to push it away.

Clive comes to sit down next to me, his face creased with fatigue, looking older than I've ever seen him. His Mohawk hangs to his ears. The black eyeliner accentuates the bags under his eyes.

He grabs my hands unexpectedly, an intensity in his eyes. "Jane . . . ," he says. "I need to ask—"

But the elevator dings, and Kieran walks out. Clive and I stand as he approaches, his shoulders sagging.

"How is she?" Clive says.

Kieran runs a hand through his hair. "She's fine."

"And the baby? How's the baby?"

Kieran exhales slowly. "She's fine, too."

Clive's face lights up. "It's a girl?"

"A very tiny girl."

Clive grabs me in a hug, and we spin. "I've always wanted a girl!" He puts me down. "Can I see her? Can I see the baby? What's her name? I've always liked the name Elizabeth for a girl, after Elizabeth Bennett, of course. Or Elinor. Just not Lydia. She's a disaster."

"No name yet. The baby is in the NICU. No visitors right now."

"Then can I see Von?" Clive asks.

Kieran shakes his head. He turns to me and says, "First, she'd like to see you."

~

Kieran and I enter the elevator. He presses the button for the third floor and steps back next to me. I can't move. As the doors close, the air is still, suspended, waiting to see what happens next. We haven't spoken a word since we almost kissed at Paudie's Pub, but what to say now?

There's too much to say. Too much to admit. If I do, I could lose Kieran. To confess to a life that doesn't exist, a life I'm starting to think I don't want, only to lose this one . . . ? I can't do it. I won't.

My hand subtly stretches at my side, reaching for Kieran's. We both watch the doors, my fingers aching to connect with his. But the elevator reaches the third floor, the doors open, and Kieran steps out.

He leads me down the hallway toward Siobhan's room. I touch his arm.

"Kieran . . ." But where to begin? I set off to find Clementine, and instead I found him. If I could carry his burden today, I would. "Do you think they serve Jell-O here?"

A vague smirk pulls on Kieran's tired face.

"That day feels like a lifetime ago," I say. "And that person I was . . . I don't feel like her anymore."

Kieran turns, continues down the hallway, and calls back to me. "This way, Bunny."

∼

Siobhan's room is cozier than mine was, but just as white. She sits propped up in bed, wearing a hospital gown, a beige blanket pulled up to her waist. With her bright pink hair and her tattoos exposed, she is the most colorful thing in the room.

A machine keeping track of her pulse is next to the bed, but muted.

"I'll just go find some tea," Kieran says.

Siobhan nods. "I won't forget my promise."

When Kieran is gone, I ask, "Promise?"

Siobhan shakes her head. "I have a track record for destructive behavior. He's just worried I'll repeat old patterns."

I laugh and fidget with my hands, willing myself not to bite my nails. Siobhan has never wanted me around. I don't know why that's changed now. So I wait.

"Do you want to know why I have so many tattoos?" she asks.

Tread lightly. "Only if you want to tell me."

"To piss off my dad." She indicates the colorful sleeve tattoo down her right arm. Imbedded in the colors is a flock of black birds. "I started this one in secondary school. I found out he was sleeping with the headmistress at my school. He'd come into town to sleep with her and never once visit me. Bloody bastard." She points to the tattoo on her left forearm that says, "We're all mad here." "It's from *Alice's Adventures in Wonderland.* I came home with poor marks in school, and he said I'd never amount to anything, just like my crazy mum."

"That's awful."

Siobhan rolls her eyes. "You don't know the half of it. Kieran bungee jumps to feel better. I get tattoos." She shows me an empty spot on her right forearm. "I've been saving this spot for the baby. When my dad hears I'm keeping her, he'll be done with me, and I won't need to get any more." She radiates a calm I haven't seen before.

"Can I do anything? Get you anything?"

Siobhan shakes her head, her eyes focused on the object in her hand—the blue sea glass I gave her rolls around on her fingertips. "Each piece reminds me that sometimes in a world of beige sand, the ocean tosses out a colorful piece of glass." She squeezes her hand into a fist. "I owe you an apology."

Taken aback, I counter, "For what? I think Clive has tortured you with enough Celine Dion. We're even."

Siobhan looks at me now, like she's not going to let this go, her demeanor serious, her hand clutching the sea glass. "You were right. I'm selfish. I don't appreciate people the way I should."

If I could take back my dreadful words, I would. "Siobhan—"

"I really wanted to hate you. But you're different than I expected. Don't get me wrong, your style is utterly boring. Your knack for saying the wrong thing at the wrong time is a real problem. But you're kind . . . funny." She gathers a breath. "I know I don't deserve it, but I need your help."

"Anything," I say.

Her voice carries the tone of disbelief. "You're going to let me off that easily?"

"I told you I want to help, and I mean it."

Siobhan keeps her eyes glued to mine. "Kieran blames himself for *my* mistakes. He's paying penance with his life. I need you to make him realize he doesn't need to do that."

I back away. "I'm not sure he'll listen to me."

"He will. You have a gift."

I laugh. "For making sugar cookies?"

"For making people fall in love with you." Siobhan says the words in such a serious tone, I freeze. "You were trouble from the beginning, I knew that. I just forgot how much Kieran likes getting into trouble. You could be the reason he changes his whole life."

"But how?"

"You weaseled your way into our lives. I'm sure you'll figure something out, *Yank*." The look of genuine connection on Siobhan's face, a bond between us, erases all the nasty comments, all the discomfort between us. And when they're gone, what's left is a hint of real friendship.

"Thank you," I say sincerely.

Siobhan sweeps her hand. "Don't get too excited. We're not going to start dyeing each other's hair or talking about our periods. Now get out and let me sleep."

CHAPTER 20

The hallway is quiet around me. An attendant walks toward me carrying a tray of food. On the tray is a container of orange Jell-O.

The past is settled. There is no changing it. But moving forward, choices need to be made. None of them will be easy, but I'm no stranger to that. Maybe it wasn't my fate to put Clementine's life together. Maybe I survived the plane crash so I could do that for Kieran. It's time someone helped him for a change.

I take the elevator down to the waiting room, where Clive sits nervously with paper teacups scattered on the chairs beside him.

"How is she?"

"Good. She's sleeping," I say. "Have you seen Kieran?"

Clive points to the door. "He said he needed a walk."

I hug Clive before racing out the door. "Wish me luck!"

The warm air and natural light hit me at once, and my eyes start watering. I shield the sun from my face, searching for Kieran, but he's nowhere to be seen. A desperate fear of losing him creeps back, but my determination overrides it. If this could all be gone, if life can change in a heartbeat, I need Kieran now.

Large emerald-green lawns surround the hospital. The ground beneath my feet is damp with rain. Clouds scatter in the sky to the east.

I circle the building, past doctors, nurses, patients, and visitors strolling casually. Kieran could be anywhere. I keep running.

When my breath tightens, I stop to catch it. Three weeks ago, I could barely move. I was brought back to life, and I'm not about to let it slip away.

Finally, when I've almost fully circled the entire building, I find him. Kieran paces the lawn, his hands in his pockets, head bowed. I pick up my speed.

He must hear me coming, because the moment I'm about to call his name, he turns. He moves toward me, clearly perplexed.

"Did you mean what you said?" he asks intently, his body now close to mine. "About not being the girl you were."

I try to catch my breath and nod at him. "I don't want to go home, Kieran. I found my life here." I take a step closer.

Kieran turns from me and begins pacing again. "You don't know what you're talking about, Bunny. I can't be responsible for your mistakes, too. You don't belong here."

"Yes, I do," I say. "It might be the only thing I do know. And they're *my* mistakes to make. You are not responsible for them."

Kieran turns back to me, his eyes bright with adrenaline and fatigue. "What about your family, your friends in America? You're being unreasonable. I can't let you do that."

"Well, it's not up to you. It's up to me."

Kieran shakes his head. "No. I won't let you. You're going home. That was the plan all along. You said a week, maybe two. I let this go on too long."

Panic tightens my throat. I need him. He can't send me away. Not now. Not when we've come this far together.

Suddenly, a memory of fire and the smell of burned plastic overrides my senses, making me feel unsteady on my feet. The feeling I had for so many restless nights of reaching for someone, but never being able to grab on, hold them, touch them, sends me into a spin.

"Please," I say to Kieran, reaching for him, feeling his arm within my grasp, knowing he's there. "You're all I have. You're all I want."

I'm begging for Kieran to hold me, to meet me halfway—so I can stop reaching, so we can do this together.

"Do you *really* mean that?" he asks. "You need to be sure."

Yes. Yes. Yes. I've never been surer about anything. Kieran lowers his forehead to mine, like he's tired of holding himself together.

"You saved me," I say.

I feel him shake his head. "You're the bravest person I've ever met. You don't need saving, Bunny."

I *am* strong—I feel that now down to my core.

"I know what I want," I say.

"Then ask me, Bunny." The frustration has melted from Kieran's eyes. All that's left is anticipation.

"Will you kiss me?"

He steps close, a fire in his eyes that he hasn't let me see before. "As long as you remember . . . you asked for this."

Kieran's lips press to mine. I want to gasp for air, but the sensation of his mouth erases the need for breath, the need to move, to do anything but feel him.

His mouth slowly pries my lips apart. Bliss runs in tingles down my arms and legs. Kieran's tongue tangles with mine, and he pulls me closer. His hands grasp at my back, knotting my shirt in his fists, pressing me to him.

I stand on tiptoes, wanting to be closer, needing it. No more backing away. Kieran lifts me off my feet, and I float above the ground. His tongue runs along my bottom lip, and I think there is no better sensation in the world. A small moan escapes my lips, euphoria making me dizzy.

But all too soon, Kieran sets me down, his body pulling back, his hands untangling from me. I lean forward, ready for more, but his mouth separates from mine. He leans in, running his lips along my cheek and settling his mouth on my ear. Shivers spread on my skin.

"People are staring, Bunny."

I step back from Kieran, embarrassed. He gives me a sly grin, and in an instant, I want to be back in his arms with his lips on mine.

"Don't give me that look, Bunny. I'm trying to control myself."

"Who said I want you to control yourself?"

Kieran groans, and for a second I think he might kiss me again, but he steps back. "Not here."

I take a step closer. "Then where?"

"Where do you want to go?"

Anywhere you'll kiss me. That's my answer. But as the ecstasy of kissing him calms to a warm hum, I remember what Siobhan said. Kieran can change his life. But he won't do it hiding out in Waterville.

"I think it's time you take me to Dublin."

CHAPTER 21

The suggestion isn't an instant hit, but when Siobhan tells Kieran to "get the hell out of the hospital" and declares that she "doesn't need a babysitter when she has a baby of her own to look after," and Clive says he's staying with her whether she likes it or not, Kieran softens to the idea.

"Get out of here!" Siobhan yells. "Before I call security and have you kicked out. I can't breastfeed a baby in front of my brother."

Kieran pats Clive on the back. "Good luck, lad. Seems like our Von is back to her usual self."

Clive responds lovingly. "Thank the Lord."

We leave them as Clive climbs into bed next to Siobhan, cradling her in his arms. I know she's in good hands. The best, really.

I should be exhausted—we both should be—but I feel electric next to Kieran as we leave the hospital.

"So how long does it take to get to Dublin from here?"

"A little over three hours."

I don't know when we'll be back in Waterville. The feeling of change is in the air—for me and Kieran, and for Siobhan and Clive. What I thought I knew is no longer. But my fear of the future doesn't exist anymore. I'm beyond that now.

"I don't have any clothes," I say.

Kieran glances over his shoulder at me as he walks up to his truck. "Who said we need clothes?" He looks different in the sunlight suddenly. Lighter. He opens the truck's passenger door. "Are you coming, Bunny?"

And I pick up my pace.

~

Dunnes department store is in the center of Tralee. The streets are tangled with everything from mobile phone stores to pubs. People are everywhere this afternoon. The streets are busy with cars and buses. If Tralee feels overwhelming, I can't imagine what Dublin will be like. Life doesn't stop here. It doesn't slow down to look back. There's a comfort in the frenetic energy.

I shop hurriedly in the ladies department, grabbing a few shirts and pants before heading over to the undergarments section. The last time I picked out underwear, my choices were limited, and I wasn't necessarily worried about who might see them. But as I peruse the racks of lacy, cotton, and silk underwear, my attention drifts to who might see them now. It convolutes my brain, so I just grab the pair closest to me. Last time I tried to dress up for Kieran, it backfired.

With clothes picked out, I make my way to the men's section. A few people toddle through the racks, but I can't find Kieran anywhere. Minutes pass. The song playing over the department store speakers changes twice, but Kieran is nowhere to be found. My heart rate picks up against my will. Back in the women's section, thinking maybe Kieran came to find me, all I see are a few clerks organizing clothes.

The enormity of Dunnes becomes apparent as I speed through the different departments, searching for Kieran. Section after section is like a maze. Eventually, I stand paralyzed in the middle of the store, clothes in hand. This is what it feels like to be without him. I try to let the feeling wash over me, but it's too awful. People become scary strangers, and I'm just drifting.

"Bunny, what are you doing?" I hear Kieran behind me.

A bag is clutched in his hand. I run toward him, grabbing him securely around the neck and pressing myself to him. My heart races, pounding into his.

Even when Kieran tells me he popped across the street to get us some proper food for the drive, that he thought I needed more time, I still can't shake the lost, unanchored feeling. Like starting all over again. Knowing that strength is what got us to this point, I push the feeling down. This isn't about me now.

We go through the checkout line. When the cashier picks up my underwear, Kieran gives me a sideways glance.

I shrug. "Do you think they'll fit?"

"Don't, Bunny."

"Don't what?"

He shakes his head. "This is going to be a long drive to Dublin."

~

"You again." The smell of fresh bread and sugar is all around me. I realize I'm in a bakery. "I thought you'd be gone by now."

"Don't most people winter in Cleveland?"

I laugh. "That's Florida."

"I'm starting to think maybe Cleveland is the hidden gem of America. Nicest people I've ever met."

"I think that's what they say about people from your country. You barely survived the Dawg Pound in that ridiculous shirt."

"A dare's a dare," he says.

"Can I get you anything? We're known for our sugar cookies, but the macaroons are a close second."

"I have heard that next to Paris, Cleveland is the place to come for a good macaroon."

"Have you been to Paris?" I ask.

"Yes. Dreadful place. Just awful. Horrible, snobbish people. We should go together." He comes to stand in front of me, his blond hair almost the color of my own—though his is natural. Mine was a rebellious mistake. My dad is still making fun of me.

"You're asking me to go to Paris with you? We just met."

"So?"

"So . . . I can't just up and leave my life to go to Paris with a stranger."

"There's only one solution then," he says, brushing his hair from his forehead. His words are as charming as his body language. "I'll just have to stay here in Cleveland until you agree."

"That's a crazy idea."

"I've done worse." He beams at me, his brown eyes holding mine. "So is that a yes? You'll go to Paris with me one day?"

I should run the other way, but something flickers inside that keeps me still—a part that itches for an adventure. I don't give him a concrete answer. Instead, I hand him a sugar cookie. "We'll see."

∼

"Bunny, wake up. We're in Dublin." Kieran touches my arm. I sit up sluggishly. The radio is fuzzy in the background. A male voice with a thick Irish accent comes through the speakers. He sounds like he's announcing a sports game.

Kieran turns off the radio. "Sorry, I needed noise to keep me awake."

My dream was clearer than the ones in the past. Others have been vague—words, feelings, people without faces, voices without feelings— but in this one I could see, feel, practically taste the sugar.

"Kieran?" His eyes are on the road, but I ask, "Will you look at me?"

Without hesitation, he turns, his blue eyes tired. "Is everything OK?"

It wasn't Kieran in my dream. Sitting next to him now gives me a different feeling—this is real. The person in my dream isn't. I could be making up memories at this point, my mind wanting to create a moment that was never there. Now is not the time to wonder. I have too much in my life to ponder the past.

"I'm fine," I say.

Buildings branch out before us. Traffic surrounds our car, honking, filling the tangled mess of streets. Kieran drives speedily, as if he's done this a million times, dodging between cars and swerving so close to them I think we might take someone's side mirror off. This is Kieran's real home. I watch him navigate, the city boy who was raised in boarding schools with fine things, who now attends Trinity College, who has tailored suits and can travel all over the world. He's comfortable here, yet it's clear in his posture that a piece of him is uncomfortable to be back, too.

"Did your friends stick around Dublin for the summer?" I ask.

"What?" Kieran concentrates on the road.

"Your friends from school? Are they around?"

"Some," he says.

"Maybe you could introduce me to them?"

Kieran pulls up to a building that is noticeably taller than the rest, and says, "Maybe." His tone makes it clear that he wants to avoid the topic. Something's happened that he won't speak about. He really *was* hiding in Waterville. But pressing the issue won't help, so I let it drop, for now.

Dublin is compact, with buildings crammed next to each other. Most can't be more than three or four stories tall. The building we've pulled up to, though, towers over the rest in the area. It's on a canal, surrounded by water on three sides.

"What is this place?" I ask. The windows that line most of the building hover above us.

"Millennium Tower," Kieran says. "It's the tallest residential building in Dublin."

Even Kieran's voice sounds tired. He's trying to hold himself together after the stress of the past two days, but now that we've arrived, I can tell his body's giving out.

We walk into the building, through the lobby, and to the elevator. After we step inside, Kieran presses the button for the tenth floor. He leans back against the wall, resting his head, like he could fall asleep standing up.

But when the elevator dings our arrival on the tenth floor, he grabs my hand and promptly leads me forward. Our intertwined fingers give me a jolt of adrenaline. Kieran has never grabbed my hand so casually before. He's always acted unsure, but now, as he unlocks the door and pulls me inside with him, it's as if any hesitation has disappeared. Almost.

His apartment startles me. One entire wall is lined with windows. The others are clean and white. The fading daylight casts a warm glow over the black accent furniture. This place is cosmopolitan. It's the opposite of Kieran, and I get the feeling he had very little to do with furnishing it. In a way, it reminds me of the suit he was wearing all those weeks ago—the one he threw out.

"This was another graduation bribe from my dad," Kieran says. "Though I don't own the place. He does. I'm just forced to live here and thank him for it."

"I take it he picked out the décor."

"My father wouldn't waste his time." Kieran grins at me. "His assistant did."

"Has his assistant ever met you?" I joke, picking up one of the decorative bowls on the coffee table. This place is more like a showroom than an apartment. Nothing speaks to Kieran's taste or personality.

He laughs. "Never."

"Why accept it?" I set the bowl down.

"It was better than one of the small apartments at Trinity." Kieran winks at me, but I know there's more.

I take a step toward the window. "Your dad chose a place this high up," I say. "I take it he doesn't know about your fear of heights?"

"He knows nothing about me." An added layer of fatigue is in Kieran's voice, but he disregards my sympathy. "I actually prefer being high up."

"That's right." I roll my eyes. "You're the guy who wants to be a pilot. You live to torture yourself."

"Flying isn't the torture in my life, Bunny." Kieran runs his hand along the leather couch. I want to shake everything out of him until all his broken pieces are on the ground, exposed. Then we can start to fix his life. But it won't be that simple. I know by now that Kieran may help others easily, but he doesn't freely hand out much about himself.

I continue toward the window, step by step, unsure how I will react being this high up. But even as small twinges of fear arise, they disappear quickly.

"No more fear of heights?" Kieran says.

"I think I was more afraid of fear itself."

Below me, the canal runs into a river that seems to cut Dublin in half. Miles and miles of streets intertwine ten stories down, but the view extends farther, past the concrete, all the way to the ocean.

"It's amazing," I say, leaning closer to the glass.

"You can see all the way across Dublin Bay from up here."

I reach my hand out to him. "Come stand next to me and look."

He takes my hand in his, wrapping his fingers around mine, our palms pressing together. My stomach pulls tight with happiness.

"You've changed, Bunny," he says.

"I told you." We step up to the glass, our noses practically touching the window, but Kieran doesn't stay long before he lets go of my hand and sits down on the couch.

I walk around the apartment. The kitchen is modern with sleek finishes and gourmet appliances. The only bedroom has a king-size bed, and there's a large bathroom. I'm tempted to scour his drawers and closets, as if his hidden secrets will reveal themselves, but that would only set us back, and I understand keeping things inside. For now, I have to let it be.

When I walk back into the living room, Kieran is resting on the couch, his eyes closed. The chaos of the past two days has finally hit him, forcing sleep whether he likes it or not. But even in a state of surrender, tension creases his face, and his hands are balled into fists.

I get a blanket from the bedroom, carefully pull Kieran's shoes from his feet, and prop him up comfortably. The blanket moves up and down with his breath. I want to memorize him. To etch his face into my memory so that no matter what happens, I will never forget the way he looks right now—his black hair falling over his forehead, his lips slightly apart. I'd give anything to kiss him again, but for tonight, I'll have to settle for a view of the bay, curling up in his bed, and wrapping myself in his sheets, as though they were his arms.

CHAPTER 22

"You did this on purpose," I say. "You tricked me, and now I'm a casualty of your bad choices."

"I knew what I wanted, plain and simple."

We're seated on a plane. I won't look at the man next to me.

"So it didn't matter what you left behind. The girl you left behind. You sound like a spoiled asshole."

"I didn't want her. She knew that. It never would have worked. I wanted you." He grabs for my hand, his touch familiar. "That's why I'm going back. To make it right."

"How?"

"I don't know, but . . . I'll think of something."

"It's too late for that. And you dragged me along for the ride. What did you think I would do when I found out? Did you think I'd actually stay with you?"

"I didn't want to lose you."

I yank my hand away. "I don't want any part in this. I'm going back home the second we land."

My stomach drops, all of me drops in a moment of startling free fall.

"Something isn't right," he says. "I smell fire."

"Nothing is right," I say, more to myself. "I wish I'd never met you."

"You can't get rid of me that easily. It doesn't work that way."

We drop again, this time for longer, and when we settle, my head flies forward and hits the seat in front of me.

"Are you OK?" he asks frantically. His hands cup my face, turning me toward him. Heat and pain sear through me. I should write his face into memory—etch it forever—his blond hair, his warm brown eyes, his hands that held mine for months. But I don't want any of it. All I want is to forget him.

"I can't believe this is how it ends," I say. "We're broken before we ever hit the ground."

"If that's the case, hold my hand," he says. "At least, until the end."

He opens his palm to me. I don't move toward him. Instead, my body lifts, like cresting over the highest roller coaster the moment before you fall toward the earth—that one second of weightlessness. But like everything else, it doesn't last. The earth pulls you down. That is the nature of all things.

I never find his hand.

And we begin to fall . . .

～

A scream rips loudly into my sleep and startles me awake. I sit up, my breath pinched and labored, my hand reaching out, grabbing for a person who isn't there. Helpless. Like I'm swimming through darkness only to find more of nothing. Disoriented and sweating, I don't know which way is up or down, which way to avoid a fall. It feels as though I'm locked in a corner of a room, and the floor will give out from under me. I'm pinned down, but frantic to escape.

I pray for it to be over, for this feeling to go away, though I'm terrified it never will. I'll be locked, chained to this forever. Nothing makes sense—the voices I hear—from people I can't remember, even myself. It's like hearing and feeling someone else's emotions. I thought I was done with this, but it had only receded, hiding in the shadows, waiting for the wrong time to come back.

Someone grabs me through the darkness. Hands wrap around my body. My heart slows down. This I know. *This* is real. I press my face into Kieran's chest. The smell of him matches the smell of his sheets.

"A nightmare," I say, breathless. "It was just a nightmare."

I ball Kieran's shirt in my fists. I want to erase this nightmare feeling from my mind and never remember it again. I pull Kieran's face down toward mine, knowing the closer he is to me, the less space my ghosts have to haunt me. He's my barrier, my distraction, right or wrong. I need him.

I force my lips on his. It only takes a breath before Kieran lets me in, lets my tongue twist with his, my mouth starved for his attention. My hands grapple with his clothes and skin as I pull him down on the bed with me, letting the weight of his body ground me back in reality. Legs and arms tangle, and with each hurried breath, I feel further from my nightmare.

My hands climb under Kieran's shirt. I try to inch it off, but he moves, pulling me down on him. He can't stop me now. We're desperate for this. I know he feels it, too, and I won't let him hold back, not anymore.

I reach for the bottom of his shirt again.

Kieran sits up on the bed, his breath fast. "Be absolutely sure, Bunny. We can't take it back once it's done."

The air in the bedroom is heavy and electric. Nothing bad lingers here. It's all been pushed from sight and mind. Forgotten for better feelings.

"I'm sure."

"Then ask me to do it," he says.

My hands push his shirt up, feeling the warm skin beneath. I peel it from his body without hurry, every inch consumed. I toss the shirt to the side of the bed.

"Your turn," I say. Kieran eyes me from lips to waist, but he doesn't move. His chest rises and falls. "This is me asking you."

The devious grin that I love so much returns to Kieran's face. "Well . . . if you insist." He grabs the bottom of my shirt, slowly pushing it higher and exposing my stomach. My heart races, but not out of nerves. Kieran pauses halfway up, as if he's drinking in the moment as much as I did.

The higher he moves, the more exposed I become. But I'm not afraid. I don't think I've ever wanted anything more.

Too soon, Kieran rids me of my shirt. His eyes travel the length of my body, but even then, he doesn't move first. Inch by inch, slowly, I close the gap between us, until I see a scar on his shoulder that I haven't noticed before. My fingers trace it. Kieran looks down at my hands on his skin.

"What's that from?" I ask.

"Spelunking."

I move in closer and whisper in his ear. "So you *have* been spelunking."

Kieran nods into my neck, his breath on my skin. I find another scar on his side, along his ribs, and let my fingers drift down to his chest.

"And this one?" I whisper in his ear.

"Rock climbing." Kieran's mouth is warm on my hair.

There's one on his back, and I let my fingers dance along the raised skin.

"Running with the bulls in Spain." His words are barely audible.

My hands travel down to the top of his jeans, my fingers edging their way beneath the fabric as Kieran sighs softly in my ear.

"Any other scars I can't see?" I unbutton the top of his pants.

"Bunny . . . ," he says in my ear. "I'm trying to be good."

I kiss the base of his neck, my lips following the line of his collarbone. Then I pull back and look in his eyes, my mouth inches away from his. "Can we have some fun instead?"

A spark lights in his eyes that turns my whole body electric. "Since you asked so nicely . . ."

The rest of the night is spent lost in a sea of sheets. We come up for air only to lose ourselves again beneath the surface. My dream disappears into the mist outside the window, hanging over Dublin Bay, the mist and my dream eventually making their way out to sea.

CHAPTER 23

The sun starts to rise, and Kieran lies next to me, asleep. The tension is gone. His breath comes naturally, the pull and push even. Peaceful. Watching him sleep, I realize how far we've come. For weeks, he was up before me, never letting me see him vulnerable. Always working. Always moving. Always helping. I realize now that he was avoiding me, but slowly that's changed.

I place my hand on his chest, needing to be convinced he won't disappear. Even after the elation of the night, fear creeps its way into my heart—the familiar feeling that life can't be trusted to work out as we think it will. I curl next to Kieran and push the feeling away—I'm used to it by now—and find a restful sleep.

Sunshine pours in the windows of the apartment when I wake up later. My clothes are strewn about the room, and delirium still fogs my brain. A memory of Kieran's lips traveling up my spine sends a wave of euphoria through me. I could wake up like this every day.

I feel around the bed but can't find Kieran. Grabbing his shirt from the floor, I put it on and go to stand at the gigantic windows. The fear he'll disappear isn't there today. It seems nothing could ruin the ecstasy I feel this morning.

Below, the water in the canal sparkles. People walk the streets. The city is laid out in front of me, all the way to the coast.

I made it to Dublin . . . and it's only the beginning.

I watch the people below, walking with purpose, leading their lives. For weeks, I've been waiting for my life to start again, and now it's here. I've made my choice, and it feels good. Better than good. It feels complete.

A clock radio sits on the nightstand. I press it on, and a song comes through the speakers—an up-tempo pop beat with more bass than guitar. It matches the feeling inside of me right now. Alive. Vibrant. The day seems brighter than usual. The only clouds linger far off to the west. I feel like I'm floating. Like all that's around me is new. The air. The sunshine. Me.

When you're floating, it's impossible to fall.

I turn up the music and sway my hips to the beat. When the song picks up pace, I do the same, bouncing on my toes and hopping around the room like a bubble that won't pop. My arms soar through the air, riding an invisible wave. My head swings back and forth, messing up my hair worse than it already is. The music wails as I dance ecstatically. Shaking myself loose. Feeling the floor beneath me, my heart beating in my chest, my skin tingly.

This is bliss.

This is happiness.

This is feeling alive.

This is freedom.

"Is that a popular dance move in America?" Kieran's voice behind me. I turn around hastily, hair in my face, shocked, out of breath. "Don't stop. I was enjoying the show immensely. Particularly the costume."

I grab the bottom of Kieran's shirt and pull it down over my legs.

He walks over to me, holding a hot cup of tea.

"You're not getting bashful on me now, are you?" He glances at the bed, a naughty grin on his face. "I think we're past that point, Bunny."

And I think to myself: *Thank God. Last night was real. It happened. I cannot, will not, forget it.*

"Good morning, Bunny." Kieran kisses me on the cheek and hands me the cup.

This is better than good.

"So what should we do today?" I ask, my eyes connecting with Kieran's and then hinting, not so subtly, toward the bed.

But he steps back, shaking his head. "You need to see Dublin."

I move closer. "We have time."

"The weather is supposed to turn this afternoon, so we need to get a move on."

I close the gap between us. "You'll be my tour guide?"

He shrugs. "I thought I'd just put you on a Hop-On, Hop-Off bus for the day while I get drunk at the pub."

"So maybe you do have a drinking problem after all." His eyes look unburdened, more alive than ever. "Hop-On, Hop-Off. Is that a bunny joke?"

I stand on my tiptoes, my lips aching for Kieran's, but he pulls back, a grin on his face like he knows he's torturing me.

"Tea. Shower." Kieran backs out of the room. "We have things to see before the rain comes."

When he's out of the room, I do one more wild dance move, shaking my hair in my face more and stifling a yelp in my throat. This feeling . . . this makes living through death worth it. I flop down on the messy bed, feeling the rumpled sheets under me, pressing my face into the pillow. A howl of glee explodes from my lips as I smell Kieran all around me. His sheets and shirt cover me. I never want this to end.

But when I catch sight of my notebook sticking out of the back pocket of my jeans on the floor, my elation freezes.

The thought of telling my dad that I won't be going home with him, that I can't, that my life is here now, scratches away a piece of my contentment. The longer I wait to tell him, the worse it will be. I've played multiple scenarios in my head—one where he slowly comes to know me as Jane, one where he visits and eventually begins to love me for who I am, not who I was. Whether he can do this is his choice. I didn't ask to be someone I'm not, and I won't do that to him. But my life belongs somewhere else now.

I press my nose to Kieran's shirt. Explaining what I've done—my past, my lies—won't be easy, but I can't focus on that right now. I came to Dublin to set Kieran free. Jane's freedom can wait.

~

It seems that every time I think I know where life will take me, I'm reminded that I really know nothing. People surprise you. Nature surprises you. Life surprises you.

After a short drive outside of the city, Kieran pulls up to Dublin's Weston Airport. Small planes are parked on the runway.

"It's a private airport," Kieran says as we pull in through the gates. "My father uses it when he brings his plane over from London."

"You have a plane?" I try to keep my voice even.

Kieran lets out a light laugh. "*He* owns a plane. I borrow the smaller planes here to log practice hours." He must see the surprise on my face, because he says, "Just because I can't actually be a pilot doesn't mean I don't pretend sometimes. Perks of being a rich kid. Flying planes is an acceptable hobby."

"Along with wrestling tigers." I try to appear calm, though my insides are jumping.

"And spelunking." Kieran winks at me.

"So when you said you were going to show me Dublin . . ."

"Don't worry, Bunny, you'll see Dublin today," Kieran says. "You'll just get a bird's-eye view."

My throat is beyond dry. Every time I swallow, it hurts. I manage to muster one word. "Grand."

We park and get out of the car, Kieran leading the way to a small plane parked on the runway. As my peripheral vision blurs, the sharp nature of this punishment becomes all too real. This is penance for all my lies. I can't blame Kieran. He doesn't know what happened to me. Dishonesty has repercussions, and this is just one in what I am sure will be a long line of them. The alternative—telling the truth—would bring everything to an end.

I stretch out my shaking hands. "Kieran . . ."

He turns to me, his eyebrows raised. "Yeah, Bunny?"

I can't bring myself to meet his eyes. My gaze drops to my shoes, the ones Stephen gave me weeks ago. I've walked as someone else for so long. How do I peel back the layers when, at the core, there's nothing but a life I don't remember?

Kieran steps closer to me. He brings his hand to my chin and lifts my face toward his. When his lips press to mine, I can feel the hunger in him, and at the same time, his restraint, only letting himself go so far. If it's my responsibility to move closer, so be it. I'll take it on gladly.

Kieran eventually brings his lips to my ear and whispers, "Is that what you needed, Bunny?"

Yes. And more.

"Tell me it's going to be OK," I say.

His nose comes to rest on mine. "I won't let anything happen to you. Do you trust me?"

I nod, hypnotically. Kieran grabs my hand and pulls me toward the airplane. Any confession I had in mind leaves with the wind.

"You're more likely to die in a car accident on the way to the airport than in a plane crash," Kieran says casually.

I'm not sure what the likelihood is of being in another plane crash, but I was hoping I wouldn't have to find out. The luck of the Irish clearly isn't on my side today.

$\sim$

We sit in the cockpit. The plane is only big enough for the two of us. Kieran messes with knobs and buttons as I sit with my hands knotted in my lap, trying to breathe through the anxiety. Kieran speaks into a radio, talking to someone on the other end, letting him know we're preparing for takeoff. Then he turns to me. "I used to be desperately afraid of flying," he says.

I blink slowly, my eyes starting to speckle with stars. "How did you get over it?"

"My father bought a plane and forced me to fly." Kieran laughs to himself. "The pilot could see how scared I was, so he took me into the cockpit and showed me how everything works. Planes are built to fly. He said, 'A plane would rather be in the air than on the ground.' It made sense to me then."

"Then why do they crash sometimes?"

Kieran says, gently, "Because no one and nothing is perfect. Mistakes happen, but I won't make any today. OK?"

I nod tightly, and Kieran turns the ignition. The engine grumbles loudly as it starts, making me jump in my seat.

Kieran pushes the throttle forward, and the plane begins to taxi toward the runway. I close my eyes and try to settle my beating heart, but I can't seem to calm down. I'm two seconds from jumping out of the plane and confessing all my sins when Kieran places a hand on my thigh.

I open my eyes to find him looking at me intently.

"I've checked and double-checked everything. Now, we're going to move fast down the runway because I need the plane to be at a certain speed to get off the ground. Then we're going to lift off into the air and ascend until we're at five hundred feet." He speaks to me the way he did when he taught me how to surf. Direct. Strong. Knowledgeable. His tone comforts me. "That's when you'll hear me retract the flaps. It's going to make a noise, but don't worry. Once we're at a thousand feet, we'll level off. I have to pull back on the engine. You'll hear it slow down. It's just me reducing the power."

"And then what?" I say.

"And then we just fly."

I sit back. The runway stretches in front of us.

Past the fear is freedom, I say to myself. At this point, there's no choice. "Just do it."

"Right." Kieran presses the throttle forward, and the engine gets louder. We begin to move. "Remember to take off, you need speed."

The plane gains momentum down the runway.

"Once I hit seventy-five miles per hour, we're OK to lift off. Right now we're at fifty . . . sixty . . ." I make fists with my hands and press them into my sides. I try to regulate my breathing, but it's inconsistent and choppy. "Sixty-five . . . seventy . . . We're almost there, Bunny. Are you ready?"

Am I ready? Am I ready to let go? Is that even possible? But the alternative is to hold on, letting fear rule my life, walking every day with a shadow over me, so that every time I look in the mirror, a piece of me is afraid of what I see. It's allowing my past to rule my future.

I don't want to live like that.

"I'm ready," I say. Fear slowly creeps up my body, rising until it crests over my head and washes back down, sending chills along my spine and tingles to my toes.

The plane lifts off the runway and into the air, and I decide, right now, to leave my fear on the ground. My body becomes buoyant as we climb. The buoyancy filters all the way down into my heart.

"We're at five hundred feet. Now, I'm going to retract the flaps." Kieran's eyes are focused on the vastness in front of us, calculating our movement through the air. My chest is no longer tight. It's expansive, like the sky.

"Did you feel it? The rush?" I ask him.

Kieran smiles. "Every time."

We get to our cruising altitude, one thousand feet. As the plane levels and Kieran pulls back on the throttle, I dare to glimpse out the window at what's below. Dublin sprawling below us and out to the west, to the ocean. My nerves aren't fully relaxed, but instead of being worried they might take control, they're more of a comfort now—they give me a sense of being alive. This is the buzz Kieran seeks, the hum of adrenaline that makes you want to yelp with excitement.

The blue ocean sparkles in the sunlight, and to the east, the city is a tangled web of streets and buildings. Bridges extending from one side of the river to the other.

"What's the name of the river?" I ask.

"The River Liffey," he says.

"Right." I make a mental note.

I see a gigantic round building that resembles a spaceship and ask him what it is.

"Aviva Stadium," Kieran says.

"Have you been there?"

"Loads of times for Rugby matches and concerts." He circles the plane around.

"Is it fun?"

Kieran grins wickedly. "What kind of fun are you talking about? Watching Rugby players bash into each other, or what we did last night?" I feel myself blush. "I will admit I've never had that kind of *fun* there . . . but there's time to change that."

Kieran's cocky expression turns me inside out, but the view needs my attention for now. I notice his apartment building towering above the rest, and to the south, far off in the distance where the buildings become sparse and the rolling hills start again, a mountain comes into view.

"And that?"

"That's Sugar Loaf."

"Have you climbed it?"

"In the dark, with a twelve pack of beer." He grins at the memory. "Maybe we could climb it someday."

Kieran nods. "If you'd like."

He points out the Guinness factory and Dublin Castle and Grafton Street, adding that at this time of year, each of them is overrun with tourists. "We're avoiding the crowd," he says.

Taking the plane around again, he shows me the expansive grounds of Trinity College. It takes up a large portion of Dublin.

"Do you like going to school there?" I ask.

"I didn't have a choice." Kieran shrugs.

"If you did have a choice, would you have done something different?"

"I would have done a lot differently." Kieran keeps his attention on the sky in front of us as he turns the plane. "I want to show you something else."

We fly off the coast and over Dublin Bay. Kieran takes the plane north, away from the city, and starts to decrease our altitude. When the plane begins to descend, my stomach jumps.

"I just want to get a little lower so you can see well," he says calmly.

"What am I looking for?"

"There are cliffs just outside of the city in Howth. When I was at school, I got in the habit of going there anytime life seemed . . . overwhelming." Kieran's eyes grow serious. "It's gorgeous, but on a windy day, there's no telling if you'll make it back alive. It always made me feel better about my life when I walked away in one piece."

The plane cruises along the coast until I see what Kieran is talking about. Steep cliffs of green line the ocean, the white foam of salt water crashing against them. The land is rugged and rolling, and the cliffs are sheer, jagged drop-offs straight down into the water below. Trails line the land, and I can see a few people out hiking.

"Will you take me on the cliff walk?" I ask.

"Sometime," Kieran agrees.

"Tomorrow!"

The gleam returns to Kieran. "Only if you promise to hold my hand the entire time."

I take it as an invitation to hold his hand now.

Kieran glances down at our interlaced fingers. "I think you're braver than me, Bunny."

"That's impossible," I say.

"You are. I'm sure of it."

Eventually, Kieran turns the plane back toward the airport. "Weather's coming in," he says. "We'll want to be back before the rain starts."

Kieran talks me through the steps he takes to land the plane safely. My nerves spike again as the nose angles down toward the ground, but they don't overwhelm me this time. The earth gets closer and closer, and when the wheels touch down, Kieran and I bounce in our seats, and I feel like I might burst with joy.

"You did it!" I yell. "We made it!"

Kieran taxis the plane back to where it was parked when we arrived and turns off the engine. But instead of climbing out, he stays in his seat, eyes on the control panels in front of him, his expression unreadable.

"What is it? Aren't you happy?" I ask.

Kieran nods. "Yes. I'm happy." But he's not telling me all of it. "You need to know . . . I didn't think this would happen when I saw you at the hospital. You were just so stubborn."

"Stubborn? Me?" I smirk at him.

"You surprised the hell out of me, Bunny."

I recall that Clive had an opinion about surprises. I place my hand on Kieran's cheek and turn his face toward mine. "Surprises make the story interesting."

Kieran takes my hand from his face and inspects it, running his fingers along mine and then inching his way up my arm, letting his fingertips inspect my skin. My stomach knots the higher his fingers travel.

"No scars," he whispers. When his hand reaches my lower lip, his thumb traces the outline of my mouth.

"None that you can see from the outside."

"And the ones I can't see?" he asks. "What about those?"

The pulse between us is alive. I place my hand on top of Kieran's. "They don't matter anymore."

In this moment, I'm desperate for the twisting of bodies, for us to lose our clothes and time and just collapse into each other. But a raindrop falls on the windshield. We both notice it.

Kieran's hand falls from my face. "We better get going. The rain's coming."

∾

Back at the apartment, rain slashes on the windows. It's dreary outside, but inside, I'm still floating. The buoyancy of flying without fear has a lasting effect. I walk straight to the windows and start pointing out all the sites we saw today, my nose pressed to the glass.

"I can see Aviva Stadium from here." I point south. "And Sugar Loaf!"

Below, the rain makes the canal murky and the rest of the city gray on gray. When I turn around, I find Kieran watching me with a keen eye.

"You impress me, Bunny."

"Why? Because I can bake without a recipe?" I joke.

"Don't do that. Don't sell yourself short." Kieran walks toward me. "You're the strongest person I've ever met." His fingers play with my purple hair. "With a somewhat impulsive side that can lead to reckless behavior."

I touch Kieran's face, the stubble on his chin. "You saved me."

"No." He shakes his head. "I had good timing. You would have saved yourself, with or without me."

Without me . . . The thought guts me. Kieran's done so much for me. He's challenged me in ways I couldn't have imagined. When he says I'm strong, I believe it, but he helped expose that in me.

Life is a collaborative effort. We can't do it on our own.

Kieran's stomach growls, lightening the moment, and we laugh. An idea comes to me then.

"Stay here," I say. I go to the closet and get a raincoat. "I'm going to the store."

"Bunny, it's pouring outside."

"I won't be gone long. There must be a place close by."

"You're crazy to go out in this. Just stay. We'll order something."

Kieran doesn't understand what he did for me today, and while the extent of it has to remain hidden for now, I can offer something back to him, piece by piece. "Just tell me where the market is."

"Three blocks down is a Tesco market."

It isn't far. I should be back shortly.

"Are you sure you want to do this?" he asks.

I open the apartment door, determined and blissful. "Definitely."

~

The rain hits me hard when I step outside of Millennium Tower. The air is cool, with a slight stench of dead fish coming off the water. I hug Kieran's raincoat around me and make my way toward the Tesco.

The wind blows, spitting rain in my face as I cross the street and take the bridge across the canal. Even with the rain, the fresh air feels nice. I breathe it in, feeling alive, and even take off my hood and turn my face upward, smiling as the rain falls on my skin. I can't help but revel in how far I've come. The streets of Dublin are laid out before me like a sign—I can choose any road to go down.

The bright lights of the Tesco are just two blocks ahead. I pick up speed, my hair now soaked, rain dripping from the ends. The gray clouds make it seem later in the evening than it really is, and the lights from the establishments seem even brighter.

I cross the last street, my destination in sight, but I stop as a vision catches my eye. The sign above the door says Dillon's Pub. Inside, TVs are on. I look through the window, and in a single moment, the world starts spinning too quickly. Seeing myself on the TV screen is disorienting. I walk into the pub, any thought of food gone.

Andy comes on the TV. He's standing in front of Paudie's Pub, his cocky face taking up most of the screen.

"I knew I'd seen her somewhere before, and then it hit me!" Andy knocks the side of his head. "She's that girl who survived the plane crash . . . just with purple hair! She even told me she was from Cleveland! She was hiding out in this boring town the whole time!" Andy holds up the picture he took of us, flashing it to the camera, a shit-eating grin on his face. "There she is—Lusty Lavender. My friends are gonna freak when they hear this."

The screen flashes to a reporter standing along the beach in Waterville and holding an umbrella in the rain.

"The girl's father and authorities have searched the town, but have yet to discover if Clementine Haas is still here. While Paul Haas has stayed quiet the month since his daughter went missing, we've just been informed that in a few minutes he will finally break his silence, making a public plea for his daughter's safe return."

I back into the door of the pub, causing a few people to turn. I bring my hood up immediately and walk out, numb all over. I can't catch my breath. The rain continues to pour on me. I lean back against the wall as my new reality sets in. Everyone knows what I look like now. They know I was in Waterville. There's nowhere to hide anymore. I can't conceal who I am from . . . anybody.

My stomach rolls with nausea, and I almost throw up, but there's nothing left in me.

I knew this might happen, but my bliss blinded me to it. As I drifted from the headlines, I didn't think about the possibility that I'd be back on the front page. Waterville was supposed to be safe, but I'm not protected anywhere now. I should have known I couldn't stay hidden forever. That at some point, my house of lies would come crashing down.

Back at Millennium Tower, the elevator takes me up to the tenth floor. I open the door to Kieran's apartment, my saturated clothes hanging heavily on me. Kieran sits in the leather chair in the living room. He stands when I walk in.

My entire body hurts, inside and out, even the tears streaming down my face. I deserve this pain. You can't avoid hurt. You're only choice is to live through it.

"Bunny, what happened? What's going on?" Kieran comes to me, taking the wet raincoat off while I stand like a statue, feeling like I'm cracking apart, one lie at a time.

"Ask me the question," I say.

For a moment, Kieran is confused. Then he understands. "Truth or dare?"

There's only one thing left to do. "Truth."

CHAPTER 24

The beginning is the only place to start—waking up in the hospital with no memory. My confession dominoes from there. The crash, my unknown life before, the lie about being mugged, the real reason I left the hospital, the real reason I dyed and cut my hair, the real reason I'm afraid of heights, the media that's been hunting for me . . . my real name. All of it . . . finally real.

The expression on Kieran's face makes me shudder. He sits still on the couch in the living room, his brows pulling tighter the more I talk. When he runs his hands through his hair, like he does when he's frustrated, my stomach tightens.

"But everything I said to you I meant," I plead. "That wasn't a lie."

"Except the part about who you really are," Kieran counters.

I grab his hand. "You have to believe me when I say I don't know who Clementine Haas is. I can't take ownership of her life. I don't want it."

"Your birthday?" Kieran asks.

"That was the truth. I read the date on my chart at the hospital."

"And your dad . . ."

This is the most shameful part. I can't bear to even glance in his direction. "He's been waiting for me in Limerick this whole time."

"How do you know?"

"I called the hospital one night, about a week after I left, and spoke with my nurse, Stephen. He said my dad was determined to stay in Ireland until I was found. At the time, it was a relief. I still thought I'd remember my life, but . . ." I drift off, knowing this is the part I need to tell him most of all. Jane's life depends on it.

"But?"

"I still don't remember anything!" I exclaim. "The memories haven't come back! I'm not any closer to being Clementine Haas than I was the first day you met me. I know it feels like I've lied to you . . . but I couldn't have told you the truth because I don't know it in the first place. If I told you I was Clementine Haas, the girl from the accident, you wouldn't have helped me. I needed to be away from the hospital and the media. Do you know how hard it's been not to pick up a newspaper and read about my life? But it's not *mine*." My heart aches. "But with you . . . I feel like a new person. Like someone who has a life to look forward to, not just a past haunting her."

"What if it comes back?"

I shake my head. "It's not coming back."

"How do you *know*?"

"It's not!" I yell, immediately regretting that I raised my voice. "My past doesn't matter anymore. I'm moving on. I'll just keep running, if that's what it takes." I breathe and try to settle my nerves, but it's no use. At this point, I'm a whisper away from cracking. "The question is: Are you moving on with me?"

My question lingers in the air, heavily, as if I could almost touch it. This day has turned upside down, but tomorrow . . . It won't take the media long to figure out where I was staying. By tomorrow, Clive and Siobhan will see the papers. My identity will be revealed on the cover of every tabloid. I can dye my hair again and again, but I can't stay hidden in Ireland forever. I gather one last ounce of courage.

"I dare you to start a new life with me."

Kieran's eyes flash with something—possibility, maybe? Or maybe just the same reaction he has to every dare—the rush of doing something wholly unsafe to remind him he's alive. It's the ultimate dare, the one he's most afraid of, but if on the other end, we can be together . . . I search his eyes for a sliver of possibility.

"I saw you flying today. I saw how happy you were." I move closer, kneeling down in front of him. "You don't need this." I gesture around the lavish apartment. "We can start over . . . together."

Kieran inhales audibly. I inch closer to him. Even now there's electric heat between us.

"We can make it work," I say, moving slowly, leaning in closer. And then closer. When Kieran shifts, I close my eyes and feel the warmth coming off his skin. My clothes are still damp, my hair wet, but right now I can't feel anything but him.

Kieran's hands grasp my arms, and for a second, I believe he's going to kiss me and this nightmare will be over. But he sets me back on the couch before standing up.

"I think you better sleep on the couch tonight." He leaves the room, and I am alone, the cold creeping back into my bones. I hear his bedroom door close with a click, our happy ending washed away with the Irish rain.

CHAPTER 25

My nightmares would be a relief. Drifting into the nothing of amnesia would feel better than shivering in the cold of reality. Lying on the couch in Kieran's living room, my teeth chatter as I try to sleep.

The end is coming. My lies have overtaken the life I tried to have. The worst part is that I can't even claim the life I lied about. Without Jane's life, I have nothing, and with Clementine's, I have nothing. I hug my knees to my chest, not wanting the sun to rise. Right now I might be miserable, but tomorrow . . .

The world will know who I am. Hiding will be impossible. I'm back where I started, except this time I don't even have Stephen here to help me.

The rain has stopped now. The air outside is quiet and still. I try to imagine what the ocean sounds like in Waterville tonight. The whoosh of water as it crashes on the shore and the slurp as it sucks rocks and sand back out to sea. I thought I could avoid continually crashing, but as it turns out, it's unavoidable. Even on the calmest day, the ocean still rolls into the beach and pulls pebbles out to sea.

My clothes are still wet. The dampness chills my bones. I don't deserve to feel bad for myself. I knew this would happen all along. I just fooled myself into thinking it would be different—that I could change the inevitable. But lies are lies, even if the truth doesn't make sense.

I hover over sleep, focusing on the dark just outside the windows. Light has to come at some point. Night can't stay here forever.

When arms grab around my waist and hoist me off the couch, I'm sure I'm dreaming. The familiar smell of Kieran fills me with comfort, and I think the nightmares have finally stopped. I curl into his chest, feeling the warmth of his body next to mine.

"My God, you're freezing, Bunny."

"No . . . I'm pig and cow parts. You thought I was a bunny, but I lied."

"You need to get out of your wet clothes." Kieran sets me down on his bed. My head swims, and my teeth chatter. He pulls my shirt off me, but there's no hint of intimacy.

"Please take a moment to locate your nearest exit," I say. "In some cases, your nearest exit may be behind you." I lie down on the bed, aching for heat. Kieran slips me out of my jeans. "But there's no exit to this story. I can't get out of it."

"Bunny, you're delirious."

I turn my face into the warm sheets, breathing in Kieran. If this is my last night here, I want to remember how it felt to be surrounded by him.

"You said it today. Planes are built to fly. They aren't built to crash," I say. "Why did it have to be *my* plane? *My* life? I survived only to lose everything."

Kieran kneels down in front of me. "I don't know why life happens the way it does."

I reach for him, almost believing that he won't be there, that I really am imagining all of this. But when my skin connects with his, my hand finding his cheek, when he turns his mouth into the palm of my hand, and I feel his breath meet my skin, I know it's real.

"I'm sorry I dragged you down with me."

"Bunny . . . ," he says. This is the most we've touched since I laid out my truth for him. I'm desperate for him to stay. Kieran takes my hand from his face. He traces my fingers with his own, as if studying my skin. When his eyes lock with mine in the dim room, the blue of his is practically iridescent.

He climbs into bed with me. My whole body is tired, but alive at the same time. I can't believe this is actually happening. He's warm as his legs edge their way between mine, his arms pulling me to his chest. I lay my ear on top of his heart and listen. That's how I know this is real.

Kieran lifts my chin toward his face. I see the boy I met in the hospital, the fearless wonder who taught me how to surf, who danced with me on my birthday, who kissed me as if breathing didn't matter, who showed me I could fly again.

"Dare accepted," he says. Kieran places his warm lips on mine, and I melt.

CHAPTER 26

It was real. I didn't dream it. The sun has returned, making my eyes squint and water as I wake up in Kieran's bed. I knew that morning had to come, but the dread I felt as I lay on the couch last night is gone.

Kieran accepted my dare. I don't know what the future will bring us, but now I know we'll be together. There are no more lies between us.

I roll over to find a hot cup of tea on the nightstand, and—just like my first days in Waterville—a note.

First tea. Then shower.

I add internally: *then forever.*

When I finish my tea, as instructed, I take a long shower. Steam fills the bathroom, the opposite of the cold rain that fell on me last night. But the rain never lasts in Ireland. The sun comes out eventually.

As I brush my hair, I contemplate what color I'll dye it next. My mind starts to wander over all the possibilities with Kieran. Maybe we'll escape to the northern part of Ireland. I haven't been there. Or west. We can find a small town, like Waterville, on the ocean. We can surf during the day and sit out at night, listening to the waves.

I dress in a fresh outfit and walk out of the bedroom, needing to see Kieran. Craving him. For too long last night I thought I lost him. I thought it was all over. But he changed his mind.

Kieran is in the living room, freshly dressed, but the picture is off. What I see is so unexpected it startles me.

He's not the only one here.

Two other people sit on the couch—one I recognize, the other I know.

Stephen and my dad sit, gazing out the window at the Dublin sunshine. When they hear my footsteps, both come to their feet. I'm paralyzed, wondering if what I see is actually happening.

The truth hits me—Kieran didn't change his mind. He tricked me into believing he did. He went behind my back. Pieces start to fit together. Kieran asking me about my dad. Me telling him about Stephen. With that information, all it would take is a call to the hospital in Limerick. But when did he do it? My stomach turns as I realize that Kieran brought me into his bed because he knew this was coming. He knew it would all be over today.

He stares at the floor. "I'm sorry, Bunny. There was no other way."

"Don't call me that," I say. My head starts to hurt, and the room spins slightly.

"He did the right thing, Clementine," Stephen says. "We've been worried sick."

Sick. That's how I feel right now. Like I'm on the world's most horrific roller coaster, with no ups, only perpetual downs. Gravity pulls, my bones ache to their core, and I can't fight it. A humming starts in my ears, like a broken engine that makes too much noise. I grab my head, just wanting it all to stop.

When Stephen and my dad take a step closer, I use all my might to move. Before anyone can stop me, I'm out the apartment door, running for my life. I press the elevator button as someone yells after me, but the elevator will take too long, so I divert to the emergency exit. That's what

I need right now—this is an emergency, and I need out. Tears fall down my cheeks as I push the stairwell door open and start down, counting the flights as I descend.

Nine . . .

"Wait! Please!" someone shouts behind me.

Eight . . .

He's gaining on me, but I pick up my pace.

"I'll just keep chasing you!"

Seven . . .

Six . . .

"Teeny, for the love of God, would you just slow down! I've got a bad knee. Running down these stairs isn't helping!"

"Well, you should have listened to the doctor when she said you needed physical therapy!" I yell back.

"You know how I feel about that!" He sounds winded.

"Yeah," I scoff, mocking my dad's voice as I run. "'The only therapy a Clevelander needs is beer. Takes care of all your pain at half the cost.'"

"I've lived in Cleveland my whole life!" he yells. "We know pain well!" I stop on the landing of the fourth floor. My dad pants behind me, clutching his side. "Jesus Christ, Teeny, are you trying to kill your old man?"

"Say my name again," I say.

"Teeny."

"That's not my name."

"I never liked Clementine, but your mother was set on naming you after food. It could have been worse, she wanted to name you—"

I cut him off. "Paprika. She wanted to name me Paprika."

"Can you imagine the nickname? *Pap?*" My dad cringes. "Your life would have been over in junior high. I did you a favor by vetoing that name."

I lean back against the wall, breathless and awestruck, the anger melting away into . . . exhilaration. "You named me Clementine because I was premature."

My dad nods. "You were so teeny-tiny with jaundice. 'Like a little orange,' your mom said."

"Like a clementine."

"It was too fluffy a name for me. I like a good, strong name. Jane was my idea."

"Jane," I say with a laugh.

"That was my pick, but I lost in the end. We compromised on the nickname."

"Teeny."

"Yes." My dad's breathing has slowed. I look at his face, at the wrinkles around his eyes from too much sun, at his salt-and-pepper hair cut short to his head and thinning, at his right pointer finger, slightly crooked from when he broke it playing a pickup basketball game and refused to go to the doctor because he didn't want the other players to think he was a wimp.

"I remember." Memories start to click in place, my heart pounds, my life—Teeny's life—comes back to me in little flashes.

"You do?" he asks, but hesitantly, like he isn't sure he can trust himself to believe it.

"I do." I throw my arms around him, hugging his now-familiar body to mine. It's as if someone turned on a light that I thought had burned out. I can see my bedroom with its old flowered wallpaper, and the single bathroom with white subway tile that my dad and I share. Our front porch with a broken swing, and the flagpole where my dad proudly flies a Browns flag every Sunday during football season. I pull back. "You own a landscaping business."

My dad huffs. "In a place that has snow half the year. Not my smartest move."

"And Grandma Rolland took over the bakery when mom died."

He touches my cheek with a look like he hasn't seen me in forever. "She didn't have the knack for baking like your mom did, but she tried, God rest her soul."

"Grandma Rolland died last year!" I say it with a little too much enthusiasm and then apologize. "That's when I took over the bakery."

"You should have gone to college like I wanted," my dad chides.

"I'm in night school at Cleveland State."

"It's not the same. I wanted you to have a real college experience, with parties and dorm rooms and friends from all over the world." He shakes his head. "You spent so many years taking care of your old man—washing my clothes, cleaning the house—you deserve a life without me in it."

"So that's why I like to clean . . ."

My dad sits down on a stair, something heavy weighing him down. I take the seat next to him.

"It's OK, Dad. I remember it now. I don't mind taking care of you. I like it, really." But he just shakes his head. "What is it?"

"I'm the reason you were on that plane, Teeny . . . Do you remember that?"

When I try to engage with that memory, it's still dark.

"It was my fault," he says. "I could never afford to send you to Europe, but I wanted you to see the world. When James gave you your birthday present, I pushed you to go."

"James?"

"He was your boyfriend, Teeny. James Mahon."

The name conjures a picture within me—a boy with blond hair, brown eyes, a charming Irish accent that would make any girl swoon. A warm but convoluted feeling comes over me as I try to pull more memories to the surface, but my head is foggy. The exhilaration of remembering starts to fade as I realize a truth about memories—they aren't all good.

James's voice echoes within me. It's so familiar. I've heard it while I've been here, confused when it's happened, thinking my mind was playing tricks on me. But my dreams . . . reaching for someone. I stand up suddenly. "Where is he? Where's James?"

"Teeny . . ." My dad grabs my hand and gently pulls me back down on the step. His eyes fill with grief. "James was on the plane with you. He didn't survive."

I think I might throw up. Nothing makes sense. "I don't remember him clearly, Dad. The plane . . . I can't . . ."

My dad hugs me. "Maybe it's for the best. Maybe you're not ready to remember everything. Just give it time. You've been through so much."

"But why was I on that plane?"

"You were on your way to Paris," my dad says in a soft tone. "It was a birthday gift from James. You weren't even supposed to be on that flight, but at the last minute, he decided to take you to Ireland first, so you could see where he was from." I hear what he's saying, but it doesn't all click into place. "I wasn't about to say no. It was your chance to see the world. I never could have afforded to take you, Teeny. But James . . . he could do that for you."

"I don't understand." My voice is pinched. I'm on the verge of tears. My memories don't all fit. Some things I can see clearly, others are faded and blurred. "Why was James in Cleveland?"

"He was traveling and came into town to stay with a cousin and see a real 'American football game.' But you know how Cleveland is . . . once it gets under your skin, it's hard to walk away from." My dad kisses me on my head. "*You're* hard to walk away from, Teeny."

His shirt smells of his minty aftershave, the smell of every morning he and I got ready for the day together. When I was little, he would let me pretend to shave with him, putting foamy cream on my face and using a covered razor to wipe it all away. Then he'd pat my cheek with a little aftershave. He still uses the same kind.

"I'm still so confused—" I begin, but my dad shushes me.

"There's time, Teeny. Give yourself time. I'm just so happy to have you back." His expression looks broken, what I put him through these past weeks showing on his face. "No more running, OK? Promise?"

I agree, my gut heavy with guilt. "Promise."

My dad helps me off the step, keeping his arm securely around me as we make our way back up the stairs. I can sense his need to keep me close. He's worried I'll run off again. I don't know how to explain to him what I did and why I did it, but like he said, there's time. Somehow I'll find a way to make it up to him.

"What do we do now?"

"We go home," he says. "I have us booked on a flight tomorrow. I miss our house, Teeny. I miss my television. I can't watch another episode of *Coronation Street*." He smiles. "The Tribe is actually winning. Can you believe that? There's still no hope for the Browns, but we'll take what we can get."

As we climb back to the tenth floor, I feel the weight of what I'm about to leave behind. Ireland. Kieran. My life here. I still can't believe he called my dad, but now that my memories are starting to come back, I'm not sure I can be mad at him. In actuality, I think I've already forgiven him. But where does that leave us? Can I really walk away? Just the thought makes me ache. And what about my life here? I don't know if I can leave, even with my memories starting to come back. Nothing about this feels . . . easy.

"I'll tell you one thing," my dad says. He points down at my bare feet. "I could have killed James when you showed up with that ridiculous tattoo."

I stiffen as we walk.

"He got you drunk one night and dared you to do it." My dad shakes his head. I'm frozen, motionless on the steps. "He was always playing that stupid game—truth or dare? You were never one to pick truth, Teeny, that's for sure."

I have to grab the railing to stop myself from collapsing. A piece of my life suddenly fits perfectly with another. I bolt up the steps, two at a time, my breath tight. I hear my dad yelling for me to slow down, but I can't. My life is barreling full speed ahead, and by now I know I can't avoid a crash. It's coming, and not the way I expected.

I slam Kieran's apartment door against the wall as I enter and hear Stephen say, "I'm Jewish and gay."

Kieran looks surprised as I run past him and into the bedroom, getting my notebook out from under the mattress.

The picture of Kieran and his friends. I fall down to my knees, my hands shaking. For unknown reasons, I couldn't let it go. But now . . . I know why.

There in the center of the picture is Kieran, and next to him, a boy with blond hair and brown eyes, dressed in a uniform, a devilish grin on his face. It's James.

Kieran stands in the doorway.

"You knew who I was the whole time," I say weakly, though I want to sound fierce.

"I was just trying to keep you safe."

"Safe?" I bark at him. "You took me flying yesterday, even though you knew what I've been through."

"You're stronger than you think." Kieran clenches his jaw. "And, yes. *Safe*. James would have wanted me to help."

"Don't say his name." I close my eyes, pushing the image of James from my mind. Somehow, I find the strength to stand up. "So you were just *helping* this whole time. Pretending."

"I told you to remember the Jell-O. You saw what you wanted to see. I just tried to play along."

"So that's why you helped me leave the hospital."

"I went that day . . . for reasons."

"Reasons?" I snap. "Even now, you're lying to me."

"Yes. *Reasons*. I knew James would have wanted me to make sure you were OK. You didn't have anyone."

"So what you said about volunteering, helping people—that was a lie. You were there, just waiting for me."

"I was helping people . . . you, in particular." Kieran takes a long breath. "You had a reckless determination to leave. I had no idea you were so stubborn. I figured better you be with me than some other stranger. I could keep track of you." And then Kieran rolls his eyes. "Little did I know that being reckless is in your nature."

"Don't." My tone is sharp. "Don't talk about me like you know me."

"I *do* know you," Kieran pleads.

"And then what? What were you going to do once I remembered who I was?"

"I didn't think it would last as long as it did. I thought I'd be taking you back to Limerick before the week was out." He runs his hands through his hair. "It all got out of control. I didn't expect . . ." He groans like the words are caught in his mouth. "I knew it was over last night. I couldn't let you run again."

The sick reality dawns on me. The whole time I was being Jane, discovering who I was, creating a new life, Kieran knew, and he always intended to hand me back, to let me go. To *leave* me. There was never any possibility that we would stay together.

"What about . . . ?" I look at his bed. "Were you just . . . pretending?"

"I never did anything you didn't ask me to do."

"But you made me think . . . Was *this* your way of keeping me safe?"

He doesn't respond to that question. His jaw tightens as if he's fighting back words. Even now, he can't reveal himself. He can't fully let me in.

"Well, you failed." Tears fall from my eyes. I feel broken and exposed, like a hole has been punched through my chest. I may have gained some of my memories, but I'm losing everything else. Kieran didn't really care about me. He was just acting. Playing a part so he could keep an eye on me. I start to piece events together in my head. "The night you came home drunk . . ."

"I don't think it's uncommon for people to get drunk after going to their best friend's funeral."

"That's why you were in Dublin." I close my eyes. James is dead. But even now, my feelings for him are like reading someone else's diary. It's as if someone else was in love with him. I can't tell if the pain I'm feeling is guilt or the realization that I fell in love with his best friend. But it was all a ruse, all based on lies.

I force myself up. For a month, I wished I could know what Kieran was thinking, why he hesitated to touch me, what his burden was. I thought it was all because of his dad, because of Siobhan and the baby, but now I see the truth.

I straighten myself out and wipe the tears from my eyes. I lay the picture of Kieran and James on the bed, next to my notebook. I don't need either anymore.

"I take back what I said. You're not a good person. You *are* responsible for all of this. You only care about manipulating people for your own benefit. Just like your father."

I leave Kieran alone in the bedroom. When Stephen, my dad, and I walk out of the apartment, the door closes behind us. Kieran doesn't come after me. We fight through reporters huddled outside of Millennium Tower, get into the car, and begin the long drive back to where I started. And I know this is the end of our story. The tabloids have found me. *I've* found me. It's time to leave Ireland for good.

CHAPTER 27

"I'll never get used to driving on the wrong side of the road," my dad says. I rest my head in Stephen's lap in the backseat of the car.

"It's not wrong to us," Stephen says.

"We'll be home before you know it, Teeny," my dad says in the rearview mirror. "Baseball games. Swimming in the lake. No more tabloids and dreary hospitals."

"Now that you're found, you'll be yesterday's news," Stephen says with a wave of the hand. "Plus, I think Prince Harry has a new girlfriend. That'll keep them busy for a while."

I should be relieved to go home, but the past month replays in my head. How could I have been so stupid? So foolish? I thought I was lying to Kieran, but really I was lying to myself. How could I have thought this would end any other way? It was a fantasy. Kieran knew it all along. I thought I was creating my own story, but really, Kieran was. And I fell in love with him, like a total idiot.

That's the part that hurts so much. My heart is broken, and I want to hate Kieran for all that he's done, to wipe him from my mind, but I know I never can. Even all the way in America, I'll think about him. Dream about him. Because that's how memories work. They come back to you, knock you down, and beg you to surrender.

"I like the new do. Looks lovely," Stephen says. I wish I was open to receiving his kindness, but my head hurts, and my heart feels worse. "Are you going to keep it like this?"

"I haven't really thought about it," I say.

"I think you should." And then he leans down and whispers so my dad can't here. "So was I right?"

"About what?"

He gives me a wicked grin. "Clementine likes sex?" I nudge Stephen. "Come on, I saw the way that boy looked at you. There was only one bed in that apartment. Was it how I thought? Like having your first kiss all over again?" Stephen gets a dreamy look about him, but his questions only threaten to bring back my tears.

Kieran confessed everything to my dad over the phone last night. How he helped me escape the hospital. How he hid me out in Waterville. How he's a friend of James's and felt obligated to help. And how he had no intention of keeping me away for so long, but the situation got out of hand.

"He thought he was helping," my dad said. "I can't fault him for trying, as misguided as it was. I remember how I was at twenty, with your mom. If she said jump, I did it, even if there was a plate of glass inches from my head. I didn't care about the consequences. I only cared about making her happy."

This isn't what happiness feels like, though. This is what it feels like when the plate of glass shatters at your feet, and all that's left is a bump on the head and regrets.

I roll onto my other side. "I don't want to talk about it."

"We have a lot to discuss," my dad says from the front seat. "I can't believe it's already mid-July."

"Like what?" I ask.

"Well . . . like college, for instance. You're a sophomore now. I think you need to consider transferring out of Cleveland State and going away to school. Ohio University, maybe? I hear Athens is lovely in the fall."

"Dad." I sit up, watching him in the rearview mirror.

"Just think about it." Then his face lights up. "Dorms . . . parties . . . football Saturdays . . . While I hate to admit it, it would be good for you to be away from home. Lord knows I've had enough practice not having you around this summer." The last bit comes out strained, and I'm reminded of the pain he must have gone through.

"I'm so sorry, Dad. I'll make it up to you."

But he waves it off. "I have you back, Teeny. That's all I want. Plus, I'm a Cleveland Browns fan. I've lived through worse, and every year I still think we have a chance. You think one month in Ireland is going to kill me?"

Stephen watches the pastures pass out the window.

I grab him in a hug. "Thank you for staying with him, and for coming to get me. You're the loveliest person I've ever met, Stephen."

Stephen holds me tightly. "I thought your dad might need reinforcements. You're a hard one to let go of, Clementine Haas. I knew it the second you woke up in the hospital. You charmed me from the get-go."

Stephen is unaware of how much his comment hurts. It just reminds me how easy it was for Kieran to let me go. He let me walk out of his life. Worse, he *forced* me out of his life.

I take a deep breath, sitting back, knowing I need to move on now, and ask my dad, "If I go off to college, what'll happen with the bakery?"

"Gail Bober's been running it all summer. She's actually pretty good at it. She offered to manage the place until you graduate, and then you can decide if you want to take over. You might find you want to do something else with your life."

What my dad is proposing is not like him. We've been a team ever since my mom died. Now he wants to break us up. "Where is this coming from, Dad?"

He pulls over to the side of the road so he can face me in the backseat. "This past month, Teeny . . . made me look at our life differently.

I kept you home because I needed you. Without your mom . . ." He takes a deep breath. "You're all I have. But that's not fair. You need a life. That's why you left the hospital, right? You wanted to find yourself?"

Tears form again as I nod. "But that was different."

"I can't imagine how scary it must have been to wake up with no memory, but you pushed through it, Teeny. You took control of your life. In a way, I couldn't be more proud of you." He shakes his head. "You can't stop now just because we're going home. You have to keep searching. Life is going to take you on a wild ride. You need to be open to that. And I need to let you experience it."

"Really?"

He agrees. "Really."

I grab him in a hug. "Thank you," I whisper.

"Just promise me you'll come home for at least one Browns game."

"Browns/Steelers. Save me a seat in the Dawg Pound?"

He nods and turns back onto the road, muttering, "I still hate Ben Roethlisberger."

As we drive, I lie back down on Stephen's lap, and he plays with my hair again. I'm going to miss him. I barely know him, but he will always be etched in my memory. He was there on the day I was born, after all. He cut my hair and fixed me up. Made me feel human when I didn't know who I was. And tomorrow, I'm leaving Ireland behind. All that will remain are the memories.

"I can tell you this," my dad says. "Heather can't wait for you to get home. She's been calling and texting me every day. At one point, I thought she might get on a plane and come here herself."

The name conjures memories—two little girls choreographing dances in my musty old basement, secretly putting on makeup at school when we weren't allowed, driving along Lake Erie in the summer with sunburns, the windows rolled down, blasting music and singing at the top of our lungs, getting drunk for the first time, and then throwing up. Heather is my best friend. The love I have for her, the connection, becomes real in an instant.

"You should probably give her a call when we get to the hotel," my dad says. "Let her know you'll be home tomorrow." His excitement to be home is written all over his face.

But my mind is elsewhere. Kieran said James was his best friend. But he can't call him anymore. Can't talk to him. Can't hug him or laugh with him. After all that Kieran has done, I don't want to feel sympathy for him, but his best friend is dead. The loss must run deep. I now understand a piece of Kieran's burden that he couldn't share, the distress I saw in him at times. He was grieving. It makes sense that Siobhan was protective.

Until now, I hadn't considered Siobhan's role in all of this. She knew who I was the whole time. She knew what Kieran had done. He asked her to lie. No wonder she didn't like me. She was forced into a game she didn't want to play.

I sit up again. "How far away is Tralee from Shannon Airport?"

"A little less than two hours," Stephen says, surprised.

"Dad . . ." I find his reflection in the rearview mirror. "Can we make a detour? I need to go to the hospital."

$\sim$

As I walk into the Tralee hospital, I try not to look in the direction of the grassy field where Kieran and I first kissed, but memories come back to me nonetheless. I press on, asking my dad and Stephen to wait in the lobby while I go up to see Siobhan.

"You're not going to run away again, are you?" my dad says nervously.

"No."

"OK, just had to check. You know what I always say—even when you're winning, you're one moment away from Earnest Byner dropping the ball on the one-yard line."

"I promise." I kiss him on the cheek and head to the elevator.

Siobhan and Clive are curled up in her bed, watching TV, when I walk into the room.

"More episodes of *Shortland Street*?" I ask.

They both sit up, surprised. Clive says, with a smile, "Please, soap operas have nothing on this story. A girl with amnesia hides out in a small town in Ireland while tabloids search for her, rocking the country with the drama of it all. I'm not even sure if Jane Austen herself could bloody well write this."

The screen displays news coverage of me walking out of Millennium Tower, surrounded by reporters.

"Is it true what they say?" I ask. "Does the camera add twenty pounds?"

Clive climbs off the bed and comes to kiss me on the cheek. "Rubbish. You look gorgeous."

"You're lying. I look awful."

"You look"—Clive gives me a sympathetic grin—"like you've survived a plane crash."

I hesitate. "Can you ever forgive me for lying?"

Clive waves away my question. "You know I love a good story, and *this* is a good story. I'm just glad I got to play a part in it." Then he leans down and adds, "I figured it out a few days ago. Your face flashed up on the screen in the waiting room while you were asleep. Surprised the hell out of me."

"I'm sorry."

"Just promise you won't forget about us when you're back in America and dating Justin Timberlake. You'll come visit, right?"

I grab Clive in a desperate hug. "I promise."

"And keep the purple hair," he whispers. "It suits you better than the bleached-out look you were sporting before."

"I promise," I whisper back. "Thank you for being my friend when I didn't have one."

"You always have a place in Ireland, *Jane*. Don't forget that." He notices Siobhan watching us with a keen eye. "I think I'll go find us some tea."

When he's gone, I walk to the bed and sit down on the end. Siobhan is still, her lips pressed together. There's a healthy glow to her skin.

"You look good," I say.

"It's all Clive's doing. He dotes on me and the baby. You'd think *he* was the father."

"You deserve to be doted on."

"He asked me to move in with him. Wants to take care of me and the baby. Like a real family. Pretty untraditional, if you ask me, but I've never been one for rules."

"Did you say yes?"

She nods, happy.

"Where will you go?"

"Belfast, maybe. Or Galway. He wants to open a new store, somewhere where people . . . will appreciate us more."

"I'm happy for you, Siobhan." And I mean it. She deserves a life filled with love. "You knew who I was the whole time. That's why you didn't like me."

Siobhan nods slowly. "I knew it would blow up in Kieran's face, but he was hell-bent on taking you in. I just didn't want to see him in any more pain."

"Him in pain?" I say it with too much sarcasm, my own self-pity and anger taking over.

"Yes," Siobhan says strongly. "He lost his best friend, Clementine."

"But he lied to me."

"And you lied to him."

I stand up, not wanting to get into this, the wound too fresh to break it open again. "I'm happy for you and Clive. I really am," I say. "I just came to say thank you. And that I'm sorry I couldn't get Kieran to change his life. He wasn't in love with me anyway. He was just pretending."

I start toward the door. It's time to leave. I'm glad I saw Clive and know they both will be OK. At least someone's story has a happy ending.

"Do you want to see the baby?" Siobhan says.

I turn back toward her, surprised. "Really?"

She stands up from the bed, dressed in black-and-white skull-and-crossbones pajama pants and a red T-shirt. Even in the hospital, Siobhan looks cooler than me. She leads me down to the NICU nursery. There are only a few babies being tended to by nurses. Siobhan talks to one and then waves me over toward one of the cradles. It has a protective shield over the top and holes to put your arms through. Inside is a small but perfect baby girl with a full head of blonde hair.

"Clive convinced me to name her Elizabeth," she says. "I call her Lizzy."

"I like that."

"He said it would guarantee she'll be a strong female who doesn't take anyone's shit."

"I think her mother will teach her that," I say. "Did she get your blue eyes?"

"No, they're gray right now, but I bet they'll turn brown like her father's." Siobhan turns to me. "She's going to need to be strong. She won't ever have her dad to hold her hand when she crosses the street or teach her how to kick a football or cry with her when her heart's broken for the first time." The emotion in Siobhan's eyes is one I've never seen before—heartache. But a perfect baby is before me—blonde fuzz covering her flawless head.

James comes to mind. His naturally blond hair was the one feature he cared most for, constantly checking his reflection in the mirror to make sure it lay perfectly across his forehead.

And then, as I look at Lizzy, the puzzle of my life comes together, and my dreams begin to make sense—though the picture is not what I expected.

"How well did you know James?" I ask.

"Well," Siobhan says. "Kieran would probably say I knew him too well."

"He's the one. James is the father."

Siobhan confirms my revelation with a small nod. A moment isn't long enough to let all of this sink in. My mind searches for clues to explain how I stumbled into this web I didn't even know existed.

"I thought he was in love with me," Siobhan says. "I should have known better when James wanted me to keep our relationship from Kieran. No one in love would do that. But I was desperate to keep him. I was so used to being left, I just wanted *someone* to stay. I begged him not to go to America."

"But he left anyway," I say.

"He wasn't the kind of person to settle down. I knew that. He wanted to travel the world." For just a second, it's as if Siobhan's wearing her broken heart. "He didn't know about the baby when he left. I couldn't bring myself to tell him. I wanted him to pick me instead of being forced to out of obligation. But he picked *you* in the end."

"I swear I didn't know—"

Siobhan waves off my explanation. "I know." She looks back toward Lizzy. "When Kieran found out I was pregnant, he made me tell James. He was sure his best friend would come home from America and take responsibility, but James refused. He'd fallen in love with some Yank by then."

"It's no wonder you hate me."

"I don't hate you." Siobhan laughs. "I quite like you now, but then . . . in the state I was in . . . left by James, sent into hiding, my dad threatening to cut me off if I didn't give the baby up for adoption . . . It was a mess. And Kieran did what he always does. He stepped in to help me. He threatened James, said he needed to come back and take responsibility or Kieran would tell his parents what happened. James kept them in the dark, of course. He didn't even tell them about you. If his parents found out he'd fallen in love with some Yank and left me behind pregnant, it would have killed them. James knew it. So did Kieran. I knew it crushed Kieran to threaten his best friend, but he was angry. We both lied to Kieran for months."

To wrap my head around all of this feels impossible, but Siobhan continues peeling back the layers of the story.

"I was the reason you were on that plane," she says.

"What?"

"Kieran's threat worked. James promised he'd set things right so long as Kieran kept his mouth shut until he got home. James said he was planning a trip to Paris this summer, but he'd come to Ireland instead, and we'd work it all out."

"The trip to Paris was my birthday present," I say, baffled. "James changed our flights at the last minute to come to Ireland first." With Siobhan filling in the missing pieces, my dreams solidify. They weren't nightmares, but memories. I knew it, but I couldn't admit it.

"He told me about you," I say. "But not until we were on the plane here. He waited until the last minute, until I couldn't go anywhere . . ."

"It doesn't matter now."

All the lies James weaved, the unknown story he didn't tell until the end . . . But my anger eases. James is dead, and anger isn't useful. My only choice is to let him go, like a ghost of my past.

I gesture to Siobhan's arms. "James dared me to get a tattoo, even though he knew I didn't want to do it. He said he 'fancied a girl with a little color.'"

Siobhan scoffs. "He always had a way of charming you into something you knew was a bad idea . . . except he wasn't ever the one to pay the consequences." Her face creases with heartache. Her eyes fall to Lizzy. "James gave me a gift, really. He left behind a piece of himself, so he's not entirely gone from us. It's kind of poetic in a sad way." She squares herself to me. "When the plane went down, Kieran felt guilty. He said it was his fault because it was his threat that put you on that plane. Ten years of friendship, burned in a field."

"But it wasn't his fault. It was just . . . an accident."

"Kieran felt responsible for you. Like maybe making sure you were OK would make up for what had happened between him and James. I warned him not to do it. He was inviting a mess into our already messy lives, but he said he couldn't leave you alone. James wouldn't want it that way."

Siobhan's convoluted story eases my fury toward Kieran. Instead, my heart breaks for him. For the friend he lost. For the pain and guilt he must have felt. "But what about all the lies?" I say.

"You were lying, too, might I remind you." Siobhan cocks her head at me. "And what was Kieran to do? Tell you the truth? Drop a load of baggage on your lap—a dead boyfriend with a pregnant ex-girlfriend? You could barely walk, let alone handle that."

"But once I got better, he kept lying to me."

"Did you *really* want to know the truth then?" Siobhan asks.

I deflate, my defenses weakening. I pull over two chairs so we can sit down.

"I'm just so confused," I say. "I don't know what's the truth and what's just a function of Kieran 'keeping me safe.'"

Siobhan shakes her head. "Why can't it be both? Love is never safe, but it's the truth. He loves you. I saw it with my own eyes."

I'm not sure any of this matters now. My life in Ireland is over. This story has come to a close, and not in the way I expected. But I can't pretend my life is here anymore. And as long as Kieran allows his dad to control his life, he'll never be free or fully happy.

"You should tell James's parents about the baby," I say.

Siobhan looks at Lizzy. "I will. Kieran's right—they deserve to know."

The Upside of Falling Down

I take a chance and hug Siobhan. It surprises her for a moment, but then she eases into my arms. "I'll miss you."

"I can't believe I'm saying this, but I'll miss you, too, my Yankee Muppet. Come visit us."

"Do you mean that?"

Siobhan nods. "You've got Ireland in your blood now. You can't stay away too long."

The little baby in front of us stretches her arms over her head as she yawns. She's so new to this world. So fragile.

"She'll be OK, won't she?" Siobhan asks.

"Don't worry," I say. "Teeny-tiny girls grow up to be the mightiest of creatures."

CHAPTER 28

Once we've said our good-byes to Stephen in Limerick, there's nothing left to do but go to the hotel and wait for tomorrow. My dad drops his bag in the room. But me . . . I have nothing to bring home, except the one thing I had lost—my memories.

My thoughts bounce between Siobhan's revelations about James and my hazy memories of a relationship that feels distant to me now, almost like it was fake. To a certain extent, maybe it was. James was lying to me the entire time. I can't help but feel the loss of him—the reality that he's dead. But tomorrow, I have to get back on a plane. Just yesterday, I was with Kieran on a flying tour of Dublin. My mind is so knotted, I worry it won't ever come undone.

My dad sits next to me, placing his hand on my knee.

"The odds that a plane will crash is one in 1.2 million."

I cock my head at him. "I think I have pretty shitty luck then."

He chuckles. "Might I remind you that you survived, Teeny. I'd say that's the best luck of all. My only regret is that I didn't get to see much of Ireland. I never even saw a leprechaun."

I laugh. "They don't really exist."

"Or kiss the Blarney Stone."

"You're more likely to get herpes than the gift of gab by doing that."

"And you know that how?"

I say his name flatly. "Kieran told me."

My dad puts his arm around me. "Can your old man tell *you* the truth about something?"

"That seems to be the theme of the day," I huff. "Go for it."

"I never really trusted James." He throws his hands in the air. "Not to speak ill of the dead. I can see that you're hurting right now. The truth is that I was glad he wanted to show you the world, but I didn't think he was *your* world. He was just someone in your orbit for a time."

"That's poetic, Dad." I nudge him playfully, but he remains serious.

"His parents didn't show up at the hospital after the crash, Teeny. I put two and two together and knew my suspicions were right. Any boy worthy of my daughter would have told his parents about you. But he kept you a secret, I'm guessing, because *he* had secrets."

I flop back on the bed, fighting tears.

My dad pats my leg. "Well, I think we'll just have to come back here sometime. You can show me all the things you did while you were here."

"I went surfing," I say with a weary smile.

"Surfing? I didn't know surfing was a thing in Ireland."

"And I drank some Guinness."

My dad pokes my knee. "Drinking Guinness sounds like a marvelous idea. Let's go to the bar."

"Pub," I say. "Let's go to the pub."

"Pub." He smirks at my correction. "Guinness still sounds like a good idea."

The hotel pub is quiet. A few people sit at tables, chatting. We take a seat at the bar. Luckily there are no TVs, but I still keep my head down. The bartender comes over and wipes down the bar. "What can I get you?" I half expect Kieran to be standing in front of me, his face lit up with a flirtatious grin.

But it's not him. This bartender is older and shorter. He assesses me.

"Do I know you? You look familiar."

I glance sideways at my dad. He laughs, and we order a Guinness each. When they come, he takes a sip with a sigh. He's been through so much.

When he sets his pint on the bar, I giggle at him.

"What?"

I wipe away the creamy foam mustache from his upper lip. "It happens all the time." But as the words come out of my mouth, the painful memory of Kieran hits me.

"What is it, Teeny? Are you sad you're leaving?"

I nod, done with lying. Exhausted by it, really.

"That boy . . . Kieran . . ." He takes another sip of his Guinness. "I like him."

"You don't even know him."

"Don't get me wrong. I'm not happy he helped you escape the hospital or kept you hidden from me. But I'm not sure I could have helped you like he did . . . in the state you were in. And when it came down to it, he did the right thing. I'm not sure James would have. But Kieran . . . I truly believe he only wanted to help you, Teeny." He takes another drink. "But don't think I didn't notice that apartment only had one bed."

I laugh, but it threatens to come out as a cry.

"Don't worry," my dad says. "You'll fall in love again. I promise."

I start to think the words, but I'm not brave enough to say them out loud—*I think I already have.* Instead, I say, "Sure."

"You *will.*" He takes another sip of his Guinness. "We're Clevelanders, Teeny. We're tough. We wait out the storm, and eventually LeBron James wins us a championship."

I can't help but feel better sitting next to my dad, his familiarity soothing my aching heart.

"Is the Tribe really doing well?" I say.

"Teeny, you wouldn't believe it. We might actually see another World Series in Cleveland this year." My dad takes a gulp of his beer. "I'm just a little concerned about the Cubs. Those bastards are always more desperate to win."

~

Shannon International Airport is bustling with people when we arrive. Stephen was right—Prince Harry has a new girlfriend, and it's all the tabloids can talk about. People still gawk at me, recognizing me from the papers, but the attention doesn't bother me anymore. With my life slowly taking shape again, it feels easier to handle the looks.

"Are you nervous?" my dad asks as he hands me my boarding pass.

"A little," I say. "But planes are built to fly."

"I'll be next to you the whole time."

We make our way to the gate. My dad takes a seat, but I stand at the windows, so close, my nose is pressed lightly against the glass. I close my eyes and live in my memories of Ireland. I know it's not my home, but Siobhan is right—Ireland is in my blood now. A piece of me will always feel desperate to return.

For a while, watching the planes land and take off gives me comfort. The coming and going . . . a metaphor for life in a way. Nothing is permanent.

"Teeny . . ." My dad touches my shoulder. "It's time."

We board the plane and take our seats. Whatever I had here, I'm leaving behind. I distract myself by unlatching and latching the tray table, in a daze. It's probably better this way, not being fully aware of what's happening.

My dad gets up at one point, mumbling words I can barely hear. I force myself further into the haze. Numb.

Latch.

Unlatch.

"Please keep your tray table in the upright position," I say to myself.

Latch.

Unlatch.

"Please take a moment to locate the nearest emergency exit," I whisper, but my eyes stay on the tray table.

Latch.

Unlatch.

"You know—people always think having red hair is an Irish trait."

My haze vanishes at the sound of Kieran's voice.

He's sitting in the seat my dad was just in—his hair messy under his Paudie's Pub baseball cap.

"There are more Scots with red hair than Irish."

My heart beats in my ears. "What about purple hair?"

"Purple hair?" Kieran says, his eyes pointed at the seat in front of him. "That is unique to bunnies."

"What are you doing here?" I ask, practically breathless.

Kieran holds up my sweatshirt—the one Stephen gave me the first day I woke up in Ireland. "You forgot this. I thought you might need a souvenir." He inspects the sweatshirt. "'When Irish eyes are smiling, they're usually up to something.' Now *that* is the truth."

He hands me the sweatshirt, his eyes locked on mine for a long, luxurious moment.

"Is that all?" I ask.

"Well, I'd be lying if I said that was the only reason I came . . ." Kieran is serious now. "And my lying days are over."

I hold back tears. "Mine, too. But that still doesn't explain what you're doing here."

"Well . . . ," Kieran says. "I've never *not* gone through with a dare, and I believe I accepted one from you. I'm here to follow through."

"You are?"

Kieran nods. "Though I have a minor problem now."

"What's that?" The shock of this moment gives way to blissful reality. Blissful optimism. Blissful freedom.

"I've spent all my money on a one-way ticket to a place I've never been before," he says. "Do you know anyone in Cleveland? It's in Ohio. On Lake Erie." I nod slowly, noticing the light's back in Kieran's eyes and the devil in his grin. Right now, I fall in love with him all over again. "Would she be willing to help a poor lost soul who has nothing? A place to stay, maybe? It won't be long, a week or so. Maybe a little more." Kieran places his hand on my lap, palm open.

"Maybe forever?" I say.

"Well . . . since you asked so nicely."

I interlace my fingers with his. The plane's engine rumbles on. My dad smiles at us from a few rows up. Kieran squeezes my hand tightly, as if to assure me that he's here, that he isn't going anywhere.

"Don't worry," I say. "Just when you think your life is over, a new story line falls from the sky and lands right in your lap."

ACKNOWLEDGMENTS

I boarded a plane bound for Ireland back in 2002 at the age of twenty-two, ready for an adventure. I had the amazing opportunity to student teach at a small all-girls school in the tiny town of Castleisland, County Kerry, in Southwest Ireland. The months I spent there rooted in me a love for the country (and sparked multiple return trips) that I carry with me to this day. I hope I have done justice to the country that embraced this American so many years ago. I wrote from a place of deep love and gratitude.

Thank you to my agent, Renee, who encouraged me to write this story, who guides me through the wacky world of publishing, and who generally puts up with my crazy. You are a goddess.

Thank you to my friend Sinead for checking and double-checking the Irish side of this story, for helping me with research, for answering my questions, and for inviting me into your life all those years ago when I was a lonely American girl just trying to find her way in Tralee. And for instilling in me a love of *Coronation Street*, *EastEnders*, *Neighbours*, and *Home and Away*.

A big, gigantic thank you to the students of Overland High School in Denver, Colorado. This book is the product of a brainstorming session I had during a visit to the school. The teachers, students, and staff have always welcomed me so warmly. This book would not be without those students. Thank you, thank you. A special thank you to Kate

Carmody, who first invited me to the school years ago. It's been a pleasure being in your classroom. You are a mighty teacher.

To my editor, Jason Kirk. You are a renaissance man. I am just happy to be in your orbit and, every once in a while, drop a book on your desk. Thank you for your hard work and for championing my novels. I feel so lucky you picked me. Your obedient servant, R dot Crane.

A huge thank you to the entire team at Skyscape—my publicists, copyeditors, proofreaders, author relations contacts—you all work so hard to help make a book successful. I'm so grateful to work with such wonderful people.

I can't write a book and not thank my beloved Kyle, for always encouraging me, loving me, and dealing with my moments of insanity. You are my best love story.

And to Jessica Park, who picks up the phone when I call, who listens when I have a meltdown, who helps fix my stories when they're headed for disaster, and who said, "Write the Irish book *now*, or I will."

ABOUT THE AUTHOR

Photo © 2014 Cara Vescio

Rebekah Crane is the author of *The Odds of Loving Grover Cleveland* and other young-adult novels. She found a passion for this genre while studying secondary English education at Ohio University. She is a former high school English teacher, a yoga instructor, and the mother of two girls. After living and teaching in six different cities, Rebekah finally settled in the foothills of the Rocky Mountains to write novels and work on screenplays. She now spends her days tucked behind a laptop at seventy-five hundred feet, where the altitude only enhances the writing experience.